# THE INVESTIGATIONS OF
# AVRAM DAVIDSON

## OTHER BOOKS BY AVRAM DAVIDSON

### NOVELS

*Joyleg* (with Ward Moore)
*And on the Eighth Day* (as Ellery Queen)
*The Fourth Side of the Triangle* (as Ellery Queen)
*Mutiny in Space*
*Rork!*
*The Enemy of My Enemy*
*Masters of the Maze*
*The Kar-Chee Reign*
*Rogue Dragon*
*Clash of Star-Kings*
*The Phoenix and the Mirror, or the Enigmatic Speculum*
*Peregrine: Primus*
*Peregrine: Secundus*
*The Island Under the Earth*
*Ursus of Ultima Thule*
*Vergil in Averno*
*Marco Polo and the Sleeping Beauty* (with Grania Davis)
*The Boss in the Wall, A Treatise on the House Devil* (with Grania Davis)

### COLLECTIONS

*Or All the Seas with Oysters*
*What Strange Stars and Skies*
*Strange Seas and Shores*
*The Enquiries of Doctor Eszterhazy* (World Fantasy Award Winner)
*The Redward Edward Papers* edited by Michael Kurland
*The Best of Avram Davidson* edited by Michael Kurland
*Collected Fantasies* edited by John Silbersack
*Crimes and Chaos* (nonfiction)
*Adventures in Unhistory: Conjectures on the Factual Foundations of
Several Ancient Legends* (nonfiction)
*The Adventures of Doctor Eszterhazy*
*The Avram Davidson Treasury* edited by Grania Davis and Robert Silverberg

### CHAPBOOKS

*And Don't Forget the One Red Rose*
*Polly Charms the Sleeping Woman*

## AVRAM DAVIDSON RESOURCES

*The Avram Davidson Website*
An evolving electronic compendium of biographical, bibliographical, and ephemeral
material. A work of love and sweat by Henry Wessells.
http://www.kosmic.org/members/dongle/henry/

*The Nutmeg Point District Mail*
(ISSN 1089-764X)
A newsletter about Avram Davidson and his work. Write to:
Temporary Culture
Post Office Box 43072
Upper Montclair, NJ 07043-0072
Also available in electronic form at the above URL.

# THE INVESTIGATIONS OF
# AVRAM DAVIDSON

EDITED BY GRANIA DAVIS
AND RICHARD A. LUPOFF

ST. MARTIN'S PRESS ❧ NEW YORK

*Design by Victoria Kuskowski*

*Edited by Corin See*

Library of Congress Cataloging-in-Publication Data
Davidson, Avram.
    The investigations of Avram Davidson / edited by Grania Davis and Richard A. Lupoff; additional lolligags by Michael Kurland.—1st ed.
        p.     cm.
    ISBN 0-312-19931-7
    1. Detective and mystery stories, American.   I. Title.
PS3554.A924A6    1999
813'.54—dc21                                          98-44012
                                                                CIP

First Edition: February 1999

10   9   8   7   6   5   4   3   2   1

To Anthony Boucher
(a.k.a. Herman W. Mudgett),
Frederic Dannay and Manfred B. Lee
(a.k.a. Ellery Queen),
and Sr. Richard Gibbons.

# CONTENTS

## STORIES

*Introductions by Grania Davis, Richard A. Lupoff,
and additional lolligags by Michael Kurland*

# THE INVESTIGATIONS OF
# AVRAM DAVIDSON

# Avram Davidson,
# My Friend, This Stranger

Richard A. Lupoff

## The Other Avram Davidson

It is almost—well, almost as if you discovered that your favorite down-and-dirty, gin-swilling, stogie-smoking, barrelhouse piano player, who performed nightly in assorted saloons and whorehouses, grinding out bawdy jingles on a variety of battered, out-of-tune uprights, each Sunday morning rose and shaved and donned a set of elegant togs and made his way to a great cathedral and there performed sacred songs in praise of God on a magnificent pipe organ.

Or as if you discovered that your favorite poet, a spinner of the most delicate, frangible imagery with a shimmering, subtle technique, had a secret passion for writing smutty limericks.

Odder still, as if there was a whole population who knew the musician only for his sacred performances, or the rhymester only for her ribald rhymes—and these persons were as astonished to learn that the musician played piano in honky-tonks or that the wordsmith wrote high-tone verse as you were to discover their "other," secret careers.

So it was with the late Avram Davidson, whom I was proud

to call my friend, and whose works continue to astonish and delight me years after his death. So it may be with you.

Avram was acclaimed in the science fiction community (although in fact more of his works are properly classified as fantasies) as a quirky, brilliant, utterly individual talent. A talent who sprang unannounced on an unsuspecting readership with a series of fancies molded in shapes that no one had ever imagined before and painted in colors that no one had ever seen or even suspected to exist.

He is fondly remembered for those stories and novels, but I would venture that not one in three grateful readers of Avram's science fiction is aware that he was a mystery writer as well. Not only that: Avram was a *terrific* mystery writer.

Many writers who build their careers in one field of literature make occasional forays into other realms; these feints are generally followed by quick retreats to familiar territory.

But Avram appeared over and over in the leading periodicals of the field, more than forty times in *Ellery Queen's Mystery Magazine* alone, and as many more in *Alfred Hitchcock's Mystery Magazine*, *The Saint Mystery Magazine*, *Manhunt*, *Bestseller Mystery Magazine*, *Shock*, *Bizarre Mystery Magazine*, *Keyhole Mystery Magazine*, and *Mike Shayne Mystery Magazine*, as well as such out-of-category periodicals as *Collier's*, *Midstream*, *Harlequin*, *Knight*, and *Playboy*. His stories were frequently anthologized, and he won prestigious awards as a mystery writer.

He never published any mystery novels under his own name, which is perhaps why he remains unlisted in major reference books on crime fiction. By contrast, he receives extensive coverage in the standard reference volumes on science fiction. In both cases, Avram was better known for his short stories than for his novels. His short stories were brightly polished and hard surfaced.

But even this point is more clouded and ambiguous than it seems. It is an open secret in the literary community that several writers ghosted for "Ellery Queen" in the latter days of Frederic Dannay and Manfred B. Lee, the ever-squabbling cousins who invented Queen and wrote under the Queen byline for many years. Among the Queens' ghosts was Avram Davidson, who penned two somewhat quirky "Queen" novels, *And on the Eighth Day* (1964) and *The Fourth Side of the Triangle* (1965).

It should be noted that Dannay and Lee had an unusual way of developing their novels. Starting with a rather minimal sketch, they would fill in more and more details until they reached their "final outline," a lengthy document that resembled a kind of condensed novel more closely than it did a conventional outline. From this, in the days when they wrote their own books, they would proceed to flesh out the text.

In the days when they used ghosts, the "Queens" still carried out the process from rough sketch to "condensed novel," with the ghost then providing the flesh. Come to think of it, to be quite fair and accurate, these books might better be called covert collaborations than outright ghost jobs.


## A LITTLE BIT OF BIOGRAPHY

BORN IN YONKERS, New York, on April 23, 1923, Avram Davidson received a conventional education and was attending New York University when he left civilian life to serve in the Second World War. There has been some confusion over the branch in which he served. In fact, he was a hospital corpsman in the United States Navy. In this capacity he was assigned to the Fifth Marine Division in Okinawa, site of one of the bloodiest and most terrible campaigns of the war. He was then detailed to serve in mainland China, and was in Beijing (then Peking) at the time of the Japanese surrender in 1945.

Avram's very first novel, *The Corpsmen*, was based on his experiences in the Second World War. It has never been published in full. The manuscript was rescued from oblivion in the stacks of Texas A&M University by Avram's tireless bibliographer, Henry Wessells. Grania Davis, Avram's onetime wife, lifetime friend, and literary executor, then placed an excerpt (titled

"Blunt") with *The Magazine of Fantasy and Science Fiction*. The full text may yet appear.

After leaving the navy and living in the United States for some time, Avram emigrated to Israel and served in the Israeli Army during that nation's war of independence, 1948–49.

He returned to the United States and attended Pierce College in southern California, where he studied the care and breeding of sheep. He traveled to Israel again, hoping to apply what he had learned at Pierce, but his ideas were not warmly received; he returned once more to the United States and shortly commenced his literary career.

He made his publishing debut, as far as is known, with several stories and verse in *Jewish Life* between 1947 and 1949. He also placed stories with *Commentary* magazine, where they appeared in 1952. These writings were Judaic in nature. (For this information and much more I am indebted to Henry Wessells.)

Avram turned to the world of popular fiction with "My Boy Friend's Name is Jello," a short story that appeared in *The Magazine of Fantasy and Science Fiction* for July 1954. His first published mystery story was "The Ikon of Elijah," in the December 1956 issue of *Ellery Queen's Mystery Magazine*. Even at this early stage of his career, he wrote with remarkable skill, subtlety, and complexity of character. In their story blurb the editors of *Ellery Queen* said, "Watch Mr. Davidson: he has the gift—the precious gift of words and insight." The story is told primarily by what the author omits rather than what he reveals—a notable achievement for any spinner-of-tales, no less for one at the outset of his career.

Although I read many of Avram's early stories, it was his first published novel, *Joyleg*, written in collaboration with Ward Moore, that initially made a strong impression on me. If you will pardon a brief autobiographical note, I will tell you how.

The year was 1962. My home at the time was on East Seventy-third Street in Manhattan. My place of employment was a somewhat decrepit office building downtown at Twenty-third Street and what was then known as Fourth Avenue (now Park Avenue South). I had bought a little paperback edition of

*Joyleg* and started reading it one evening as I rode home on the Lexington Avenue IRT.

The book so gripped me that I forgot where I was. Totally engrossed, I finally looked up only to realize that I had ridden past my stop. I left the subway at the next station, walked over to Second Avenue and boarded a downtown bus.

Captivated again by the book, I rode past my stop.

I climbed from the bus and, vowing to avoid further humiliation, set out on foot, paperback book clutched in hand, happily reading *Joyleg*. And after a few minutes, for the third time engrossed in the book, I felt a terrific wallop. The impact sent a shuddering shock through my body. I staggered back, literally seeing stars, dizzy and disoriented, my ears ringing.

Had I been mugged?

Had a taxi jumped the curb and plowed into a mass of pedestrians?

Alas, I had become so absorbed by the book that I forgot to watch where I was going and had stridden headlong into an iron stanchion.

When at last I found my apartment and stumbled into the vestibule my darling wife screamed in alarm. Here was her husband, home from work more than an hour late, dirty, disheveled, far from steady on his feet, and with an ugly blue bruise rising on his forehead.

"What happened to you?" she cried.

"Well, I was reading this really, really good book," I explained. . . .

At about this time Avram began a tour of duty as editor at *The Magazine of Fantasy and Science Fiction* (1962–64). He impressed his distinctive personality on the magazine during his tenure, and issues from this era are fondly remembered, but he gladly returned to full-time writing. He did, nonetheless, edit three more-than-worthwhile anthologies of material from the magazine. A fourth anthology, *Magic for Sale* (1983), is even more noteworthy, both for its fine selection of stories and for Avram's extensive editorial notes.

It was in this era of the early 1960s that I also met Avram for the first time. I must say that you would not take him for a veteran of the Okinawa campaign and the Israeli war of independence, nor for a rough-hewn sheep rancher. He was, in fact, a rotund fellow, slightly shorter than average. He had large, dark eyes that could switch from a piercing intensity to a jolly twinkle in an instant. His hair was curly and black, with increasing suggestions of gray as the years passed. He wore a distinctive spade-shaped beard that expanded over time to cover more and more of his face.

He had a comfortable air about him, and was popular in New York literary circles (at least those to which the then so-young Dick Lupoff was able to gain entree). The pleasant sight of Avram on a Sunday morning, strolling benignly down a hotel corridor and cheerfully handing out fresh bagels, must remain in many a store of fond recollections.

Avram was fond of good food, generally of a plain and hearty nature, as many of his stories indicate. He was not a heavy drinker, but he took an occasional glass of schnapps with considerable pleasure, especially if it was of superior quality.

He was not unappreciated as a writer. His short story "The Necessity of His Condition" won the Ellery Queen Award for 1957. "Or All the Seas with Oysters" won a Hugo Award in 1958. "The Affair at the Lahore Cantonment" won an Edgar Award in 1962. His story-cycle *The Enquiries of Dr. Eszterhazy* won the World Fantasy Award in 1976. "Crazy Old Lady" was a 1977 Edgar nominee. *The Redward Edward Papers* was nominated for a World Fantasy Award in 1979. "Naples" won the World Fantasy Award in 1979. And the World Fantasy Convention presented him with a Lifetime Achievement Award in 1986.

Honors aplenty!

His stories appeared in nearly fifty "best of" anthologies. These included both mystery and science fiction volumes, not unexpectedly, but also others ranging from *Year's Best Fantasy Stories* to *Best Horror Stories*—thereby confounding categorization once again.

Several of his mystery stories were adapted for the small screen. Particularly notable was "Thou Still Unravished Bride," featured on *Alfred Hitchcock Presents* in 1965. It was directed by

David Friedkin from a script by Friedkin and Morton Fine; the cast included Sally Kellerman and David Carradine.

And Avram was an essayist and critic of no mean talent as well as a writer of fiction.

But like many talented authors, he was perhaps too good for his own good. His works were often a trifle (all right, more than a trifle) esoteric. And he kept doing different things. One Avram Davidson story would be a dark and cleverly constructed tale of crime; the next, a gossamer fantasy. In his novels he tried space opera (with little success), barbarian adventure (less), and finally a more textured variety of historical fantasy, redolent almost of the spirit of Thomas Burnett Swann (and this with far better results).

He was recognized by the academic world with a series of appointments under such titles as "visiting lecturer," "writer in residence," or "visiting distinguished writer" at such institutions as the University of California at Irvine, the College of William and Mary, the University of Texas at El Paso, the University of Washington, and the University of Michigan.

Respected and appreciated by critics, academics, and above all by his colleagues—the appellation "writer's writer" comes unavoidably to mind—he somehow failed to achieve the mass acceptance and consequent financial rewards of countless other writers, many of them, as the expression would have it, not fit to sharpen his pencils. The frustration which he must have felt comes out in his almost painfully hilarious—and accurate—story, "The Captain M. Caper" (1970).

He published at least fifteen novels in his lifetime, not counting the "Ellery Queen" books, and no fewer than an astonishing 218 short stories. Selections of these latter have been in and out of print in countless anthologies, as well as a dozen single-author collections.

A man of widely ranging tastes, and fascinated by history and myth, Avram wrote numerous essays on the ancient world and its more mysterious aspects. They were collected in the volume, *Adventures in Unhistory: Conjectures on the Factual Foundations of Several Ancient Legends* (1993). Rambling, erudite, and discursive, the essays are not to every taste, but to me each of them is like a delightful visit with the shade of Avram Davidson, from the reading of which I emerge buoyed, stimulated, and enlightened. This book, issued by Owlswick Press, was the last volume of Avram's work to appear in his lifetime.

Every admirer of Avram has his own favorite piece, and I will not attempt to "prove" that this work or that is superior to that work or this. I will merely state that my personal favorite, or at least my "most favorite of favorites," is *The Adventures of Doctor Eszterhazy*. Originally published as *The Enquiries of Doctor Eszterhazy* in an easily overlooked and undistinguished-looking paperback (which nonetheless won the World Fantasy Award in 1976), this splendid book has since been reissued in a handsome hardbound edition. This "new" *Eszterhazy*, still available from Owlswick, contains several stories written after the original edition was published.

Engelbert Eszterhazy, Doctor of Medicine, Jurisprudence, Philosophy, Science, and Literature, is a droll and magnificent *mitteleuropean* Sherlock Holmes whose base of operations is Number 33 Turkling Street in the city of Bella, capital of Scythia-Pannonia-Transbalkania. The years of Eszterhazy's flourishing are not specified, but clearly his best work in unraveling mysteries was done before the assassination of the Archduke Ferdinand in Sarajevo, that bloody act which, in the opinions of some historians, at least sparked if it did not fuel the cataclysmic Great War and the century of tragedies that followed.

But to anybody who would prefer "The Necessity of His Condition," or "The Cobblestones of Saratoga Street," or "The Importance of Trifles," or any other of Avram's ten-score-and-more stories, or any of his novels, or his nonfiction, I will simply say, *No debate. No argument. In this embarrassment of riches there lie pleasures aplenty for all who would seek them out.*

Of Avram's own reading habits a fair amount is known. For obvious reasons we know that he was familiar with the works of Ellery Queen. It is also clear from references in his works and from conversations or correspondence with him, that he was thoroughly conversant with such pop-culture icons as Sir Arthur

Conan Doyle and that doyen of eldritch horror tales, Howard Phillips Lovecraft.

Perhaps less obvious is Avram's interest in the works of Edgar Rice Burroughs. At the time of our first acquaintanceship I was working as an editor at Canaveral Press in New York, busily guiding the newly released, hitherto unpublished manuscripts of Burroughs into print. Avram wrote to me, inquiring about the possibility of his adding new works to Burroughs's "John Carter of Mars" saga. Nothing came of this plan, alas, and one can only speculate on what a Barsoomian yarn by Avram Davidson would have been like.

After Avram's death, Grania Davis recovered much of his personal library from the tiny apartment where he had been living. Avram's books are for the most part well read, his library clearly intended for use, not exhibition.

There are very few volumes of literary fiction among his books, these few including *Crome Yellow* by Aldous Huxley and *Canal Town* by Samuel Hopkins Adams. Further, Avram reserved places of honor for the works of his many writer friends.

Most of his library consisted of reference books on history, geography, and the esoteric, and of classics. He owned a complete annotated set of the works of Pliny the Elder. He owned a copy of *Ships and Seamanship in the Ancient World*. He owned *The Golden Game: Alchemical Engravings of the Seventeenth Century*, by Stanislas Klossowski de Rola. He owned Ovid's *Metamorphoses*, Samuel Pepys's diary, the biography of Helen of Troy, *The Song of Roland*, *Arcana Mundi: Magic and the Occult in the Greek and Roman Worlds*, *The Catalan Chronicles* of Francisco de Moncada, *Italian Towns* by Henry James, Boswell's *Life of Johnson*, and *The Golden Ass* as translated by Robert Graves.

According to Grania Davis he owned "a mountain of books on Africa," which he planned to use as research materials for a work based on the African legend of the Pygmies and the Cranes.

He never stopped working, even after a series of strokes left him disabled and partially paralyzed.

Still, at the end, he was forced to rely on his veteran's benefits to eke out a meager existence. He died on May 8, 1993. He gave us a great deal, and deserved better in return than he received.

## REASSESSMENT TIME

THE LATE LIN Carter, himself one of the more talented—albeit quirky and underachieving—writers of my generation (and Avram's), developed an intriguing theory about the lives—or afterlives—of authors. If an author is sufficiently noteworthy during his career, Carter opined, an increase in interest will follow the author's death. After a while, as the demands of curious readers are met, and as literary historians, biographers, and critics have had their say and exhausted their store of comment, interest flags and the author's books lapse from print once again.

Then—and this, I believe, was Carter's key idea—after the passage of some years, the author is rediscovered. Some if not all of his works are reprinted, the academics and critics murmur their magical spells, and the author is either crowned with the laurels of at least conditional and temporary immortality (for ultimately, only God is truly immortal) . . . or he is tossed onto the trash heap of literary history, and his works with him.

Carter unburdened himself of this theory a good many years ago, late at night while a winter log crackled in the fireplace and after many delicious libations had been consumed, so my recollection of the event is somewhat fuzzy-edged; but I do believe that Lin suggested a considerable lapse of time, possibly as long as a century, before that final reassessment took place.

In Avram's case, the time is drastically shortened. He died in 1993, aged just over seventy. Tragically neglected and justly embittered in his last years, Avram lives through his works. Even now a renaissance is under way with the recent publication of *The Avram Davidson Treasury* and *The Boss in the Wall: A Treatise on the House Devil.*

The former volume, issued by Tor Books, is a huge collection of Avram's stories, primarily of his science fiction and fantasy but including several criminous tales as well. His unique talent yielded many works which can be listed under the rubrics of several categories. More appropriately, I should say that they are uncategorizable, but at least some taxonomy, the practice of sorting and labeling, is often useful. So I will speak of Avram's mystery fiction, his science fiction, his fantasies, as in fact I have already done in this modest essay.

There are several stories in the *Treasury* that Grania Davis, who co-edited both collections, would have liked to include in *The Investigations* as well. I especially call to your attention "The Affair at the Lahore Cantonment," which won the 1962 Edgar Award for short story, and "Crazy Old Lady," which was a 1977 Edgar nominee. I suggest that once you have finished reading *The Investigations of Avram Davidson*, you proceed to the *Treasury*.

*The Boss in the Wall* is another matter. Carved out of a sprawling unpublished Davidson manuscript, it appears under the joint byline of Avram Davidson and Grania Davis. It was Grania who rescued the huge manuscript from oblivion and prepared *The Boss in the Wall* for publication. The longer manuscript may someday be published. The shorter version was issued by Tachyon Publications of San Francisco, and I commend it to your attention.

We may be jumping the gun, in terms of Lin Carter's reassessment theory, but it is my confident belief that the issuance of these three books will remind many thousands of Avram Davidson's old readers of what a gem of a writer he was, and will bring him to the attention of even more thousands of readers.

Avram was, in his unique way, a throwback to the old school of tale-spinners. He could tailor his style to the setting and theme of a story. He was the master of the *mot juste*, the "right word." With a mere handful of syllables he could transport a reader to the deck of an ancient sailing vessel as it plied the waves of the sun-dappled Mediterranean, to a musty and mysterious little shop in a shadowy byway of Victorian London, to the spartan executive offices or the clattering production line of a modern corporation.

From time to time he lapsed into the naturalistic prose that is the hallmark of the modern short story, but more often his own voice was clearly audible, and rather than being an intrusion upon the story he was telling, his presence remained (and remains) a welcome and reassuring constant.

Grania Davis has commented that Avram's normal mode of storytelling is the mystery. "Whether the story is classified as a crime story or a fantasy, there is usually a puzzle to be solved, a mystery to be investigated." Avram Davidson transcended the usual boundaries of categories, and simply told Avram Davidson stories.

If this is truly reassessment time, I have no doubt that Avram Davidson will not only gain entrance to Parnassus, but will be greeted by cheering crowds and by rows of graceful maidens strewing his pathway with sweet-smelling blossoms.

And a glass of good schnapps.

Avram deserves no less.

*—Richard A. Lupoff, 1998*

# The Necessity of

# His Condition

———◆◆❋◆●———

"The Necessity of His Condition" was first published in 1957, and won the Ellery Queen Award for best short fiction published that year.

It is considered one of Avram Davidson's most important stories. The topic is American slavery. An early rejection letter for the story said, "I'm glad you sent it to me. But we couldn't touch it because of its theme." The irony of the story is that it takes no sides. It simply draws the legal consequences of slavery to their awful conclusion.

Davidson's own story notes said, "Really, I have, in part, to thank *Life* magazine for first implanting in my mind a certain detail of the Slave Code on which this story is based. This detail came to my attention years later during my long research into the institution of slavery in the United States as background for a projected article on the Dred Scott decision. The research produced much that was new to me, all of it of course unpleasant: did you know, for instance that (I believe) numerous Free Negroes themselves owned slaves?—And it also produced this story.

"It also produced the Queen's Award (Ellery, not Elizabeth), the first large sum of money I had ever made. This story marks the turning point in my career as a writer."

*—GD*

holto Hill was mostly residential property, but it had its commercial district in the shape of Persimmon Street and Rampart Street, the latter named after some long-forgotten barricade stormed and destroyed by Benedict Arnold (wearing a British uniform and eaten with bitterness and perverted pride). Persimmon Street, running up-slope, entered the middle of Rampart at right angles, and went no farther. This section, with its red brick houses and shops, its warehouses and offices, was called The T, and it smelled of tobacco and potatoes and molasses and goober peas and dried fish and beer and cheap cook-shop food and (the spit-and-whittle humorists claimed) old man Bailiss's office, where the windows were never opened—never had *been* opened, they said, never were *made* to be opened. Any smell off the street or farms or stables that found its way up to Bailiss's office was imprisoned there for life, they said. Old man Bailiss knew what they said, knew pretty much everything that went on anywhere; but he purely didn't care. He didn't have to, they said.

J. Bailiss, Attorney-at-Law (his worn old sign said), had a large practice and little competition. James Bailiss, Broker (his newer, but by no means new, sign), did an extensive business; again, with little competition. The premises of the latter business were located, not in The T, but in a white-washed stone structure with thick doors and barred windows, down in The Bottom—as it was called—near the river, the canal, and the railroad line.

James Bailiss, Broker, was not received socially. Nobody expected that bothered him much. Nothing bothered old man Bailiss much—Bailiss, with his old white hat and his old black coat and his old cowhide shoes that looked old even when they were new—turned old on the shoemaker's last (the spit-and-whittle crowd claimed) directly they heard whose feet they were destined for.

It was about twenty-five years earlier, in 1825, that an advertisement—the first of its kind—appeared in the local news-paper.

"*Take Notice!* (it began). James Bailiss, having lately pur-chased the old arsenal building on Canal Street, will henceforth operate it as a Negro Depot. He will at all times be found ready to purchase all good and likely young Negroes at the Highest Price. He will also attend to Selling Negroes on Commission. Said Broker also gives Notice that those who have Slaves ren-dered unfit for labor by yaws, scrofula, chronic consumption, rheumatism, & C., may dispose of them to him on reasonable terms."

Editor Winstanley tried to dissuade him, he said later. "Folks," he told him, "won't like this. This has never been said out open before," the editor pointed out. Bailiss smiled. He was already middle-aged, had a shiny red face and long mousy hair. His smile wasn't a very wide one.

"Then I reckon I must be the pioneer," he said. "This isn't a big plantation State, it never will be. I've give the matter right much thought. I reckon it just won't pay for anyone to own more than half a dozen slaves in these parts. But they will multiply, you can't stop it. I've seen it in my lawwork, seen many a planter broke for debts he's gone into to buy field hands—signed notes against his next crop, or maybe even his next three crops. Then maybe the crop is so good that the price of cotton goes way down and he can't meet his notes, so he loses his lands *and* his slaves. If the price of cotton should happen to be high enough for him to pay for the slaves he's bought, then, like a dumned fool"—Bailiss never swore—"why, he signs notes for a few more. Pretty soon things get so bad you can't *give* slaves away round here. So a man has a dozen of them eating their heads off and not even earning grocery bills. No, Mr. Winstanley; slaves must be sold south and southwest, where the new lands are being opened up, where the big plantations are."

Editor Winstanley wagged his head. "I know," he said, "I know. But folks don't like to say things like that out loud. The slave trade is looked down on. You know that. It's a necessary evil, that's how it's regarded, like a—well . . ." He lowered his voice. "Nothing personal, but . . . like a sporting house. Nothing personal, now, Mr. Bailiss."

The attorney-broker smiled again. "Slavery has the sanction of the law. It is a necessary part of the domestic economy, just like cotton. Why, suppose I should say, 'I love my cotton, I'll only sell it locally'? People'd think I was just crazy. Slaves have become a surplus product in the Border States and they must be disposed of where they are not produced in numbers sufficient to meet the local needs. You print that advertisement. Folks may not ask me to dinner, but they'll sell to me, see if they won't."

The notice did, as predicted, outrage public opinion. Old Marsta and Old Missis vowed no Negro of *theirs* would ever be sold "down the River." But somehow the broker's "jail"—as it was called—kept pretty full, though its boarders changed. Old man Bailiss had his agents out buying and his agents out selling. Sometimes he acted as agent for firms whose headquarters were in Natchez or New Orleans. He entered into silent partnerships with gentlemen of good family who wanted a quick return on capital, and who got it, but who still, it was needless to say, did not dine with him or take his hand publicly. There was talk, on and off, that the Bar Association was planning action not favorable to Bailiss for things connected with the legal side of his trade. It all came to nought.

"Mr. Bailiss," young Ned Wickerson remarked to him one day in the old man's office, "whoever said that 'a man who defends himself has a fool for a client' never had the pleasure of your acquaintance."

"Thank you, boy."

"Consequently," the young man continued, "I've advised Sam Worth not to go into court if we can manage to settle out of it."

"First part of your advice is good, but there's nothing to settle."

"There's a matter of $635 to settle, Mr. Bailiss." Wickerson had been practicing for two years, but he still had freckles on his nose. He took a paper out of his wallet and put it in front of them. "There's this to settle."

The old man pushed his glasses down his nose and picked up the paper. He scanned it, lips moving silently. "Why, this is all correct," he said. "Hmm. To be sure. 'Received of Samuel Worth of Worth's Crossing, Lemuel County, the sum of $600 cash in full payment for a Negro named Dominick Swift, commonly called Domino, aged thirty-six years and of bright complexion, which Negro I warrant sound in mind and body and a slave for life and the title I will forever defend. James Bailiss, Rutland, Lemuel County.' Mmm. All correct. And anyway, what do you mean, six hundred and *thirty-five* dollars?"

"Medical and burial expenses. Domino died last week."

"Died, now, did he? Sho. Too bad. Well, all men are mortal."

"I'm afraid my client doesn't take much comfort from your philosophy. Says he didn't get two days' work out of Domino. Says he whipped him, first off, for laziness, but when the doctor—Dr. Sloan, that was—examined him, Doctor said he had a consumption. Died right quickly."

"Negroes *are* liable to quick consumptions. Wish they was a medicine for it. On the other hand, they seldom get malaria or yella fever. Providence."

He cut off a slice of twist, shoved it in his cheek, then offered twist and knife to Wickerson, who shook his head.

"As I say, we'd rather settle out of court. If you'll refund the purchase price we won't press for the other expenses. What do you say?"

Bailiss looked around the dirty, dusty office. There was a case of law books with broken bindings against the north wall. The south wall had a daguerreotype of John C. Calhoun hanging crookedly on it. The single dim window was in the east wall, and the west wall was pierced by a door whose lower panels had been scarred and splintered by two generations of shoes and boots kicking it open. "Why, I say no, o' course."

Wickerson frowned. "If you lose, you know, you'll have to pay *my* costs as well."

"I don't expect I'll lose," the old man said.

"Why, of course you'll lose," the young man insisted, although he did not sound convinced. "Dr. Sloan will testify that it was *not* 'a quick consumption.' He says it was a long-

17

standing case of Negro tuberculosis. And you warranted the man sound."

"Beats me how them doctors think up long words like that," Bailiss said placidly. "Inter'sting point of law just come up down in N'Orleans, Ned. One of my agents was writing me. Negro brakeman had his legs crushed in an accident, man who rented him to the railroad sued, railroad pleaded 'negligence of his fellow-servant'—in this case, the engineer."

"Seems like an unassailable defense." The younger lawyer was interested despite himself. "What happened?"

"Let's see if I can recollect the Court's words." This was mere modesty. Old man Bailiss's memory was famous on all matters concerning the slave codes. "Mmm. Yes. Court said: 'The slave status has removed this man from the normal fellow-servant category. He is fettered fast by the most stern bonds our laws take note of. He cannot with impunity desert his post though danger plainly threatens, nor can he reprove free men for their bad management or neglect of duty, for the necessity of his condition is upon him.' Awarded the owner—Creole man name of Le Tour—awarded him $1300."

"It seems right, put like that. But now, Dr. Sloan—"

"Now, Neddy. Domino was carefully examined by *my* doctor, old Fred Pierce—"

"Why, Pierce hasn't drawn a sober breath in twenty years! He gets only slaves for his patients."

"Well, I reckon that makes him what they call a specialist, then. No, Ned, don't go to court. You have no case. My jailer will testify, too, that Domino was sound when I sold him. It must of been that whipping sickened him."

Wickerson rose. "Will you make *partial* restitution, then?" The old man shook his head. His long hair was streaked with gray, but the face under it was still ruddy. "You *know* Domino was sick," Wickerson said. "I've spoken to old Miss Whitford's man, Micah, the blacksmith, who was doing some work in your jail awhile back. He told me that he heard Domino coughing, saw him spitting blood, saw you watching him, saw you give him some rum and molasses, heard you say, 'Better not cough till I've sold you, Dom, else I'll have to sell you south where they don't coddle Negroes.' This was just before you *did* sell him—to my client."

The old man's eyes narrowed. "I'd say Micah talks over-much for a black man, even one of old Miss Whitford's—a high and mighty lady that doesn't care to know me on the street. But you forget one mighty important thing, Mr. Wickerson!" His voice rose. He pointed his finger. "It makes no difference what Micah heard! Micah is property! Just like my horse is property! And property can't testify! Do you claim to be a lawyer? Don't you know that a slave can't inherit—can't bequeath—can't marry nor give in marriage—can neither sue nor prosecute—and that it's a basic principle of the law that a slave can never testify in court except against another slave?"

Wickerson, his lips pressed tightly together, moved to the door, kicked it open, scattering a knot of idlers who stood around listening eagerly, and strode away. The old man brushed through them.

"And you'd better tell Sam Worth not to come bothering me, either!" Bailiss shouted at Wickerson's back. "I know how to take care of trash like him!" He turned furiously to the gaping and grinning loungers.

"Get away from here, you mud-sills!" He was almost squeaking in his rage.

"I reckon you don't own the sidewalks," they muttered. "I reckon every white man in this state is as good as any other white man," they said; but they gave way before him. The old man stamped back into his office and slammed the door.

———❖———

IT WAS BAILISS's custom to have his supper in his own house, a two-story building just past the end of the sidewalk on Rampart Street; but tonight he felt disinclined to return there with no one but rheumaticky old Edie, his housekeeper-cook, for company. He got on his horse and rode down toward the cheerful bustle of the Phoenix Hotel. Just as he was about to go in, Sam

Worth came out. Worth was a barrel-shaped man with thick short arms and thick bandy legs. He stood directly in front of Bailiss, breathing whiskey fumes.

"So you won't settle?" he growled. His wife, a stout woman taller than her husband, got down from their wagon and took him by the arm.

"Come away now, Sam," she urged.

"You'd better step aside," Bailiss said.

"I hear you been making threats against me," Worth said.

"Yes, and I'll carry them out, too, if you bother me!"

A group quickly gathered, but Mrs. Worth pulled her husband away, pushed him toward the wagon; and Bailiss went inside. The buzz of talk dropped for a moment as he entered, stopped, then resumed in a lower register. He cast around for a familiar face, undecided where to sit; but it seemed to him that all faces were turned away. Finally he recognized the bald head and bent shoulders of Dr. Pierce, who was slumped at a side table by himself, muttering into a glass. Bailiss sat down heavily across from him, with a sigh. Dr. Pierce looked up.

"A graduate of the University of Virginia," the doctor said. His eyes were dull.

"At it again?" Bailiss looked around for a waiter. Dr. Pierce finished what was in his glass.

"Says he'll horsewhip you on sight," he muttered.

"Who says?" Bailiss was surprised.

"Major Jack Moran."

Bailiss laughed. The Major was a tottery veteran of the War of 1812 who rode stiffly about on an aged white mare. "What for?" he asked.

"Talk is going around you Mentioned A Lady's Name." Pierce beckoned, and at once a waiter, whose eye old man Bailiss had not managed to catch, appeared with a full glass. Bailiss caught his sleeve as the waiter was about to go and ordered his meal. The doctor drank. "Major Jack says, impossible to Call You Out—can't appear on Field of Honor with slave trader—so instead will whip you on sight." His voice gurgled in the glass.

Bailiss smiled crookedly. "I reckon I needn't be afraid of

him. He's old enough to be my daddy. A lady's name? What lady? Maybe he means a lady who lives in a big old house that's falling apart, an old lady who lives on what her Negro blacksmith makes?"

Dr. Pierce made a noise of assent. He put down his glass. Bailiss looked around the dining room, but as fast as he met anyone's eyes, the eyes glanced away. The doctor cleared his throat.

"Talk is going around you expressed a dislike for said Negro. Talk is that the lady has said she is going to manumit him to make sure you won't buy him if she dies."

Bailiss stared. "Manumit him? She can't do that unless she posts a bond of a thousand dollars to guarantee that he leaves the state within ninety days after being freed. She must know that free Negroes aren't allowed to stay on after manumission. And where would she get a thousand dollars? And what would she live on if Micah is sent away? That old lady hasn't got good sense!"

"No," Pierce agreed, staring at the glass. "She is old and not too bright and she's got too much pride on too little money, but it's a sis"—his tongue stumbled—"a singular thing: there's hardly a person in this town, white or black or half-breed Injun, that doesn't *love* that certain old lady. Except you. And *no*body in town loves *you*. Also a singular thing: here we are—"

The doctor's teeth clicked against the glass. He set it down, swallowed. His eyes were yellow in the corners, and he looked at Bailiss steadily, save for a slight trembling of his hands and head. "Here we are, heading just as certain as can be towards splitting the Union and having war with the Yankees—all over slavery—tied to it hand and foot—willing to die for it—economy bound up in it—sure in our own hearts that nature and justice and religion are for it—and yet, singular thing: nobody likes slave traders. Nobody likes them."

"Tell me something new." Bailiss drew his arms back to make room for his dinner. He ate noisily and with good appetite.

"Another thing," the doctor hunched forward in his seat, "that hasn't added to your current popularity is this business of

21

Domino. In this, I feel, you made a mistake. *Caveat emptor* or not, you should've sold him farther away from here, much farther away, down to the rice fields somewhere, where his death would have been just a statistic in the overseer's annual report. Folks feel you've cheated Sam Worth. He's not one of your rich absentee owners who sits in town and lets some cheese-paring Yankee drive his Negroes. He only owns four or five, he and his boy work right alongside them in the field, pace them row for row."

Bailiss grunted, sopped up gravy.

"You've been defying public opinion for years now. There might come a time when you'd want good will. My advice to you—after all, your agent only paid $100 for Domino—is to settle with Worth for five hundred."

Bailiss wiped his mouth on his sleeve. He reached for his hat, put it on, left money on the table, and got up.

"Shoemaker, stick to your last," he said. Dr. Pierce shrugged. "Make that glass the final one. I want you at the jail tomorrow, early, so we can get the catalogue ready for the big sale next week. Hear?" The old man walked out, paying no attention to the looks or comments his passage caused.

On his horse Bailiss hesitated. The night was rather warm, with a hint of damp in the air. He decided to ride around for a while in the hope of finding a breeze stirring. As the horse ambled along from one pool of yellow gaslight to another he ran through in his mind some phrases for inclusion in his catalogue. *Phyllis, prime woman, aged 25, can cook, sew, do fine ironing . . .*

When he had first begun in the trade, three out of every five Negroes had been named Cuffee, Cudjoe, or Quash. He'd heard these were days of the week in some African dialect. There was talk that the African slave trade might be legalized again; that would be a fine thing. But, sho, there was always such talk, on and off.

The clang of a hammer on an anvil reminded him that he was close to Black Micah's forge. As he rounded the corner he saw Sam Worth's bandy-legged figure outlined against the light. One of the horses was unhitched from his wagon and awaited the shoe Micah was preparing for it.

A sudden determination came to Bailiss: he would settle with Worth about Domino. He hardly bothered to analyze his motives. Partly because his dinner was resting well and he felt comfortable and unexpectedly benevolent, partly because of some vague notion it would be the popular thing to do and popularity was a good thing to have before and during a big sale, he made up his mind to offer Worth $300—well, maybe he would go as high as $350, but no more; a man had to make *some*thing out of a trade.

As he rode slowly up to the forge and stopped, the blacksmith paused in his hammering and looked out. Worth turned around. In the sudden silence Bailiss heard another horse approaching.

"I've come to settle with you," the slave trader said. Worth looked up at him, his eyes bloodshot. In a low, ugly voice Worth cussed him, and reached his hand toward his rear pocket. It was obvious to Bailiss what Worth intended, so the slave trader quickly drew his own pistol and fired. His horse reared, a woman screamed—did *two* women scream? Without his meaning it, the other barrel of his pistol went off just as Worth fell.

"Fo' gawdsake don't kill me, Mister Bailiss!" Micah cried. "Are you all right, Miss Elizabeth?" he cried. Worth's wife and Miss Whitford suddenly appeared from the darkness on the other side of the wagon. They knelt beside Worth.

Bailiss felt a numbing blow on his wrist, dropped his empty pistol, was struck again, and half fell, was half dragged, from his horse. A woman screamed again, men ran up—where had they all come from? Bailiss, pinned in the grip of someone he couldn't see, stood dazed.

"You infernal scoundrel, you shot that man in cold blood!" Old Major Jack Moran dismounted from his horse and flourished the riding crop with which he had struck Bailiss on the wrist.

"I never—he cussed me—he reached for his pistol—I only defended myself!"

Worth's wife looked up, tears streaking her heavy face.

"He had no pistol," she said. "I made him leave it home."

23

"You said, 'I've come to get you,' and you shot him point-blank!" The old Major's voice trumpeted.

"He tried to shoot Miss Whitford, too!" someone said. Other voices added that Captain Carter, the High Sheriff's chief deputy, was coming. Bodies pressed against Bailiss, faces glared at him, fists were waved before him.

"It wasn't like that at all!" he cried.

Deputy Carter came up on the gallop, flung the reins of his black mare to eager outthrust hands, jumped off, and walked over to Worth.

"How was it, then?" a scornful voice asked Bailiss.

"I rode up . . . I says, 'I've come to settle with you' . . . He cussed at me, low and mean, and he reached for his hip pocket."

In every face he saw disbelief.

"Major Jack's an old man," Bailiss faltered. "He heard it wrong. He—"

"Heard it good enough to hang you!"

Bailiss looked desperately around. Carter rose from his knees and the crowd parted. "Sam's dead, ma'am," he said. "I'm sorry." Mrs. Worth's only reply was a low moan. The crowd growled. Captain Carter turned and faced Bailiss, whose eyes looked at him for a brief second, then turned frantically away. And then Bailiss began to speak anxiously—so anxiously that his words came out a babble. His arms were pinioned and he could not point, but he thrust his head toward the forge where the blacksmith was still standing—standing silently.

"Micah," Bailiss stuttered. "Ask Micah!"

*Micah saw it,* he wanted to say—wanted to shout it. *Micah was next to Worth, Micah heard what I really said, he's younger than the Major, his hearing is good, he saw Worth reach . . .*

Captain Carter placed his hand on Bailiss and spoke, but Bailiss did not hear him. The whole night had suddenly fallen silent for him, except for his own voice, saying something (it seemed long ago) to young lawyer Wickerson.

*"It makes no difference what Micah saw! It makes no difference what Micah heard! Micah is property! . . . And property can't testify!"*

They tied Bailiss's hands and heaved him onto his horse.

*"He is fettered fast by the most stern bonds our laws take note*

24

*of . . . can't inherit—can't bequeath . . . can neither sue nor prose-*
*cute—"*

Bailiss turned his head as they started to ride away. He looked at Micah and their eyes met. Micah knew.

*". . . it's basic principle of the law that a slave can never testify in*
*court except against another slave."*

Someone held the reins of old man Bailiss's horse. From now on he moved only as others directed. The lights around the forge receded. Darkness surrounded him. The necessity of his condition was upon him.

# THOU STILL UNRAVISHED BRIDE

ALMOST AS REMARKABLE as Avram Davidson's startling originality was his ability to take the familiar, even the hackneyed, and make it new once again. The story of the disappearing bride dates at least as far back as Guy de Maupassant (nor would it surprise me should some scholar trace this theme still further), and has been revisited by such distinguished authors as Cornell Woolrich.

But in "Thou Still Unravished Bride" (*Ellery Queen's Mystery Magazine*, October 1958), Avram gave the story at least *two* startling twists and made this new version entirely his own.

The editors of *EQMM* said that the story takes place in a "big city in the United States." Grania feels that Avram had Yonkers in mind. While I am willing to defer to her judgement, I must say that to me the story *feels* more like one of those middle-size New Jersey towns: Teaneck, or Elizabeth, or East Orange. When the story was adapted for the *Alfred Hitchcock Presents* television series (March 1965), the producers moved the setting to England; the superb cast included Sally Kellerman, Ron Randall, Michael Pate, and David Carradine. It was directed by David Friedkin. Perhaps these different readings arise from the universality of the story's themes.

"Thou Still Unravished Bride" introduces Police Captain Foley and Detectives Bonn and Steinberg. I don't know of any classic-type, contemporary police procedural stories among Avram's output, but he could use the paraphernalia of convention when it suited his purpose . . . as it did in this search for the so-missing Miss Sally Benner.

*—RAL*

I t used to be said, in some circles, that "a lady" had her name in the newspapers exactly three times: when she was born, when she was married, and when she was buried. It was never altogether true, for "a lady" was entitled to be mentioned when she became a mother, too.

Of course, there are ladies who, even today, are not likely to be seen in the public print at all. This is not because they are hyper-ladylike; it is because they live in large cities and are obscure—and poor. Sally Benner was certainly a lady of this class. And yet she received attention enough in the newspapers because—it appeared—she was not going to be married, and perhaps not buried, either.

Mrs. Benner heard Sally stirring at six in the morning. At seven Sally started to get up, but her mother pushed her back. "There's plenty of time," Mrs. Benner said. "You didn't get to bed till late, and you need your rest. I'll tell you when to get up." So the young woman said, "Yes, Mother."

She was a very obedient daughter. That was what made it all so odd.

At eight Mrs. Benner let her get up. Sally took a shower and came down to breakfast, kissed her father, kissed her mother. The two women clung to one another, shed a few tears. Old Joe Benner looked up from his coffee and waffles and growled a bit. "Women," he said, addressing the canary. "The way they cry about weddings makes you wonder why they bother about 'em at all."

"You shut up," said his wife, without malice. "You were so pale at your own wedding that the minister didn't know whether to marry you or bury you." And she gave a little whimper of laughter.

"I've often wished it was the last," Joe said—and pretended to duck as Mrs. Benner gave him a light smack on the cheek with her hand. "That's for being so fresh," she said. He captured his wife's hand and held onto it and told Sally that he hoped she'd be as happy with her Bob as he and her mother had been with each other.

That was the way the start of the day went. No sparkling dialogue, exactly, no dramatics. The Benners were respectable working-class people. They had four children. The other girl, Jeannie, the eldest, had been married off long enough ago for Mr. B. (he said) to recoup his fortunes for the wedding of his youngest.

There was going to be a reception at the church, then a family supper at Leary's Restaurant, then a big reception (with dancing) at Anderson Hall. After that the newlyweds would take off on their honeymoon at—but of course no one presumably knew where that was to be except Sally and Bob. Mrs. Mantin, Sally's mother-in-law-to-be, had thrown out some pretty strong hints that *Someone* ought to know Where (meaning: *She* ought to).

"Suppose there's an emergency of some sort comes up?" Mrs. Mantin had asked her son more than once, with a snivel standing by in case her son—whom she was now about to Lose Forever—should talk sharply to her.

"Keep the old man out of the bottle and there won't be no emergency," Bob said. But he told her after a while that his older brother Eddie was privy to the secret, and she had to be content with that.

After Sally went in to dress and her mother attacked the dishes and her father (he had his own plumbing business) prepared to just step around and check up on the arrangements, Mrs. Benner remarked, "Well, never let it be said again in my presence that the Lord don't answer prayers. How many years I been praying for Sally to find a nice fellow!"

"He took His time, though, didn't He? Seeing how Bob

lives right down the block here. But," Mr. Benner hastened, as Peg Benner turned on him ready for battle, "I'm not complaining. Long as they're suited, *I'm* suited." But he didn't get off that easily; his wife let him know that it was seldom enough that *he* went to church, and it wasn't *him* who had the heartbreak all these years waiting and watching and worrying, and it was all for the best because early marriages weren't near as likely to last.

After he left, his married daughter Jeannie came over, and so did their two daughters-in-law, and so did Sally's best friend, and also Mrs. Benner's sister Emma. They examined the bridal gown and the guest list and the presents and they hugged Sally and started crying a little, to warm up for the evening. Suddenly it was ten o'clock and they looked up as the church clock started chiming and there was Sally, dressed to go out.

"And where do you think *you're* going?" Aunt Emma demanded, in a mock-ferocious tone. "You better behave—you're not too big to be hit, you know!"

Sally said she was just going out to pick up a few things at the store. She was a tall, quiet girl; pink and slow and sweet. The failure of the male race to snap her up years ago had long been held against it by all distaff branches of the Benner family.

"*What things?*" demanded Aunt Emma. "What could you buy that ain't been bought already?"

Her best friend said she'd go with Sally. Her sister Jeannie said to wait just a minute, she'd drive them down. But Sally, for all her quiet and obedience, had a mind of her own. She said, "No, I'll just go by myself."

"Ah, let her go," said her mother. "Let her get a breath of air and take a little walk. Here's the whole lot of us jabbering away—let the girl alone." She waved at her daughter, who waved back as she walked off down the street.

It was lined with two-story wooden houses; they were set right next to one another. They were all kind of on the small side, but each had a back yard and a front yard, a tree and a little garden and some potted plants, and some had a swing on the porch and stained glass in the front door. It was a comfortable neighborhood, a quiet one, known to even the older generation from childhood. It was safe, it was home.

"Listen here, Peg," Aunt Emma demanded. "I wanna see that seating list. If you've put me and Sam next to Maymie Johnson like you did at *Jeannie's* wedding—"

Mrs. Benner gave the sigh of one who has—or as nearly as makes no difference—married off her last child, a daughter aged thirty, and for whom life holds no further problems; and she said to her sister, "Oh, if you didn't have something to complain about, Emma, I honestly believe you'd *die*. Maymie Johnson, poor thing, hasn't set foot out of her house in *munce*." Emma said, No! and asked what was wrong, and Mrs. Benner said, "Well, she had like what they used to call dropsy, but nowadays the doctors gave it another name. . . ."

---

SALLY ROUNDED THE corner and came face to face with Bob Mantin, on his way back from the barber shop with his brother Eddie. She said, "Oh!" and blushed. Eddie cried, "Hey, you ain't supposed to see your bride the day of the wedding, it's bad luck!" and he playfully put his hand over Bob's eyes.

Bob pushed aside the hand. He and Sally gazed at each other. Neither, it seemed, could think of anything to say. Finally Eddie asked Sally where she was going, and she said, to the store to get a few things. He said, "Oh."

Bob broke silence at last. "Well, I'll, uh, see you tonight, honey."

Sally nodded, and they parted.

---

"—SO I SAID to her, 'Well, it's up to them, Mrs. Mantin,' I said. 'Joe and me, we put it up to them,' I said. 'We let them choose. Do you want a big wedding or would you rather have the money to buy furniture?' we asked them. And they talked it over and the decision was entirely theirs. 'I know it's very nice of you and Bob's father to move all your things off of the second floor and put in a kitchen and all,' I said. 'But if they want to buy furniture, I mean such expensive furniture, that they have to do it on time, why, that's up to them,' I said. 'That's up to *them*.' " Mrs. Benner's sister, her older daughter, her daughters-in-law, and her younger daughter's girl friend, all listened to Mrs. Benner and nodded. Occasionally they punctuated her recital with Believe *Me* or *I'll* Say and Imagine *That!*

And then the church clock began to chime eleven. The expression on Mrs. Benner's face (at once combative and self-excusing) changed immediately. "Why, what's happened to Sally?" she exclaimed.

At first her emotion was one of mere affectionate annoyance. By half-past eleven she had begun to feel vexed. By twelve she was experiencing a definite anxiety. Jeannie got into her car and went to look for her sister. Mrs. Benner got on the telephone and began calling places where it was possible Sally might have stopped off, to get so engrossed in conversation as to forget this was her wedding day. The girl friend (a thin girl with a skin condition, named Agnes, who had—after the first outburst of joyful congratulations—begun to moan that after the wedding Sally wouldn't want her around any more) left to call on a few people who had no telephone. One of the sisters-in-law went around the corner to Mr. Benner's shop, as his line was busy.

"What is he doing there, anyway, so long?" fretted his wife. "He should of been back here long ago—hello, Sadie? Peg. Is Sally there? Oh . . . Well, *was* she there? This morning. I mean. She wasn't? All right, Sadie, I'll see you this—no, no, it's all right, I just thought she might of dropped by. Tonight, then, Sadie. 'Bye."

And so it went. Sally hadn't been to anybody's house, even the Mantins'. Bob's brother Eddie answered the phone. He told of their having met on her way to "the store." When? Oh . . . a little after ten. No, she didn't say which store. "Should I tell Bob? I mean, I will right now if you want me to, but—I mean, she'll prob'ly turn up any minute now, so why get him nervous for nothing? But if you want me to—" Mrs. Benner said, no, he was right, there was no point in getting Bob upset, too.

By half-past one they had canvassed all the stores in the neighborhood. The only one where Sally had been seen was Felber's Pharmacy. She had bought some things, the druggist said, at about ten or fifteen minutes after ten. She had seemed okay. When Mr. Felber said to her, handing over the package (cosmetics, hairpins, chewing gum), "Well, today's the big day, eh, Sally?" she had smiled and said, "I'm so happy, Mr. Felber." He had wished her all the luck in the world.

By now it was half-past two. Suddenly Aunt Emma, who had been saying, "Oh, I wouldn't *worry*, Peg, she's prob'ly just wandering around in a kind of sky-blue-pink daze"—Aunt Emma suddenly burst into tears and said, "Well, I don't care what *anybody* says: *I* think we oughta call the *police!*"

And all the women broke down and began to wail, and so Mr. Benner found them when he returned. And after he got them quieted down, that was what he did. He phoned the police.

---

THE WEDDING WAS called off, but quite a number of guests turned up anyway—some, because they hadn't got the word, others because they thought Sally might turn up in time for the wedding to take place after all. Naturally, they all made their way to the house; and the police decided not to turn them away because—who knows?—one of them might know something that would shed light on the matter.

But no one knew anything.

Late that night Detectives Bonn and Steinberg were talking about it with Captain Foley. "Everybody says the same thing," Bonn observed. "She was a nice, sweet, quiet girl. She was a homebody. She's had no broken engagements, no troublesome ex-boy friends. She never even went steady before. So far as anybody knows, the girl was perfectly happy with the marriage. Except for the fiancé, his brother, and the druggist, though, nobody seems to have seen her once she left the old lady's sight."

Steinberg took up the tale. "The fiancé seems to be okay. Nobody knows anything against him, and even if they did, he's been with some member of his own family all day long—brother, mother, father. *He* says she *couldn't've* run off by herself. Crying like a baby, the guy was. At the same time he doesn't want to admit she maybe met with foul play. So he says it's got to be amnesia."

Bonn was dark and thin, Steinberg was red-haired and stocky. Captain Foley, who was pale and bald, asked, "What about the druggist? And don't give me that line. He sold her vanishing cream."

Bonn said, "Well, as a matter of fact, Captain, he did. Vanishing cream, face powder, deodorant, hairpins—and a pack of chewing gum."

Foley shook his head. "That don't sound like no suicide to me. I know, I know—people have committed suicide on the eves of their weddings before. But a girl who's going to kill herself don't buy deodorants and chewing gum. Even if the river *is* only five blocks away, I'm not buying suicide. No, either she made a voluntary disappearance—in which case she ought to have her butt smacked, not letting the family know—or else it was foul play. And if she was attacked, she's most likely dead by now. They've been through every empty building in the neighborhood?"

"Not only in the neighborhood, but in that whole section of the city," said Steinberg. "How could she be the victim of violence in broad daylight, at ten o'clock in the morning, in a place where everybody knew her?" But Captain Foley said the violence needn't have occurred in the neighborhood. A car pulls up to the curb, a guy offers her a ride, she gets in—what's to notice? he asked. And then the car drives off. She wasn't the kind of girl to accept a ride from a stranger? Then maybe it wasn't a stranger. . . .

THE STORY WAS in the morning papers, and the usual crowd had gathered (or rather, was circulating; the police wouldn't let them stop) near the Benners' house. Mrs. Benner was in her room, having failed to fight off the effects of a sedative the doctor made her take. Joe Benner and Bob, red-eyed, were sitting together in the kitchen drinking black coffee.

"It was amnesia," Bob repeated for the thousandth time. "She wouldn't run off. Not Sally. Her picture's in the papers, somebody's bound to see her."

"Sure," Sally's father repeated, his face reflecting no such optimism. "Sure."

Bonn and Steinberg mingled with the crowd. They looked and listened.

"They ought to call in the FBI."

"Can't do that unless there's evidence of a kidnapping."

"They oughta drag the river."

"Evidence—whadayacall evidence?"

"They must of had a quarrel. Don't tell *me*. They had a lover's tiff, and the boy friend's ashamed to say."

"They oughta drag the river."

"My cousin he run out on his own wedding once. But a guy, that's a different thing. Know what I mean?"

The next day Mrs. Benner went on television and appealed to her daughter to return home, or—if for any reason she was unwilling to do this—at least to communicate with her family. For the afternoon and evening news she was joined by Bob Mantin. He begged Sally's forgiveness if he had offended her in any way. He asked only that she notify them if she was all right. The minister of the Benners' church issued a statement.

But no one heard a word from her. The usual flow of evil communications began, by mail and phone. Sally's body was in an alley on the other side of town. Sally was being held for ransom. A woman had seen her from the window of a bus in another state; she was coming out of a bar.

"Speaking of bars," suggested Bonn, "let's circulate in a few of them. For all I know the girl is what they say she is, but maybe she isn't. If there's any dirt, you hear it over the bar." Steinberg nodded.

Perhaps it is because Americans have guilt feelings about drinking during daylight hours that almost all bars are dark and dim. When the first place fell into focus after the bright street, the detective partners observed that there was a moderate gathering in the bar-cavern. An elderly woman with wild white hair and a cracked-enamel face was crooning into her beer, "I don't care, you go ahead 'n laugh if you wahnoo, but I say, in my opinion, all these young girls disappearing: it's the white slave trade. What I think."

"Naa," said a sharp-looking young man a few stools down. "That's all a thinga the past. No mystery in *my* opinion. Girl changed her mind. Woman's privulidge, is'n it, Mabel? And she's afraida go home."

The man to his right met this suggestion with such an insufferable smirk that the sharp-looking fellow was nettled. "All right, Oscar," he said, "whadda *you* think?"

"I think they oughta drag the river," said Oscar. Bonn looked up. He saw out of the corner of his eye that his partner had caught it, too.

"Weren't you over by the Benners' place yesterday?" Steinberg asked Oscar.

Oscar said, "Yeah, he'd went over to a take a look. But the cops kept moving everybody on."

"*You* saw that, did'n ya? Howdaya like that? 'Move along, keep moving,' " he mimicked. "No wonder they ain't found nothing out yet. Waste all their time like that."

Bonn said, "Yeah, well, I heard you make the observation at that time that they ought to drag the river."

"And I *still* say it."

Mabel ordered another beer. The sharp-looking young man took a look at Bonn, observed Steinberg, affected a startled glance at the clock, and was suddenly gone. Steinberg moved into his place. "Well, now, Oscar, that's a long, long river," he said. "Where do you think they ought to start dragging? Because unless they pick the right spot, they could spend a year and not find anything. Where would you imagine is the best place?"

Oscar studied his face in the mirror. Bonn moved in from the other side. "From the Point, maybe?" Bonn suggested.

Oscar snorted. Bonn, seemingly offended, said, "What's the matter with the Point?"

Steinberg said, "Well, where then? Come on, Oscar. I'm really interested."

"You guys reporters or sumpthing?"

Bonn nodded. Oscar brightened, turned to face him. "No kidding?" he exclaimed. "You writing up this story?"

"I've got my car outside," Bonn said. "Why don't we take a ride down by the river?" Oscar thought that was a fine idea. He and Bonn went out.

Steinberg said to the bartender, "And who might that guy be?"

The bartender shrugged. "One of old man Portlin's nephews. Old lady died maybe a month back, Portlin don't like to live alone so he invites Oscar to move in with him. What does Oscar do? Well, matter of fact, I don't b'lieve he does *anything*. Except play cards, drink beer, and watch the TV. And shoot off his big mouth, like for instance just now."

THERE WERE PARKS along the river, wastes, factories, and docks, some of them abandoned. Bonn and Oscar Portlin walked along one of the docks. "Look how dangerous it is," said Oscar. "Girl could of come down for a walk, tripped, and—zing!—in she goes. See what I mean? Maybe hit her head going over. Then she wouldn't come up or yell for help or nothing. You hadda lotta experience with incidents like that. Whadda *you* think?"

It was a pleasant day, the breeze whipping the water lightly. Sea gulls swooped and skimmed low, creeing to one another. Out in the river a tug passed slowly by with a string of barges. "I think," said Bonn, after a pause, "that it sounds very possible. I think we ought to tell the police." Oscar's reply to this was a short, blunt syllable. "Don't like the police much, huh?" Oscar's lip went *psshh!* "They give you a hard time? A bum rap, maybe?"

That did it. "Boy, you can say that again!" Oscar burst out. His rather nondescript face darkened.

Sympathetically, Bonn asked what the rap was. "Off the record, of course."

Oscar smirked. "Off the record? Statchatory Rape. It was a bum rap. She *said* she was eighteen. How was *I* supposed to know? She was a tramp, anyway. Everybody knew that."

Bonn said, gee, that was too bad. But he still thought they ought to see the cops.

When Oscar still demurred, Bonn took out his badge. Then—in silence—they went back to his car.

---

"SHE WAS ALWAYS such a *good* baby," said Mrs. Benner in a tear-choked voice to a lady reporter. "See, this picture here. When she was only eight months old . . ." She showed the reporter photos and locks of hair and letters and school books—her daughter's life from infancy to womanhood.

What did Sally like to read when she was young? the lady reporter asked.

"Poetry," said Mrs. Benner. "She always liked high-class poetry." She blew her nose. "This little book here, now, she bought this with her own money." Mrs. Benner belonged to a class and generation which did not buy books; that fact alone would have served to grace the small volume even if it were not hallowed by having belonged to her missing daughter. "It's the poems of John Keats. She always used to say to me, 'Oh, Mama, they're so beautiful!' She particularly liked this one—I know the name the minute I see it—Oh. Here. This one." She moistened her lips and prepared to read, following the line with her finger.

*"Thou still unravished bride of quietness . . ."*

Her voice was measured and proud. As the meaning of what she had just read penetrated her awareness, she looked up at the reporter, then over at her daughter's picture on the piano. Then she raised her hands, and screamed, and dropped her face into her hands and cried again and again in her grief and fear and anguish.

"ALL RIGHT," SAID Steinberg, "so it was a bum rap, she was a tramp, she said she was eighteen. So let's forget that one. What else you been sent up on? We'll find out soon enough."

Oscar mumbled that he was never convicted of anything else.

"So you weren't convicted. What were you tried for, besides this one? Nothing? Sure? Okay. Ever charged with anything else? What were you charged with?"

The man looked around the small cubicle. He tried to smirk again, but failed. "Ah, that was a bum rap, too. Wouldn't even press charges."

"What was it?"

Oscar swallowed, took another long look around. Then, not meeting anyone's eyes, he said loudly, "Rape. But she did'n' even press the charge!"

Bonn said, "What makes you so sure the girl's in the river? Did you put her there?"

"No. Naa. I never even seen her."

"You kept saying that the police ought to drag the river," Steinberg hammered away. "Why? You put her in the river, didn't you? She resisted you and you killed her. Isn't that what happened?"

"Or maybe," Bonn suggested persuasively, "it was an accident? You didn't mean to kill her? So maybe you made a pass— what the hell, it could happen to anybody!—only she was a dumb kid, she got scared. . . ."

Oscar nodded slowly, his lips beginning to settle into their habitual smirk.

Bonn went on, "She started to run, tripped on that rotten old dock, fell, and hit her head. Maybe it was like that, huh? It could've happened to anybody. Why don't you tell us, kid? Then we can wrap this up, you cop a plea, get a few months which you can do them standing on your head! Give us the details, that's all we want. We find the body, settle the whole matter. Let's have the story. The stenographer takes it down, we order in some lunch—you hungry, huh?—we get some steak and some French fries—"

The smirk was in full reign now. Oscar shook his head, slowly, admiringly. "I got to hand it to you," he said. "Boy, you must have eyes in the back of your head. Yeah, that's just how it happened. She trips and falls and hits her head. I feel for the pulse—there's no pulse. The dame's dead. So, I mean, I panicked. I figured, who'd believe me? With my record. You know what I mean? So I threw her in the river." He looked up at the two detectives.

Bonn asked, very softly, "Where did you throw her in? Right where you showed us?" Oscar nodded. Bonn's sigh was echoed by Steinberg. For a minute no one spoke. Then Bonn said, "Well, I better go tell them so they can start dragging. And then I guess the family has to be told. Okay, Steinberg, you get the truth out of this monkey—"

"But I told you the truth," Oscar protested. He was bewildered; the tone of the last remark had frightened him. "That's just how it happened, like you said. 'Accident.' "

His face bleak, the officer said, "That story wouldn't convince my six-year-old daughter, and she still believes in Santa Claus. You know what I think of when I meet characters like you? Suppose when *she* grows up—" Abruptly he turned and said, "Take care of him, Steinberg," and walked out.

———◆◆◆◆———

BONN DROVE HIS car three times around the block where the Benners lived. Finally he parked and started up the steps. "They ought to have the police chaplains take care of things like this," he muttered. His finger hesitated on the bell. A noise, a babble of voices, that he had unconsciously assumed was a neighbor's television, was coming from the Benner house.

He tried the door. It was open. He walked in.

The apartment was crowded, everyone shouting and crying and laughing. *Hysteria!* he thought. *It's finally hit them!* Mrs. Benner and a young woman were sobbing and clutching each other, rocking back and forth. Bonn turned to old Joe Benner, who was crying, tears running down his face. "Mr. Benner," he began.

"Oh Lord, the police!" someone said. "We didn't tell the police!"

"Tell us *what?*" Bonn demanded. And then they all started yelling at once and Mrs. Benner released the young woman, who turned around to face him; and he saw that it was her daughter Sally.

Bonn sat down abruptly.

"Oh, I feel so ashamed," Sally said, starting to cry again.

Bob Mantin hugged her and sniffled. "Never mind, honey; never mind, honey."

"Why?" asked the detective. "Why did you do it, Miss Benner? Where were you?"

"Oh, it was such a silly thing—I'm so ashamed. It was just this awful impulse. It started in the drug store when Mr. Felber said, 'Well, today's the big day,' and I said, 'I'm so happy, Mr. Felber.' And then I got outside and it was like I heard another person saying, 'Are you *really* happy? Do you *really* love him?' And I said to myself, 'Gee, I don't know! I don't really know. Maybe I don't love him. Maybe I was only desperate because here I am thirty years old and no one else ever asked me to marry him.' And I thought, 'Oh, wouldn't it be terrible to get married if I wasn't sure?' I was like in a daze. So I got on the bus and rode to the station and I took this train to Chicago. And when I got there, I read in the papers about how nobody knew what had happened to me, so I just took the train back. Oh, I feel so ashamed! I'm sorry if I caused you any trouble."

The detective stared at her. She didn't look very bright, but even so— "You just took the train back," he repeated. "You didn't even bother about a phone call or a telegram! No, Sis, you didn't give us any trouble. You only had every police officer on the force working overtime for four days, that's all! You only—"

But he was interrupted. A fat woman in eyeglasses (Aunt Emma) said, "Well, aren't you the brave one, yelling at this poor little girl! I s'pose you're disappointed she isn't dead, huh?"

Bonn stared at her. "Well, excuse me, lady," he said. "But

41

that's just exactly what I did think, and you know why? Because some psycho down at the jail just confessed killing her and dumping her body in the river!" And Bonn snatched the telephone and dialed headquarters. "Steinberg? Listen, this is all for nothing. Call off dragging the river—"

His partner said, "What do you mean, call it off? Where are you? At the Benners? Better bring one of them down to identify the body."

Bonn said, "*What* body?"

Steinberg said impatiently, "The *girl's* body. They found it first thing. She was right where he dumped her in, poor kid. Her dress was snagged on a spike, that's why the body didn't come up. Bring one of them down to identify her. Better make it the brother-in-law."

Bonn hung up, feeling that he needed time to set Steinberg straight. All he could do was look at Sally Benner and tell himself that her disappearance had not been "all for nothing" after all.

# THE COST OF
# KENT CASTWELL

———◆◆◆◆———

"THE COST OF KENT CASTWELL" was published in 1961, and
won an Alfred Hitchcock Special Award for that year.

This clever story makes one think about the cost of crime
and punishment—not the social cost, or the hidden cost, but
the actual tax dollars coming out of your pocket and mine to
build vast institutions and lock up many people—especially
nonviolent offenders—for long periods of time. Is there a less
costly way to deal with crime and justice? Can we afford the cost
of Kent Castwell?

*—GD*

———◆◆◆◆———

Clem Goodhue met the train with his taxi. If old Mrs. Merriman were aboard he would be sure of at least one passenger. Furthermore, old Mrs. Merriman had somehow gotten
the idea that the minimum fare was a dollar. It was really
seventy-five cents, but Clem had never been able to see a reason for telling her that. However, she was not aboard that morning. Sam Wells was. He was coming back from the city—been
to put in a claim to have his pension increased—but Sam Wells

wouldn't pay five cents to ride any distance under five miles. Clem disregarded him.

After old Sam a thin, brown-haired kid got off the train. Next came a girl, also thin and also brown-haired, who Clem thought was maybe the kid's teenage sister. Actually, it was the kid's mother.

After *that* came Kent Castwell.

Clem had seen him before, early in the summer. Strangers were not numerous in Ashby, particularly strangers who got ugly and caused commotions in bars. So Clem wouldn't forget him in a hurry. Big, husky fellow. Always seemed to be sneering at something. But the girl and the kid hadn't been with him then.

"Taxi?" Clem called.

Castwell ignored him, began to take down luggage from the train. But the young girl holding the kid by the hand turned and said, "Yes—just a minute."

"Where to?" Clem asked, when the luggage was in the taxi.

"The old Peabody place," the girl said. "You know where that is?"

"Yes. But nobody lives there any more."

"Somebody does now. Us." The big man swore as he fiddled with the handle of the right-hand door. It was tied with ropes. "Why don't you fix this thing or get a new one?"

"Costs money," Clem said. Then, "Peabody place? Have to charge you three dollars for that."

"Let's go dammit, let's go!"

After they'd started off, Castwell said, "I'm giving you two bucks. Probably twice what it's worth, anyway."

Half-turning his head, Clem protested. "I told you, mister, it was three."

"And I'm telling you, mister," Castwell mimicked the driver's New England accent, "that I'm giving you two."

Clem argued that the Peabody Place was far out. He mentioned the price of gas, the bad condition of the road, the wear on the tires. The big man yawned. Then he used a word which Clem rarely used himself, and never in the presence of women and children. But this young woman and child didn't seem to notice.

"Stop off at Nickerson's Real Estate Office," Castwell said.

———◆◆◆◆———

LEVI P. NICKERSON, who was also the County Tax Assessor, said, "Mr. Castwell. I assume this is Mrs. Castwell?"

"If that's your assumption, go right ahead," said Kent. And laughed.

It wasn't a pleasant laugh. The woman smiled faintly, so L.P. Nickerson allowed himself an economical chuckle. Then he cleared his throat. City people had odd ideas of what was funny. Meanwhile, though—

"Now, Mr. Castwell. About this place you're renting. I didn't realize—you didn't mention—that you had this little one, here."

Kent said, "What if I didn't mention it? It's my own business. I haven't got all *day*—"

Nickerson pointed out that the Peabody place stood all alone, isolated, with no other house for at least a mile and no other children in the neighborhood. Mrs. Castwell (if, indeed, she *was*) said that this wouldn't matter much, because Kathie would be in school most of the day.

"School. Well, that's it, you see. The school bus, in the first place, will have to go three miles off what's been its regular route, to pick up your little girl. And that means the road will have to be plowed regular—snow gets real deep up in these parts, you know. Up till now, with nobody living in the old Peabody place, we never had to bother with the road. Now, this means," and he began to count off on his fingers, "first, it'll cost Ed Westlake, he drives the school bus, more than he figured on when he bid for the contract; second, it'll cost the County to keep your road open. That's besides the cost of the girl's schooling, which is third."

Kent Castwell said that was tough, wasn't it? "Let's have the keys, Nick," he said.

A flicker of distaste at the familiarity crossed the real estate man's face. "You don't seem to realize that all this extra expense to the County isn't covered by the tax assessment on the Peabody place," he pointed out. "Now, it just so happens that there's a house right on the outskirts of town become available this week. Miss Sarah Beech passed on, and her sister, Miss Lavinia, moved in with their married sister, Mrs. Calvin Adams. 'Twon't cost *you* any more, and it would save *us* considerable."

Castwell, sneering, got up. "What! Me live where some old-maid landlady can be on my neck all the time about messing up her pretty things? Thanks a lot. No thanks." He held out his hand. "The keys, kid. Gimme the keys."

Mr. Nickerson gave him the keys. Afterwards he was to say, and to say often, that he wished he'd thrown them into Lake Amastanquit, instead.

———————

THE INCOME OF the Castwell ménage was not large and consisted of a monthly check and a monthly money order. The check came on the fifteenth, from a city trust company, and was assumed by some to be inherited income. Others argued in favor of its being a remittance paid by Castwell's family to keep him away. The money order was made out to Louise Cane, and signed by an army sergeant in Alaska. The young woman said this was alimony, and that Sergeant Burndall was her former husband. Tom Talley, at the grocery store, had her sign the endorsement twice, as Louise Cane and as Louise Castwell. Tom was a cautious man.

Castwell gave Louise a hard time, there was no doubt about that. If she so much as walked in between the sofa, on which he spent most of his time, and the television, he'd leap up and belt her. More than once both she and the kid had to run out of the house to get away from him. He wouldn't follow, as a rule, because he was barefooted, as a rule, and it was too much trouble to put his shoes on.

Lie on the sofa and drink beer and watch television all afternoon, and hitch into town and drink bar whiskey and watch television all evening—that was Kent Castwell's daily schedule. He got to know who drove along the road regularly, at what time, and in which direction, and he'd be there, waiting. There was more than one who could have dispensed with the pleasure of his company, but he'd get out in the road and wave his arms and not move until the car he got in front of stopped.

What could you do about it? Put him in jail?

Sure you could.

He hadn't been living there a week before he got into a fight at the Ashby Bar.

"Disturbing the peace, using profane and abusive language, and resisting arrest—that will be ten dollars or ten days on each of the charges," said Judge Paltiel Bradford. "And count yourself lucky it's not more. Pay the Clerk."

But Castwell, his ugly leer in no way improved by the dirt and bruises on his face, said, "I'll take jail."

Judge Bradford's long jaw set, then loosened. "Look here, Mr. Castwell, that was just legal language on my part. The jail is closed up. Hasn't been anybody in there since July." It was then November. "It would have to be heated, and illuminated, and the water turned on, and a guard hired. To say nothing of feeding you. Now, I don't see why the County should be put to all that expense on your account. You pay the Clerk thirty dollars. You haven't got it on you, take till tomorrow. Well?"

"I'll take the jail."

"It's most inconvenient—"

"That's too bad, Your Honor."

The judge glared at him. Gamaliel Coolidge, the District Attorney, stood up. "Perhaps the Court would care to suspend sentence," he suggested. "Seeing it is the defendant's first offense."

The Court did care. But the next week Kent was back again, on the same charge. Altogether, the sentence now came to sixty dollars, or sixty days. And again Castwell chose jail.

"I don't generally do this," the judge said, fuming. "But I'll let you pay your fine off in installments. Considering you have a wife and child."

"Uh-uh. I'll take jail."

"You won't like the food!" warned His Honor.

Castwell said he guessed the food would be up to the legal requirements. If it wasn't, he said, the State Board of Prison Inspectors would hear about it.

Some pains were taken to see that the food served Kent during his stay in jail was beyond the legal requirements—if not much beyond. The last time the State Board had inspected the County Jail it had cost the tax-payers two hundred dollars in repairs. It was costing them quite enough to incarcerate Kent Castwell, as it was, although the judge had reduced the cost by ordering the sentences to run concurrently.

All in all, Kent spent over a month in jail that winter, at various times. It seemed to some that whenever his money ran out he let the County support him, and let the woman and child fend for themselves. Tom Talley gave them a little credit at the store. Not much.

——◆·····◆——

ED WESTLAKE, WHEN he bid again for the school bus contract, added the cost of going three miles out of his way to pick up Kathie. The County had no choice but to meet the extra charge. It was considered very thoughtless of Louise to wait till *after* the contract was signed before leaving Castwell and going back to the city with her child. The side road to the Peabody place didn't have to be plowed so often, but it still had to be plowed *some*. That extra cost, just for one man! It was maddening.

It almost seemed—no, it *did* seem—as if Kent Castwell was deliberately setting himself in the face of New England respectability and thrift. The sacred words, "Eat it up, wear it out, make it do, or do without," didn't mean a thing to him. He wasn't just indifferent. He was hostile.

Ashby was not a thriving place. It had no industries. It was not a resort town, being far from sea and mountains alike, with only the shallow, muddy waters of Lake Amastanquit for a pleasure spot. Its thin-soiled farms and meagre woodlots produced a scanty return for the hard labor exacted. The young people continued to leave. Kent Castwell, unfortunately, showed no signs of leaving.

All things considered, it was not surprising that Ashby had no artists' colony. It *was* rather surprising, then, that Clem Goodhue, meeting the train with his taxi, recognized Bob Laurel at once as an artist. When asked afterwards how he had known, Clem looked smug, and said that he had once been to Provincetown.

The conversation, as Clem recalled it afterwards, began with Bob Laurel's asking where he could find a house which offered low rent, peace and quiet, and a place to paint.

"So I recommended Kent Castwell," Clem said. He was talking to Sheriff Erastus Nickerson (Levi P.'s cousin) at the time.

" 'Peace and *quiet'?*" the sheriff repeated. "I know Laurel's a city fellow, and an artist, but, still and all—"

They were seated in the bar of the Ashby House, drinking their weekly small glass of beer. "I looked at it this way, Erastus," the taxi-man said. "Sure, there's empty houses all around that he could rent. Suppose *he*—this artist fellow—suppose *he* picks one off on a side road with nobody else living on it? Suppose *he* comes up with a wife out of somewhere, and suppose *she* has a school-age child?"

"You're right, Clem."

" 'Course I'm right. Bad enough for the County to be put to all that cost for *one* house, let alone two."

"You're right, Clem. But will he stay with Castwell?"

Clem shrugged. "That I can't say. But I did my best."

Laurel stayed with Castwell. He really had no choice. The big man agreed to take him in as lodger and to give over the front room for a studio. And, holding out offers of insulating the house, putting in another window, and who knows what else, Kent Castwell persuaded the unwary artist to pay several months' rent in advance. Needless to say, he drank up the money and did nothing at all in the way of the promised improvements.

Neither District Attorney Gamaliel Coolidge nor Sheriff

Nickerson, nor, for that matter, anyone else, showed Laurel much sympathy. He had grounds for a civil suit, they said; nothing else. It should be a lesson to him not to throw his money around in the future, they said.

So the unhappy artist stayed on at the old Peabody place, buying his own food and cutting his own wood, and painting, painting, painting. And all the time he knew full well that his leering landlord only waited for him to go into town in order to help himself to both food and wood.

Laurel invited Clem to have a glass of beer with him more than once, just to have someone to tell his troubles to. Besides stealing his food and fuel, Kent Castwell, it seemed, played the TV at full blast when Laurel wanted to sleep; if it was too late for TV, he set the radio to roaring. At moments when the artist was intent on delicate brush-work, Castwell would decide to bring in stove-wood and drop it on the floor so that the whole house shook.

"He talks to himself in that loud, rough voice of his," Bob Laurel complained. "He has a filthy mouth. He makes fun of my painting. He—"

"I tell you what it is," Clem said. "Kent Castwell has no consideration for others. That's what it is. Yep."

Bets were taken in town, of a ten-cent cigar per bet, on how long Laurel would stand for it. Levi Nickerson, the County Tax Assessor, thought he'd leave as soon as his rent was up. Clem's opinion was that he'd leave sooner. "Money don't mean that much to city people," he pointed out.

Clem won.

When he came into Nickerson's house, Levi, who was sitting close to the small fire in the kitchen stove, wordlessly handed over the cigar. Clem nodded, put it in his pocket. Mrs. Abby Nickerson sat next to her husband, wearing a man's sweater. It had belonged to her late father, whose heart had failed to survive the first re-election of Franklin D. Roosevelt, and it still had a lot of wear left in it. Abby was unraveling old socks, and winding the wool into a ball. "Waste not, want not," was her motto—as well as that of every other old-time local resident.

On the stove a kettle steamed thinly. Two piles of used envelopes were on the table. They had all been addressed to the Tax Assessor's office of the County, and had been carefully opened so as not to mutilate them. While Clem watched, Levi Nickerson removed one of the envelopes from its place on top of the uncovered kettle. The mucilage on its flaps loosened by steam, it opened out easily to Nickerson's touch. He proceeded to refold it and then reseal it so that the used outside was now inside; then he added it to the other pile.

"Saved the County eleven dollars, this way, last year," he observed. "Shouldn't wonder but what I don't make it twelve, this year, maybe twelve-fifty." Clem gave a small appreciative grunt. "Where is he?" the Tax Assessor asked.

"Laurel? In the Ashby Bar. He's all packed. I told him to stay put. I told them to keep an eye on him, phone me here if he made a move to leave."

He took a sheet of paper out of his pocket and put it on the table. Levi looked at it, but made no move to pick it up. To his wife he said, "I'm expecting Erastus and Gam Coolidge over, Mrs. Nickerson. County business. I expect you can find something to do in the front of the house while we talk."

Mrs. Levi nodded. Even words were not wasted.

A car drove up to the house.

"That's Erastus," said his cousin. "Gam should be along— he *is* along. Might've known he wouldn't waste gasoline; came with Erastus."

The two men came into the kitchen. Mrs. Abby Nickerson arose and departed.

"Hope we can get this over with before nightfall," the sheriff said. "I don't like to drive after dark if I can help it. One of my headlights is getting dim, and they cost so darned much to replace."

Clem cleared his throat. "Well, here 'tis," he said, gesturing to the paper on the table. "Laurel's confession. 'Tell the sheriff and the D.A. that I'm ready to give myself up,' he says. 'I wrote it all down here,' he says. Happened about two o'clock this afternoon, I guess. Straw that broke the camel's back. Kent Castwell, he was acting up as usual. Stomping and swearing out

there at the Peabody place. Words were exchanged. Laurel left
to go out back," Clem said, delicately, not needing to further
comment on the Peabody place's lack of indoor plumbing.
"When he come back, Castwell had taken the biggest brush he
could find and smeared paint over all the pictures Laurel had
been working on. Ruined them completely."

There was a moment's silence. "Castwell had no call to do
that," the sheriff said. "Destroying another man's property.
They tell me some of those artists get as much as a hundred dollars for a painting. . . . What'd he do then? Laurel, I mean."

"Picked up a piece of stovewood and hit him with it. Hit
him hard."

"No doubt about his being dead, I suppose?" the sheriff
asked.

Clem shook his head. "There was no blood or anything on
the wood," he added. "Just another piece of stove wood . . . But
he's dead, all right."

After a moment Levi Nickerson said, "His wife will have to
be notified. No reason why the County should have to pay burial expenses. Hmm. I expect she won't have any money, though.
Best get in touch with those trustees who sent Castwell his
money every month. *They*'ll pay."

Gamaliel Coolidge asked if anyone else knew. Clem said no.
Bob Laurel hadn't told anyone else. He didn't seem to want to
talk.

This time there was a longer silence.

"Do you realize how much Kent Castwell cost this County,
one way or the other?" Nickerson asked.

Clem said he supposed hundreds of dollars. "Hundreds and
*hundreds* of dollars," Nickerson said.

"*And,*" the Tax Assessor went on, "do you know what it will
cost us to try this fellow—for murder in any degree or
manslaughter?"

The District Attorney said it would cost thousands. "Thousands and *thousands* . . . and that's just the trial," he elaborated.
"Suppose he's found guilty and appeals? We'd be obliged to
fight the appeal. More thousands. And suppose he gets a new
trial? We'd have it to pay all over again."

Levi P. Nickerson opened his mouth as though it hurt him to do so. "What it would do to the County tax-rate . . ." he groaned. "Kent Castwell," he said, his voice becoming crisp and definite, "is not worth it. He is just not *worth* it."

Clem took out the ten-cent cigar he'd won, sniffed it. "My opinion," he said, "it would have been much better if this fellow Laurel had just packed up and left. Anybody finding Castwell's body would assume he'd fallen and hit his head. But this confession, now—"

Sheriff Erastus Nickerson said reflectively, "I haven't read any confession. You, Gam? You, Levi? No. What you've told us, Clem, is just hearsay. Can't act on hearsay. Totally contrary to all principles of American law . . . Hmm. Mighty nice sunset." He arose and walked over to the window. His cousin followed him. So did District Attorney Coolidge. While they were looking at the sunset Clem Goodhue, after a single glance at their backs, took the sheet of paper from the kitchen table and thrust it into the kitchen stove. There was a flare of light. It quickly died down. Clem carefully reached his hand into the stove, took out the small corner of the paper remaining, and lit his cigar with it.

The three men turned from the window.

Levi P. Nickerson was first to speak. "Can't ask any of you to stay to supper," he said. "Just a few left-overs, is all we're having. I expect you'll want to be going on your way."

The two other County officials nodded.

The taxi-man said, "I believe I'll stop by the Ashby bar. Might be someone there wanting to catch the evening train. Night, Levi. Don't turn on the yard light for us."

"Wasn't going to," said Levi. "Turning them on and off, that's what burns them out. Night, Clem, Gam, Erastus." He closed the door after them. "Mrs. Nickerson," he called to his wife, "you can come and start supper now. We finished our business."

# THE IKON OF ELIJAH

AVRAM DAVIDSON TRAVELED far and wide, and his experiences provided inspiration for many lifetimes' worth of writing. He was in Israel during the 1948 war of independence and afterward journeyed through Europe to London. His wanderings included Cyprus, where "The Ikon of Elijah" is set. Cyprus is a small island in the eastern Mediterranean where Greeks, Turks, and other ancient cultures live in a constant state of simmering conflict—and there are always opportunists who are ready to make a profit from conflict.

"The Ikon of Elijah" appeared in 1956 and was one of Avram's first published stories. The editor at *Ellery Queen's Mystery Magazine* commented: "Watch Mr. Davidson: he has the gift—the precious gift of words and insight."

*—GD*

On a wet afternoon in early winter a small and mud-splashed automobile entered Nicosia through the Paphos Gate and made its way through Sultan Solyman Square, Queen Irene Street, Ledra Street, and, finally, through a back alley which had neither name nor paving to speak of. Very few people in

Cyprus were feeling cheerful in the cold rain, and the driver of the car—a heavy-jowled man with snowy hair—was certainly not one of them. He cursed the rain and the people thronging the narrow streets of the capital city, Greeks and Turks and Armenians and British, with superb impartiality, but in a low voice. Drawing to a stop about halfway up the alley, he blew two short, hard blasts on his car horn, and struggled out, breathing heavily.

A door opened in the stone wall to the right, and a man wearing the high boots and baggy black pantaloons still favored by Cypriotes of the older generation hurried out. He had few teeth and gray stubble covered his cheeks and chin.

"More floods in the foothills, *Kyrios!*" he said. "People and cattle drowned, houses washed away—"

"I wish the whole damned island would wash away. Be quiet. Park the car. I won't need it again today."

"Yes, Mr. Carpius." The houseman folded himself into the little vehicle and maneuvered it slowly away, while Mr. Carpius entered the back garden of his house and closed the door behind him. The garden was not well kept, the interests of the master of the house presumably lying elsewhere; tiles clinked loosely under his rapid feet, unpruned shrubs grew to the size of small trees, moss was everywhere. The ground-floor windows were barred, as were the second-floor windows. There was no third floor, but if there were and if it had windows, they would certainly have been barred, too; for Mr. Carpius was a cautious man.

He let himself into the house with two keys, and passed through an enormous and shadowy kitchen, where an old woman dressed all in black was feeding chestnut wood into an ancient stove. She mumbled a greeting over her shoulder and Mr. Carpius, sniffing the aroma of lamb pilaf and stuffed grape leaves, permitted himself a little smile of anticipation, and blessed her fulsomely.

After unlocking and locking the doors of three more rooms, and passing through, Mr. Carpius came at length to a small shop fronting on a fairly busy street. His eyes flickered rapidly around it, looking for a moment with pleasure on the window:

M. CARPIUS
ANTIQUES AND OBJETS D'ART

and came to rest on a small, dark Maltese, who at once broke into a smile of obsequious welcome.

"What news, Paul?" Mr. Carpius asked, sitting in a rush-bottomed chair.

"Another terrible flood, sir—"

"Oh, damn that! Besides, I've already heard it from the houseman. What *news?*"

"Yes, sir, I understand, sir. Pray excuse me. Ah. Mr. Harari has bought the bronze camel-bells. All of them. He says he can use many more. Camel-bells are popular now—in Israel, he says. They hang them on the walls. . . . Why, sir?"

"Who cares why? Let them hang them around their necks, if they please, as long as they buy them. What else?"

"The parchment *sanjek*-map."

"Good, good." Mr. Carpius moved slightly a De Lusignan–period dagger which lay near the edge of a table. "What else?"

"And all six of the silver *denarii* of Tiberius, sir."

"*Ex*-cellent! I am very pleased, Paul," Mr. Carpius said benignly. Paul writhed in gratification. A sudden afterthought struck his employer. "At the prices marked?" he snapped.

"Oh, yes, sir!" Paul assured him, in haste. "Minus the usual ten per cent deduction for dealers," he added nervously; but Carpius waved aside the usual ten per cent deduction.

"That's all right."

"And you, sir, Mr. Carpius? Did you have good luck?"

Mr. Carpius's heavy, square face, usually pink, now darkened to a mulberry-red. He scowled, and clenched his teeth.

"No, damn it! I didn't." Paul backed away and began to arrange a trayful of strings of amber beads, the sort which pious Moslems use to recite the nine-and-ninety Attributes of the Almighty, beginning with His Compassion, a quality in which Mr. Carpius was lamentably deficient. "Let them alone!" Carpius barked. Paul dropped one, then fell to his knees.

After swallowing what seemed to be something large and dry, and beating his stubby-fingered hand on his knee several times, Carpius finally composed himself.

"I arrived there with the twenty pounds that Yohannides had agreed on," he said, "although I was naturally prepared to go much higher. The situation appeared made to order: the chapel had been closed for so many years he'd had to break the lock to get in. The place hadn't been entered since the Diocese leased the estate to the Agricultural Department before the First World War. Imagine it!"

Carpius leaned forward, furious, then went on: "An ikon of Saint Mamas riding his lion, Eleventh Century work, and the silver cover, showing details of his life, from the reign of Isaac Comnenus, the last Greek ruler of Cyprus! Fabulous! Priceless! One dare hardly estimate the value. . . . I should have forced him to let me take it away the first time I saw it. A petty clerk in the Agricultural Department, how dared he refuse to trust me? And what happened when I got back there, after driving to the end of the island? *It was gone!*

"I could have throttled him. 'What do you mean, gone? You've sold it, you scoundrel!' I said. But by and by I saw that he was telling me the truth. *The Bishop took it!* 'For safekeeping'! For forty years the Bishops didn't even know it was there, didn't think about it, care about it—now, just when I take an interest, so does the Bishop. . . . What we need Bishops for at all is something I can't see. It is just this sort of thing which causes anti-clericalism."

Carpius sat back, breathing heavily, while Paul hardly breathed at all. Gradually the angry color ebbed from the antique dealer's face.

"Tomorrow," he said calmly, "I shall see what can be done about arranging to have it stolen. If nothing can be done—and, sometimes, alas, such is the case—I shall be obliged," he sighed, "to offer to sell it on commission."

He rose, flicked on the lights, and walked over to the windows. He removed a small painting of a meditative bull in a peeling gilt frame and replaced it with a set of ivory and ebony chessmen, and had just stepped back to consider the effect when two men arrived in front of the shop. Mr. Carpius muttered something short and rapid, then smiled broadly as the two men entered.

"My dear, *dear* Mr. Calloost Chiringirian!" he sang out. *"And Major—Major—?"*

"Parslow," said the Major, a thick-set, ruddy-faced man whose bulging chest was covered with rows of ribbons.

"Hello, Carpius," said Mr. Calloost Chiringirian negligently. He was a tall man in a gray astrakhan hat, and the same pelt showed at the cuffs and collars of his coat. He turned a clever, sallow, eagle-face to the shop owner. "I've brought you a customer. Major Parslow is his Regiment's treasurer and he is looking for a piece of silver suitable for a farewell present to Colonel Eggerton, who is being retired. Something heavy and hideous— the Colonel's taste leans towards the Edwardian, if not to say, the Victorian. Nymphs, with huge bosoms and massive buttocks, supporting an inkwell in the form of St. Paul's Cathedral—*that* sort of rubbish, Carpius. *Your* sort of rubbish."

"Mr. Chiringirian's sense of humor is famous," Carpius said bleakly.

"Quite," said Major Parslow.

Carpius snapped his fingers. "Paul," he said. Paul jumped, began to climb up a small ladder and take things down from shelves. Behind Carpius's face various emotions seethed and bubbled. He hated the suave Armenian, who had got the better of him in many a deal, and he hated him none the less for now deriding him through his merchandise. And yet he envied him with all his heart for daring to speak before Major Parslow with a boldness which he, Carpius, would never dare employ.

"Offer him a fifth of what he asks, my dear Major," the tall man was saying. "And certainly do not pay more than a third."

"I am happy," said Carpius, "to be of service to the Major. We British—"

*"You?"* the Major asked. Paul came up holding, or rather clutching, an object consisting of two silver Scotchmen in kilts,

standing on a slab of marble, and supporting a clock with several dials on its enormous face.

"I was born, of all places, in Hong Kong," Carpius tittered, "and, naturally, my being a British subject by birth is my most precious possession."

"Next, of course, to your virtue," Chiringirian said. "Examine it well, Major. It is gruesome enough to please even Colonel Eggerton, and it tells the time, the day and month, the year, and the phases of the moon. . . . I have just returned today, Carpius, from a visit to Thallassaöpolis, where I paid my respects to the Bishop. A delightful man. He had me to tea."

Carpius glared, quivering.

"He wanted my advice and counsel. Would you believe it, Carpius—an ikon of St. Mamas of the Eleventh Century, and a silver cover dating from the reign of the Emperor Isaac Comnenus . . . Lovely, lovely. He had removed it, on my advice, from a neglected chapel in the hills. We—ah—came to terms. It is now in a bank vault. How lucky I heard of it . . . dear me, Carpius, you are pale." The Armenian smiled coldly.

Carpius stared at him, livid, but he soon composed himself.

Chiringirian gestured. "This sort of rubbish you have here," he said, "would have sold well to the old Turks. They had an unfailing taste for the worst in Western Art—if, indeed, one may call it art. The Imperial Turks, the Imperial Russians, Major, they were faulty and even wicked—but when I recall the blood bath and holocaust which followed their overthrow—" He sighed deeply.

Carpius shrugged. *He* remembered the unrest in Russia and Asia Minor with affection. Business had never been so brisk, before or since. The loot of a thousand churches and monasteries passed through his hands. Perhaps those days might come again. Carpius gazed with sudden disgust around the crowded shop. It *was* rubbish—Chiringirian was right. He thought of jeweled crosses and golden communion spoons. One never knew what might happen, with half the peoples of Asia ready for one another's throats.

He let Major Parslow have, with barely a struggle, and at only four hundred per cent profit, a silver snuff-mull in the shape of a ram's head, with carnelian eyes: when the top was lifted a concealed music box played *Rule, Britannia.*

"Adio, Carpius," Chiringirian said, with a crooked smile. "We shall meet at Philippi—though I, personally, prefer the Riviera. After you, dear Major."

It was then time to close the shop. Paul put up the iron shutters and locked them, and was dismissed to the comfort of home and fireside, represented by his elder sister, a sharp-tongued spinster with a black mustache. Carpius turned his thoughts to old Eleftheria in the kitchen—or, more exactly, to the lamb pilaf and the stuffed grape leaves. Briefly he reflected that his dislike of his tall rival had put him in such emotional confusion that he had committed a great breach of custom: he had neglected to offer coffee—the sweet, thick, black coffee of the Levant, served in tiny cups with beaten-brass lids—without which scarcely any business deal or social call in Cyprus is conducted. But his mind quickly left this embarrassing recollection, and returned to supper and to the bottle of Commandaria which was to accompany it; and at this moment someone knocked on the shop door.

Carpius, about to switch off the lights, hesitated. Then he shrugged. "Who is there?" he called out.

"The monk Theodoros," was the answer.

"And what is it you wish?"

"I have . . . that is . . . Do you buy ikons?"

"One moment." Carpius began to unbolt the door. The chances were that the monk had some wretched modern daub to offer, in the worst style of cigar-box art; but one never knew, and besides, it was always well to make as many contacts with custodians of church property as possible.

Carpius opened the door. The monk Theodoros entered diffidently. His blue cassock was worn and patched, but the long, dark hair gathered in a bun at the back was glossy with health, and the fresh blood of youth was on his cheeks where as yet an untrimmed beard grew sparsely. Looking into the monk's eyes, Carpius received a startling impression: they were not the eyes of social man; they were like the eyes of some untamed bird of the hills or seas—clear and bright and focused afar off.

In the Greek Church, whose priests may marry, the term of "monk" is applied to all celibate priests, including those in parish positions; but Carpius felt certain that Theodoros was not one of these.

"Which is your monastery?" the dealer asked.

"Saints Barnabas and Basil," the monk replied in a low voice.

Carpius knit his forehead in thought. "I don't believe I have ever heard of it," he said, and almost at once a vague shadow of memory arose, only to fade quickly.

"It is a small monastery. It . . . here is the ikon." The young monk began to unwrap it from a piece of oilcloth. Carpius took it. His eyes widened, then narrowed. He lifted it close to his eyes, then to his nose, then examined it again. The style was Early Byzantine, or late Hellenistic, and depicted the Prophet Elijah lifting a hand in benediction while standing in a fiery chariot drawn by fiery horses. The hands and face were that shade of gray which in the Eastern Church indicates sanctity. Across the top, in old Greek minuscules, was written: "*Prophetas Elias* ascending unto Heaven." The legend along the bottom read: "Painted by the hermit Prokopios to the glory of the Thrice-Holy and for the salvation of his soul."

"Why, the paint is hardly dry on it!" Carpius said.

"Yes, it is newly done," the monk admitted, "but surely the paint is quite dry? Yes." He tested it. Carpius ignored the gesture. His mind moved warily, searching for the right words. He must not startle this shy creature, he must move warily. If what he thought was true—

"I trust," he said cautiously, "that proper care is being taken of the original. It is very old. And very holy," he added hastily.

"Oh, very holy," the monk agreed. "In all Cyprus there is no holier ikon. It is never left alone for a single moment—one monk is always engaged in prayer before it."

"Very proper. . . . What is the price of this copy?"

The price was low enough, but Carpius automatically knocked a few piasters off it. He let the young monk depart, but not without asking his blessing. It was not the dealer's intention to make too great an impression this first time, but he wanted the impression to be a favorable one. That night, after supper, and while leisurely smoking a yellow Egyptian cigarette, he questioned old Eleftheria.

The Monastery of Saints Barnabas and Basil? Oh, yes, she had heard of it, but she hardly knew what to say about it. It had not been built as a religious retreat; originally it was only a large farmhouse. She supposed that the monks were devout: they were always keeping fast days and fast periods to commemorate events everyone else had forgotten; they ate no meat, no fish, no eggs, no milk, no cheese; and they also mortified themselves with long vigils spent either on their feet or knees. But the fact was, they were heretics! Yes, they had thrown off the discipline of the Holy, Orthodox, and Autocephalic Church of Cyprus, if such a thing could be believed. And why? Because of the calendar. When the Archbishop had followed the Four Patriarchs in directing that the Gregorian Calendar should be adopted so that the religious date should agree with the civil date, these monks had defied him. What, adopt the innovation of a "Latin" Pope? Abandon the ancient Julian Calendar always used by the Church? Never! So, of course, they had been put under the ban, and had retreated to their Monastery. They were very poor, few in number, and, worst of all, they were said to have opposed the *enosis* movement; they had not desired union with the Motherland because the Greek government had outlawed the Julian Calendar Sect in Greece.

Carpius listened, outwardly—but only outwardly—not very interested. But after Eleftheria had tottered off to bed, he took from the bookshelf a large illustrated volume, Spendlove's *The Iconography of Cyprus*, and rapidly turned the pages. Yes, it was mentioned there. Spendlove, the greatest authority on the religious art of the island, had seen it in 1905. He described the ikon faithfully, but the monks—the ikon had then been located in a monastery near Paphos—had not permitted him to photograph it or any of their other ikons: ". . . being as yet unconvinced [wrote Spendlove] that the camera is not an invention of the devil. They have very little sense of time—all the events of

Christian history seem almost contemporary to them. Constantinople has fallen only yesterday, and Alexandria (I attribute this ikon of Elijah to the Alexandrian School) only the day before. Hence the reason why they do not seem to value this particular ikon more than any other, despite its unquestionable age."

Carpius wondered how it had got from where it was then to where it is now, but the point was not important; probably it had simply been taken by one of the dissident monks—since he was not going to buy it he need not bother about a clear title. Carpius did wonder, though, why its present custodians obviously valued it more than its former owners did. He thought he knew the answer and decided to waste no more time—to leave the next day.

——◆◆◆——

THE MONASTERIES OF CYPRUS, where so many traditions of earlier times still linger, are as open for travelers to lodge in as churches are open for them to pray in. Rooms are always kept for visitors' convenience. There is no charge made for this, or for meals, but it is customary for travelers to drop something in the pyx on leaving.

Carpius, not particularly desiring to adopt the ascetic diet of the monks, brought along an ample supply of provisions—canned delicacies, smoked meats, sweets, a bottle of rum. He did not know how long his stay would last, but business had fallen off so much because of the rains (Mr. Harari and Major Parslow had been the only decent customers in days) that his absence could hardly make things worse. He had not told Paul where he was going. Paul was dependable, but only up to a point: he babbled to his sister, and his sister had the longest tongue in Nicosia. Carpius would not be surprised if the sale of the ikon of St. Mamas had not contributed quite a few pounds toward her dowry—trust Chiringirian for that. Nor did Carpius desire to make himself conspicuous by taking his own car. He regretted that the railroad had been discontinued, but regrets were useless.

Jolting from side to side in the small and crowded bus, the antique dealer regretted the absence of the railroad still more. The day was misty, the curves on the mountain roads were exceedingly sharp, and the driver's habit of taking one hand off the wheel to cross himself while making each turn did nothing at all for Carpius's peace of mind. The only gratification of the ride was that the other passengers were all too busy talking to one another to notice him. There was little logic in his desire to be inconspicuous, but he felt that in order to avoid the bad luck of the St. Mamas incident he ought to go about this matter differently. There was so much more at stake this time. If the ikon of the Eleventh Century were so valuable, then the price of this earlier one almost transcended the power of estimation.

For a while Carpius managed to forget the bus. He thought of a villa in the South of France, a well-furnished flat in Paris, and a certain hotel in Switzerland, where he had once stayed briefly—not a large hotel, but admirably appointed. In this pleasant dream (in which Cyprus, with its rains and mud, its turbulent population, and its few good resorts crowded during the brief season with rich and vulgar Egyptians, played no part) Carpius remained until the bus stopped suddenly and jerkily at a crossroads store. All the passengers got off, chattering loudly—some to stretch their legs, some to use the sanitary facilities, some to get coffee, some because this was their stop. Carpius got off not quite last, his bundle under his arm. He suddenly realized he had been here before. The vague memory which the monk's words, "Saints Barnabas and Basil," had aroused in his mind was based on this single visit.

While en route to the mountains one summer to sell a genuine forged Alma-Tadema to a cotton pasha at one of the hotels, he had stopped here briefly. The day had been especially clear. Some distance down the smaller road a path branched off and led to a large stone house a mile or so away. Idly he had asked what house it was and had been told, "The Monastery of Saints Barnabas and Basil." (The pasha had bought the Alma-Tadema. It was crowded with decorously semi-nude young men and women, the pasha's own taste tending rather toward the latter, though by no means excluding the former.)

While the passengers trooped into the combination shop and café, Carpius faded away into the mist. He had bought his ticket to the end of the line, but he did not think his absence would be noted. Sticking closely to the side of the road, he came presently to the path he remembered. He was not used to carrying bundles, or, indeed, to walking more than very short distances. It was fortunate that the route lay downhill. In less time than he would have thought, the world lay wrapped in silence. No sound from the road reached him. The trees and bushes crowded close to the path, discharging part of their moist burden upon him as he brushed by. Head down, he trudged along, and hardly noticed when he entered the monastic grounds. He came face to face with the house and stopped abruptly.

It was old and heavy and made of stone. The windows were few and narrow. Architecture was not Carpius's forte, but he thought that at least part of the structure dated from the reign of the De Lusignan dynasty, the "Latin" kings of Cyprus, before the days in the island of Genoa and Venice, and poor lost Othello. Later additions to the house had copied the same style. The roofs, which were on several levels, were mostly large slabs of mossy stone (the walls would have to be thick to support their weight), and partly tiles, black with age. Carpius knew that he could not expect plumbing, running water, electric lights, or other features he had found in up-to-date, more prosperous monastic establishments. He viewed the lack of these conveniences with philosophical detachment. He could enjoy them later—in the South of France, in Paris, in the Berne-Oberlandt.

To the monk who received him he explained that he wanted to see the Archimandrite, or Father Superior. Only after presenting Carpius with a tray on which were a glass of water and a small dish of preserves—traditional symbols of hospitality—did the monk depart, his feet echoing on the stone floors until the sound of them died away. After a long time the sound began again. The Father Superior was an old man with a vast gray beard. Carpius stood up and bowed. The old man inclined his head.

"Yesterday, Archimandrite, I bought from your monk, Theodoros, an ikon of the Prophet Elijah."

"Brother Theodoros? He has not yet returned. There was nothing wrong with the ikon? Brother Constantine painted it."

"Oh, no," Carpius hastened to assure him. "It is a very good ikon. But it has troubled me that he asked so little for it."

The Archimandrite said nothing, so Carpius decided to skip the gambit of offering to add to the price, and continued.

"In fact, I scarcely slept the whole night. I kept thinking of the holy Prophet and how he fled into the wilderness to escape the wickedness of the priests of his day, and of the government." The old man looked up. There was a gleam of interest in his eyes. "Surely, in a place where the priests do evil and the government supports them, the people are corrupted as well." The old man nodded slowly. "When I considered the action of the Archbishop in changing the calendar," Carpius went on, "I was troubled. But I said to myself, 'Surely what this venerable and holy man does cannot be wrong?'"

The Archimandrite frowned, and Carpius hastily resumed: "But last night it came to me, as if in a vision, that he *was* wrong. What right had he to tamper with the ancient traditions of the Church, with the Julian Calendar that was good enough for the Fathers of the Church—Origen, Polycarp, Ephraim of Edessa, and the others? And I was obliged to admit—no right at all! The Established Church of Cyprus is now in a state of heresy, of apostasy! Its festivals are all on the wrong days, and hence are no festivals at all. Most reverend Archimandrite, I have come here to seek the true religion from you."

The old man's face was illuminated with joy. He stretched out his hands.

"My son," he said, in a voice tremulous with emotion, "you speak with the tongue of angels. You have not come here in vain."

---

LATE THAT NIGHT, while Carpius was trying to compensate for the frugal supper of the monks with a late snack of deviled ham, biscuits, and brandy, he reviewed the situation. How right, how lucky and right, he had been in his guess as to why the ikon of Elijah was so venerated here. In the prophet of Israel, the short-tempered Tishbite, the dissident clerics of the monastery saw the forerunner of their own order. As Elijah had denounced false worship, so had they. As Elijah had been obliged to flee into the wilderness from the anger of authority, so had they. The only thing Carpius had not calculated was the vision which the Archimandrite had had: With tears running from his eyes, and protestations of his unworthiness, the old man described how, in a dream, Elijah appeared before him, chariot and all, holding out his mantle with the words, "Thou art cold. Cover thyself."

Actually, the monks were retreating from more than a change in calendar. They were retreating from the airplane and the jazz band and the hand grenade, the tumult and weary unrest of the present troubled age—retreating from it and turning back to the long and deep slumber of Byzantium. Off on their side road they need never even smell the fumes of an automobile. And deep in the cellar where the ikon reposed, in a special tiny chapel all to itself, no bigger than a dungeon cell, each monk in turn venerating upon his knees, they found the peace they sought—sweet and silent and heavy.

Carpius took the copy of the ikon from its wrapping and mentally compared it with the original. As to whether or not Spendlove had been correct in calling it Alexandrian, he could not say; but certainly it was Hellenistic. It had nothing of the rigidity or formalized stiffness which characterized later iconography; it was purely natural. Perhaps the Monk Prokopios, before his turning to the religious life, had painted many a late Roman patrician or tribune or matron; perhaps he had even done bacchanalian scenes for the walls of some pagan tavern or villa.

Putting speculation aside, Carpius rose and removed his shoes. Finding the stone floors cold to his feet, he added a second pair of socks. In one pocket went the copy painted by Brother Theodoros. In the other went a small bottle and a thick gauze pad; this might not be necessary: very likely the monk on vigil would be dozing at this hour, in which case it would be the work of a few moments to make the exchange. But just in case . . . And if the bottle and gauze were needed, what then? They were always having visions, these monks; let him make the most of this one when he recovered. In the dim light cast by the tiny lamp, no one could tell the difference between the old ikon and the new.

Silently Carpius went through the corridors and down the steps, flashlight in hand. Here and there a monk snored, or breathed heavily in his sleep. Down, farther down, deep into the cellar, along a cold, cold hall—at last he saw ahead of him the pale glow of the tiny chapel lamp. He switched off his flashlight and crept slowly ahead. In the cell a monk crouched on his knees, elbows resting on the floor, head buried in his hands. His breath came and went, smooth and even.

"Asleep," Carpius thought, inching forward. He reached out his hand for the ikon, and in a moment—so swiftly that his eye retained no image of an intermediate picture—the monk was on his feet, howling wildly and grappling with him.

"Satan!" the monk shrieked. "Father of lies, and of thieves!"

He's an old man, Carpius thought; how does he have the strength to shout like that? And with his free hand Carpius lifted the heavy flashlight and struck.

Then, looking at the monk lying there, another thought came to him—lines from something he had once read, something an Englishman had written: *Who would have thought the old man had so much blood in him?*

Perhaps the struggle had taken longer than it seemed; perhaps he stood there longer than he thought; but when he looked up he saw them at the door. Carpius stood there, stupidly, motionless. He heard their voices, saw them lift the body, felt the cold seeping through his stockinged feet. One syllable began to beat in his head like a pulse. *Why? . . . Why? . . . Why? . . .*

"Why?" asked the Archimandrite. "Why did you kill Brother Damianos?"

"I didn't mean to . . . He saw me reach for the ikon . . . I didn't mean to. I am very sorry, believe me—" His mind was clearing now, swiftly; it darted this way and that, seeking a point of escape. "I only wanted to look at the ikon, but he thought I came to steal it. He took me by the throat and I was frightened."

He dropped to his knees and clutched the Father Superior's hand. "Do not turn me over to the police! It was an accident!"

"An accident," murmured the old man. The monks muttered and crossed themselves. "Moses appointed cities of refuge for the manslayer to flee to," the Archimandrite said. "Sanctuaries for those who had killed accidentally. You say you are sorry . . . I shall choose to believe you." The Archimandrite disengaged his hands.

"Oh, thank you, thank you," Carpius said.

The monks moved backward—moved away from him, away from the blood.

"We shall not call the police," the old man said. "But you must pray—pray for Divine forgiveness. You must repent. Pray without ceasing."

"I shall." Carpius rose.

It *had* been easy, after all. He turned to pick up the ikon, hiding it by standing between it and the monks. The copy lay on the floor beside the original. He slipped the real one in his pocket. A grating noise interrupted him. He turned to see the door swing shut. A key clattered in the lock. He looked through a small opening in the door. It was a thick door, bound with iron. He pressed his face to the opening, not understanding.

"Pray without ceasing," the Archimandrite repeated. "We shall bring you food and water twice a day, and oil for the lamp. We shall feed you as the ravens fed Elijah. As long as you live we shall feed you, and you must pray for forgiveness."

They moved away.

Carpius stared at the walls around him. The roof was made of stone—he had noticed that; in order to support such a heavy roof, the walls must be very strong and thick. . . .

# THE COBBLESTONES

## OF SARATOGA STREET

ALTHOUGH AVRAM DAVIDSON was born in the nearby suburb of Yonkers, and in his seventy years lived in many corners of the globe, from Belize to Beijing and from Jerusalem to Amecameca, I suspect that "Little Old New York" was really his favorite city. He studied its history and geography, as many of his stories show.

"The Cobblestones of Saratoga Street" (*Ellery Queen's Mystery Magazine*, April 1964) takes place in a thinly disguised version of the tiny, tidy, very-very, upper-upper neighborhood surrounding Gramercy Park, located at the lower end of Lexington Avenue in Manhattan. If you've never been there and you get a chance, you should make it your business to amble through this quiet enclave where the New York of Stanford White's era (or earlier) survives amidst the noise, dirt, and bustle of The City That Never Sleeps.

As you stroll beside the park (you won't be able to stroll *in* it unless you have a key!) you may wonder how this odd revenant persists in the modern world. It is not by chance, believe me, but by means of the determined efforts of the neighborhood's well-to-do and tradition-loving residents.

Avram Davidson was a man fascinated with the past; at times he affected deliberately anachronistic mannerisms and

words. I think that his heart is truly in this warm and affectionate story.

—*RAL*

❖•❖•❖

*C*obblestones to Go said the headline. Miss Louisa lifted her
eyebrows, lifted her quizzing-glass (probably the last one in
actual use anywhere in the world), read the article, passed it to
her sister. Miss Augusta read it without eyeglass or change of
countenance, and handed it back.

"They shan't," she said.

They glanced at a faded photograph in a silver frame on the
mantelpiece, then at each other. Miss Louisa placed the newspaper next to the pewter chocolate-pot, tinkled a tiny bell. After
a moment a white-haired colored man entered the room.

"Carruthers," said Miss Augusta, "you may clear away
breakfast."

❖•❖•❖

"WELL, *I* THINK it is outrageous," Betty Linkhorn snapped.

"My dear," her grandfather said mildly, "you can't stop
progress." He sipped his tea.

"Progress my eye! This is the only decently paved street in
the whole town—you know that, don't you, Papa? Just because
it's cobblestone and not concrete—or macadam—or—"

"My dear," said Edward Linkhorn, "*I* remember when several of the streets were still paved with wood. I remember it
quite particularly because, in defiance of my father's orders, I
went barefoot one fine summer's day and got a splinter in my
heel. My mother took it out with a needle and my father
thrashed me . . . Besides, don't you find the cobblestones difficult to manage in high-heeled shoes?"

Betty smiled—not sweetly. "I don't find them difficult at
all. Mrs. Harris does—but, then, if *she'd* been thrashed for going
barefoot . . . Come on, Papa," she said, while her grandfather

maintained a diplomatic silence, "admit it—if Mrs. Harris hadn't sprained her ankle, if her husband wasn't a paving contractor, if his partner wasn't C. B. Smith, the state chairman of the party that's had the city, county, *and* state sewn up for twenty years—"

Mr. Linkhorn spread honey on a small piece of toast. " 'If wishes were horses, beggars would ride—' "

"Well, what's wrong with that?"

" '—and all mankind be consumed with pride.' My dear, I will see what I can do."

———✦✦✦✦———

His Honor was interviewing the press. "Awright, what's next? New terlets in the jail, right? Awright, if them bums and smokies wouldn't of committed no crimes they wouldn't be in no jail, right? Awright, what's next? Cobblestones? *Cob*blestones? Damn it, *again* this business wit the cobblestones! You'd think they were diamonds or sumpthin'. *Awright.* Well, om, look, except for Saratoga Street, the last cobblestones inna city were tore up when I was a *boy*, for Pete's sake. Allathem people there, they're living inna past, yaknowwhatimean? Allathem gas lamps in frunna the houses, huh? Hitching posts and carriage blocks, for Pete sakes! Whadda they think, we're living inna horse-and-buggy age? *Awright*, they got that park with a fence around it, private property, okay. But the streets belong to the City, see? Somebody breaks a leg on wunna them cobblestones, they can *sue* the City, right? So—*cobblestones?* Up they come, anats all there is to it. Awright, what's next?"

His comments appeared in the newspaper (the publisher of which knew what side his Legal Advertisements were buttered on) in highly polished form. *I yield to no one in my respect for tradition and history, but the cobblestoned paving of Saratoga Street is simply too dangerous to be endured. The cobblestones will be replaced by a smooth, efficient surface more in keeping with the needs of the times.*

As the Mayor put it, "What's next?"

Next was a series of protests by the local, county, and state historical societies, all of which protests were buried in two- or three-line items in the back of the newspaper. But (as the publisher put it, "After all, C.B., business is business. And, besides, it won't make any difference in the long run, anyway.") the Saratoga Street Association reprinted them in a full-page advertisement headed *PROTECT OUR HERITAGE,* and public interest began to pick up.

It was stimulated by the interest shown in the metropolitan papers, all of which circulated locally. *BLUEBLOODS MAN THE BARRICADES,* said one. *20TH CENTURY CATCHES UP WITH SARATOGA STREET,* said another. *BELOVED COB-BLESTONES DOOMED, HISTORICAL SARATOGA STREET PREPARES TO SAY FAREWELL,* lamented a third. And so it went.

And it also went like this: *To the Editor, Sir, I wish to point out an error in the letter which claimed that the cobblestones were laid down in 1836. True, the houses in Saratoga Street were mostly built in that year, but like many local streets it was not paved at all until late in the '90s. So the cobblestones are not so old as some people think.*

And it went like this, too:

Mr. Edward Linkhorn: Would you gentlemen care for anything else to drink?

Reporter: Very good whiskey.

Photographer: Very good.

Linkhorn: We are very gratified that a national picture magazine is giving us so much attention.

Reporter: Well, *you* know—human interest story. Not so much soda, Sam.

Photographer: Say, Mr. Linkhorn, can I ask you a question?

Linkhorn: Certainly.

Photographer: Well, I notice that on all the houses—in all the windows, I mean—they got these signs, *Save Saratoga Street Cobblestones.* All but one house. How come? They *against* the stones?

Reporter: Say, that's right, Mr. Linkhorn. How come—?

Linkhorn: Well, gentlemen, that house, number 25, belongs to the Misses de Gray.

Reporter: de Gray? de Gray?

Linkhorn: Their father was General de Gray of Civil War fame. His statue is in de Gray Square. We also have a de Gray Avenue.

Reporter: His *daughters* are still living? What are they like?

Linkhorn: I have never had the privilege of meeting them.

———◆◆◆◆◆———

MISS ADELAIDE TALLMAN's family was every bit as good as any of those who lived on Saratoga Street; the Tallmans had simply never *cared* to live on Saratoga Street, that was all. The Tallman estate had been one of the sights of the city, but nothing remained of it now except the name *Jabez Tallman* on real estate maps used in searching land titles, and the old mansion itself— much modified now, and converted into a funeral parlor. Miss Tallman herself lived in a nursing home. Excitement was rare in her life, and she had no intention of passing up any bit of attention which came her way.

"I knew the de Gray girls well," she told the lady from the news syndicate. This was a big fib; she had never laid eyes on them in her life—but who was to know? She had *heard* enough about them to talk as if she had, and if the de Gray girls didn't like it, let them come and tell her so. Snobby people, the de Grays, always were. What if her father, Mr. Tallman, *had* hired a substitute during the Rebellion? *Hmph.*

"Oh, they were the most beautiful things! Louisa was the older, she was blonde. Augusta's hair was brown. They always had plenty of beaux—not that I didn't have my share of them, too, mind you," she added, looking sharply at the newspaper lady, as if daring her to deny it. "But nobody was ever good enough for *them.* There was one young man, his name was Horace White, and—oh, he was the *hand*somest thing! I danced with him myself," she said complacently, "at the Victory Ball after the Spanish War. He had gone away to be an officer in the Navy, and he was just the most handsome thing in his uniform that you ever saw. But *he* wasn't good enough for them, either. He went away after that—went out west to Chicago or some

75

such place—and no one ever heard from him again. Jimmy Taylor courted Augusta, and William Snow and Rupert Roberts—no, Rupert was sweet on Louisa, yes, but—"

The newspaper lady asked when Miss Tallman had last seen the de Gray sisters.

Oh, said Miss Tallman vaguely, many years ago. *Many* years ago . . . (Had she really danced with anybody at the Victory Ball? Was she still wearing her hair down then? Perhaps she was thinking of the Junior Cotillion. Oh, well, who was to know?)

"About 1905," she said firmly, crossing her fingers under her blanket. "But, you see, nobody was *good* enough for them. And so, by and by, they stopped seeing *anybody*. And that's the way it was."

———◆◈◆———

THAT WAS NOT quite the way it was. They saw Carruthers.

Carruthers left the house on Sunday mornings only—to attend at the A.M.E. Zion Church. Sunday evenings he played the harmonium while Miss Louisa and Miss Augusta sang hymns. All food was delivered and Carruthers received it either at the basement door or the rear door. The Saratoga Street Association took care of the maintenance of the outside of the house, of course; all Carruthers had to do there was sweep the walk and polish the brass.

It must not be thought that because his employers were recluses, Carruthers was one, too; or because they did not choose to communicate with the outside world, he did not choose to do so, either. If, while engaged in his chores, he saw people he knew, he would greet them. He was, in fact, the first person to greet Mrs. Henry Harris when she moved into Saratoga Street.

"Why, hel-lo, Henrietta," he said. "What in the world are *you* doing here?"

Mrs. Harris did not seem to appreciate this attention.

Carruthers read the papers, too.

"What do they want to bother them old stones for?" he asked himself. "They been here long as I can remember."

The question continued to pose itself. One morning he went so far as to tap the cobblestones story in the newspaper with his finger and raise his eyebrows inquiringly.

Miss Augusta answered him. "They won't," she said.

Miss Louisa frowned. "Is all this conversation necessary?"

Carruthers went back downstairs. "That sure relieves my mind," he said to himself.

---

"THE NEWSPAPERS SEEM to be paying more attention to the de Gray sisters than to the cobblestones," Betty Linkhorn said.

"Well," her grandfather observed, "people *are* more important than cobblestones. Still," he went on, *"House of Mystery* seems to be pitching it a little stronger than is necessary. They just want to be left alone, that's all. And I rather incline to doubt that General M. M. de Gray won the Civil War all by himself, as these articles imply."

Betty, reading further, said *Hmmm.* "Papa, except for that poor old Miss Tallman, there doesn't seem to be anyone alive—outside of their butler—who has ever *seen* them, even." She giggled. "Do you suppose that maybe they could be *dead?* For years and *years?* And old Carruthers has them covered with wax and just dusts them every day with a feather mop?"

Mr. Linkhorn said he doubted it.

---

COMPARISONS WITH THE Collier brothers were inevitable, and newsreel and television cameras were standing by in readiness for—well, no one knew just what. And the time for the repaving of Saratoga Street grew steadily nearer. An injunction was obtained; it expired. And then there seemed nothing more that could be done.

"It is claimed that removal would greatly upset and disturb the residents of Saratoga Street, many of whom are said to be elderly," observed the judge, denying an order of further stay; "but it is significant that the two oldest inhabitants, the daughters of General M. M. de Gray, the Hero of Chickasaw Bend, have expressed no objection whatsoever."

Betty wept. "Well, why *haven't* they?" she demanded. "Don't they realize that this is the beginning of the end for Saratoga Street? First the cobblestones, then the flagstone sidewalks, then the hitching posts and carriage blocks—then they'll tear up the common for a parking lot and knock down the three houses at the end to make it a through street. Can't you *ask* them—?"

Her grandfather spread his hands. "They never had a telephone," he said. "And to the best of my knowledge—although I've written—they haven't answered a letter for more than forty years. No, my dear, I'm afraid it's hopeless."

Said His Honor: "Nope, no change in plans. T'morra morning at eight A.M. sharp, the cobblestones go. Awright, what's next?"

At eight that morning a light snow was falling. At eight that morning a crowd had gathered. Saratoga Street was only one block long. At its closed end it was only the width of three houses set in their little gardens; then it widened so as to embrace the small park—"common"—then narrowed again.

The newsreel and television cameras were at work, and several announcers described, into their microphones, the arrival of the Department of Public Works trucks at the corner of Saratoga and Trenton Streets, loaded with workmen and air hammers and pickaxes, at exactly eight o'clock.

At exactly one minute after eight the front door of number 25 Saratoga Street, at the northwest corner, swung open. The interviewers and cameramen were, for a moment, intent on the rather embarrassed crew foreman, and did not at first observe the opening of the door. Then someone shouted, *"Look!"* And then everyone noticed.

First came Carruthers, very erect, carrying a number of items which were at first not identifiable. The crowd parted for him as if he had been Moses, and the crowd, the Red Sea. First he unrolled an old, but still noticeably red, carpet. Next he unfolded and set up two campstools. Then he waited.

Out the door came Miss Louisa de Gray, followed by Miss Augusta. They moved into the now absolutely silent crowd without a word; and without a word they seated themselves on the campstools—Miss Louisa facing south, Miss Augusta facing north.

Carruthers proceeded to unfurl two banners and stood—at parade rest, so to speak—with one in each hand. The snowy wind blew out their folds, revealing them to be a United States flag with 36 stars and the banner of the Army of the Tennessee.

And while at least fifty million people watched raptly at their television sets, Miss Louisa drew her father's saber from its scabbard and placed it across her knees; and Miss Augusta, taking up her father's musket, proceeded to load it with powder and ball and drove the charge down with a ramrod.

After a while the workmen debated what they ought to do. Failing to have specific instructions suitable to the new situation, they built a fire in an ashcan, and stood around it, warming their hands.

———◆◆◆◆———

THE FIRST TELEGRAM came from the Ladies of the G.A.R.; the second, from the United Daughters of the Confederacy. Both, curiously enough, without mutual consultation, threatened a protest march on the City Hall. In short and rapid succession followed indignant messages from the Senior Citizens' Congress, the Sons of Union Veterans, the American Legion, the B'nai Brith, the Ancient Order of Hibernians, the D.A.R., the N.A.A.C.P., the Society of the War of 1812, the V.F.W., the Ancient and Accepted Scottish Rite, and the Blue Star Mothers. After that it became difficult to keep track.

The snow drifted down upon them, but neither lady, nor Carruthers, moved a thirty-second of an inch.

At twenty-seven minutes after nine the Mayor's personal representative arrived on the scene—his ability to speak publicly without a script had long been regarded by the Mayor himself as something akin to sorcery.

"I have here," the personal representative declared loudly, holding up a paper, "a statement from His Honor announcing his intention to summon a special meeting of the Council for the sole purpose of turning Saratoga Street into a private street, title to be vested in the Saratoga Street Association. *Then*—" The crowd cheered, and the personal representative held up his hands for silence. "*Then*, in the event of anyone sustaining injuries because of cobblestones, the City won't be responsible."

There were scattered boos and hisses. The representative smiled broadly, expressed the Municipality's respect for Tradition, and urged the Misses de Gray to get back into their house, please, before they both caught cold.

Neither moved. The Mayor's personal representative had not reached his position of eminence for nothing. He turned to the D.P.W. crew. "Okay, boys—no work for you here. Back to the garage. In fact," he added, "take the day off!"

The crew cheered, the crowd cheered, the trucks rolled away. Miss Louisa sheathed her sword, Miss Augusta unloaded her musket by the simple expedient of firing it into the air, the Mayor's representative ducked (and was immortalized in that act by twenty cameras). The Misses de Gray then stood up. Reporters crowded in, and were ignored as if they had never been born.

Miss Louisa, carrying her sword like an admiral as the two sisters made their way back to the house, observed Betty and her grandfather in the throng. "Your features look familiar," she said. "Do they not, Augusta?"

"Indeed," said Miss Augusta. "I think he must be Willie Linkhorn's little boy—are you?" Mr. Linkhorn, who was seventy, nodded; for the moment he could think of nothing to say. "Then you had better come inside. The girl may come, too. Go home, good people," she said, pausing at the door and addressing the crowd, "and be sure to drink a quantity of hot rum and tea with nutmeg on it."

The door closed on ringing cheers from the populace.

"Carruthers, please mull us all some port," Miss Louisa directed. "I would have advised the same outside, but I am not sure the common people would *care* to drink port. Boy," she said, to the gray-haired Mr. Linkhorn, "would you care to know why we have broken a seclusion of sixty years and engaged in a public demonstration so foreign to our natures?"

He blinked. "Why . . . I suppose it was your attachment to the traditions of Saratoga Street, exemplified by the cobble—"

"Stuff!" said Miss Augusta. "We don't give a hoot for the traditions of Saratoga Street. And as for the cobblestones, those dreadful noisy things, I could wish them all at the bottom of the sea!"

"Then—"

The sisters waved to a faded photograph in a silver frame on the mantelpiece. It showed a young man with a curling mustache, clad in an old-fashioned uniform. "Horace White," they said, in unison.

"He courted us," the elder said. "He never would say which he preferred. I refused Rupert Roberts for him, I gave up Morey Stone. My sister sent Jimmy Taylor away, and William Snow as well. When Horace went off to the Spanish War he gave us that picture. He said he would make his choice when he returned. We waited."

Carruthers returned with the hot wine, and withdrew.

The younger sister took up the tale. "When he returned," she said, "we asked him whom his choice had fallen on. He smiled and said he'd changed his mind. He no longer wished to wed either of us, he said. The street had been prepared for cobblestone paving, the earth was still tolerably soft. We buried him there, ten paces from the gas lamp and fifteen from the water hydrant. And there he lies to this day, underneath those dreadful noisy cobblestones. I could forgive, perhaps, on my deathbed, his insult to myself—but his insult to my dear sister, that I can *never* forgive."

Miss Louisa echoed, "His insult to *me* I could perhaps forgive, on my deathbed, but his insult to my dear sister—that I could *never* forgive."

She poured four glasses of the steaming wine.

"Then—" said Mr. Linkhorn, "you mean—"

"I do. I pinioned him by the arms and my sister Louisa shot him through his black and faithless heart with Father's musket. Father was a heavy sleeper, and never heard a thing."

Betty swallowed. "Gol-*ly.*"

"I trust no word of this will ever reach other ears. The embarrassment would be severe. . . . A scoundrel, yes, was Horace White," said Miss Augusta, "but—and I confess it to you—I fear I love him still."

Miss Louisa said, "And I. And I."

They raised their glasses. "To Horace White!"

Mr. Linkhorn, much as he felt the need, barely touched his drink; but the ladies drained theirs to the stem, all three of them.

# CAPTAIN PASHAROONEY

<br>

"CAPTAIN PASHAROONEY" WAS published in 1967, when Davidson's son, Ethan, was five years old. Avram Davidson loved children, and always spoke to them with grave respect. He regarded
children as small people, deserving the same consideration as
big people. This touching story captures the speech and
thoughts of a child. Although the story has a neat plot twist, it
was written right from Avram's heart.

*—GD*

<br>

The great big Cadillac drew up in front of the school in the
middle of the morning. A uniformed chauffeur was at the
wheel, and a man all dressed up in striped pants and a derby hat
got out from in front and opened the door of the back. Children
in the schoolyard were already gathering and looking through
the wire-mesh fence.

"Hey, look at the Rolds-Royst!"

"It ain't a Rolds-Royst—it's a Caddy."

"How much you wanna bet it's a Rolds-Royst?"

"Ah, you haven't got anything to bet. And besides, a
Caddy's just as good as a Rolds-Royst."

The man who got out of the door held open for him was tall
and broad-shouldered, though rather pale. A thin mustache rode

his short upper lip. He wore a dark overcoat with a velvet collar and had an astrakhan cap cocked slightly to one side of his head.

"Thank you, Jarvis," he said.

"Very good, sir."

The tall man trotted nimbly up the front steps of the school, vanished inside.

"Gee, will ya look at the butler!"

"Ah, hoddaya know he's a butler?"

"Lookit the way he's dressed! Didn'tcha ever see a butler in the movies or television? And besides—and besides— didn'tcha hear him say, 'Very good, sir'? That's what butlers *al- ways* say."

"Gee!"

"Gee!"

---

A JANITOR LEANING on his broom looked up in surprise at the rapid, brisk sound of adult male feet. The man in the astrakhan cap tossed two words at him without slowing down.

"The office?"

"Yes, sir. Right to the left a them stairs as ya come t'the top, sir, right to—"

The tall man nodded curtly, tossed something that glittered. The janitor lunged for it, "—the left a them stairs—" caught it. The tall man went out of sight, though not sound. Another, younger janitor, came up, bent over to look.

"Whah did he give ya, Barney?" Barney held it up. "Hey, a silver dollar! I haven't seen one of those in a *long* time . . . Who was he, d'ya know?"

Barney nodded. "He was a gentleman," he said. "And I haven't seen one of *those* in a long time, either. . . ."

---

THE TALL MAN walked into the office, smiled at the squat ugly woman at the desk, bowing slightly as he did so, sweeping off the astrakhan cap. "I'm Major Thompson," he said.

"Oh," she said. *"Oh.* Yes. Why—"

"I believe the Principal is expecting me."

"Oh, *yes.* Yes, he *is,* Major." She smiled back, blushed. "Mr. Buckley!" she called, trying to push back a recalcitrant chair. "Mr. *Buck—*"

Major Thompson said, "Allow me, ma'am," as he gave the chair a no-nonsense tug . . . and the lady a helpful hand under her elbow. She blushed again.

The frosted glass on the door of the inner office quivered a second before the door itself opened, and a thin little man with pince-nez spectacles, a few strands of greying sandy hair combed optimistically over his bald spot, came bustling out. *"Yes,* Miss Schultz—what—Oh."

Very tall, very broad-shouldered, Major Thompson held out his arm straightly. "Major Thompson," Miss Schultz said, in a loud whisper; and "Dr. Buckley," said the Major, taking and pumping the hand of the Principal. "A pleasure, sir."

The thin little man beamed. Then his face quivered. "It's *Mr.* Buckley," he said. "Of course, I have my M.A., and I always intended . . . but . . ."

Major Thompson smiled. "Confidentially," he said, in a lower tone. "Confidentially, I never even took my A.B." He chuckled. "What do you think of that? Too much celebrating— Harvard-Yale game—my senior year—suspended me." He laughed, a hearty laugh. Mr. Buckley laughed back. "I *could* have returned the year after that, but, well, it so happened that by that time I had other interests. Well, well," he concluded, on a note neatly blending regret and satisfaction. "How's the boy?" he asked, abruptly, seriously.

Mr. Buckley cocked his head and raised his eyebrows. "Jimmy, hmmm, how shall I put it, Major—? Jimmy has, I think, I believe I am justified in saying, mmmm, a very considerable potential—"

Softly, gravely, Major Thompson said, "But he isn't realizing that potential; is that it, sir?"

The Principal was almost distressed. He hoped that Major Thompson would not misunderstand him. He had discussed the matter with Mrs. Morley, very fine woman, Mrs. Morley, he had just hung up the phone on her call telling him to expect the Major the minute he walked in the door, almost. He had discussed the matter with Mrs. Morley once or twice, after all, she was the boy's foster-mother in a way—

Major Thompson said, "Have you met my sister?"

"No. No, I never have. I *wrote* to her—"

"But she never replied. I know. She never replies to *my* letters, either. If my wife were still alive . . ."

There was a silence. Then Mr. Buckley, in some embarrassment, said, "You see, *one* of the difficulties about Jimmy, besides the matter of his schoolwork, is, well, humm, how shall I put it, his, mmm, tendency to exaggerate?"

The Seth Thomas clock on the office wall ticked loudly. "Such as . . . for example?"

Mr. Buckley's thin face reddened ever so slightly. He looked down, he looked around. But the other man was implacable. "Such as what, sir?"

The Principal took a deep breath. "Well . . . he told us he told everybody, his teachers, his friends, Mrs. Morley, *me* . . . that . . ."

Major Thompson smiled. "Told you, perhaps, that his father had a ranch in South America with ten thousand horses . . . eh?"

"*Yes!*" exclaimed Mr. Buckley.

Still smiling, the Major said, "Mr. Buckley, I have *no* idea how many horses there are on my various South American properties." The little man's ear caught the plural, his eyelids fluttered with dawning understanding. "There may be well over that number, all told. We just don't count them, down there. Horses. Now, as to *cattle*—I can give you without any difficulty—" he reached into an inner pocket "—the latest statistics on *them* . . . if you like . . ."

Just as Mr. Buckley was assuring Major Thompson that it wasn't necessary, wasn't in the least necessary, the outer door opened and Miss Schultz came back in, shepherding a small and most reluctant little boy in front of her. The boy observed Mr. Buckley's ear-to-ear smile with some misgivings, and started to turn away. But Miss Schultz blocked the way.

"Do you know who this is, Jimmy?" she asked, pushing him

forward. The tall man bent over, slowly, and slowly put his hand on Jimmy's shoulder. The boy looked up at him in utter astonishment. He opened his mouth, shook his head. Miss Schultz tittered, joyfully, gave him a friendly little shove forward.

"Who is it that lives in South America," asked Mr. Buckley, archly, "and has many, many horses—" The boy blushed scarlet. "—on several ranches; hey? Guess!"

At first Jimmy would not lift his head. Then he did. His expression was almost defiant. He stared up at the tall man in front of him. Then his mouth opened. He pointed.

"I remember you!" he cried. "Now I remember! At my mother's! We had green ice-cream!"

Major Thompson said, gently, "Yes. It was pistachio."

The strange word seemed to throw the boy off balance. "I don't remember that . . . it was green."

Mr. Buckley said, still beaming, "Pistachio *is* green."

Angrily, Jimmy said, "Well, I don't remember! How could I? I was only about four years old!" His voice had risen to a shout. He burst into tears.

Major Thompson went down on one knee and took him in his arms.

"I didn't remember that you were my father," the boy sobbed. "I didn't remember it. . . ."

His father patted him gently, while Miss Schultz blew her big nose and Mr. Buckley took off his glasses and wiped the inner corners of his eyes with thumb and forefinger.

◆•••◆

THE PRINCIPAL OF the school agreed, not only without reluctance, but even eagerly, that Jimmy might take the day off to be with his father. "Why, under the circumstances, certainly, Major, certainly," he said. "I understand. Perfectly. What a shame, though, after all these years away, that you have to go back so soon." He clicked his tongue. "I wish," he said.

"I wish, too. But I have to be in Washington very shortly; and then—well, back to South America. Things aren't too well down there, as I'm sure you know."

Mr. Buckley did know. It was the heritage of Spain, he supposed. All those generations of fighting the Moors had made the Spanish so bellicose. . . . Jimmy came back with his coat and cap and an expression on his face both incredulous and self-important. "I gave the note to Miss Humphreys and she said Of Course. She said she hoped you'd be able to give the class a talk about South America. And *I* said: Maybe." He looked up at his father rather uncertainly.

Miss Schultz gave a little gasp and Mr. Buckley brightened. "That would be a wonderful thing, yes," he exclaimed. Half-turning to his secretary, then turning back to his visitor, he said, "Perhaps at a special assembly—? It would be wonderful for the children and . . ." He stopped. Major Thompson pursed his lips, first cocked his head, dubiously, then shook it, remarking that he doubted there would be time.

At a gesture from him, the boy began rapidly to button the coat. "What—you won't mind my asking, I'm sure—what," Mr. Buckley inquired, "is the educational system like down there?"

The Major said that it left something to be desired. "That's one of the reasons I've never sent for Jimmy." ("Ahah, ah," the principal made quick noises of understanding.) "Another was, that I wanted him to grow up in his own country. He'd always be a foreigner down there, why should he return and feel like one in the United States? Which is how it would be, you know? No, no. Much as I have missed him—and will continue to . . . Someday he'll understand."

The corridors were crowded with children coming back from their recess, and Jimmy—holding his father's hand—walked with head up, proud, darting looks from side to side. Major Thompson subdued his own long strides. Whenever he passed a teacher, he made a very short bow. Even the big boys of the sixth grade were impressed, and looked enviously at Jimmy.

"That's his *father*—"

"—big black car with a *sho*fer and a—"

"He's a *major!*"

Jimmy's head went higher. Automatically, he started to turn towards the small side door which the children generally used;

but Barney, the short-tempered old janitor, saw them coming. Almost at a run, he reached the big front doors, gestured father and son onward, and swung the door open.

"This is my father, Barney."

It was not an introduction but a declaration. Barney's head went back, his mouth opened, closed, opened. "*Now* I know where you get them high spirits from!" he exclaimed. "Some a these people," he said to the major, "are always crabby and complaining, but *I* tell 'm, I tell 'm, 'It's only high spirits.' See, reason I understand, I used to be in the Service myself. *Oh,* yes. With General John 'Black Jack' Perzhing down in Mexico when we was chasing that guy Pancho Villa."

"But he ran too fast for you," Major Thompson said. He and Jimmy went out the door.

Barney's laughter cackled behind them. He trotted to the top of the steps and called after them. "You come down to my room there behind the furnace during lunch time or after school some day, young fella, and I'll show you my pitchers and souvenirs!"

Jimmy grinned with delight. "I will, Barney, I will," he called back. "Tomorrow, maybe."

"Jarvis," the major said, "This is James, Junior."

"Good morning, Master James."

"Gee!"

---

THEY FOUND MRS. Morley, assisted by a neighbor, struggling with her hair. "I was so excited," she said, "that I just had to ask Mrs. Marks, here—she's lived next door to me for years—I had to ask her to come over and make me some coffee and help me get dressed. *My Lord!* After all these years, not so much as a letter; Mrs. Gibson—"

Major Thompson cleared his throat. "I hope you appreciate my sister's situation, Mrs. Morley. Not that I excuse her. Do you know that she didn't even inform me of her marriage?" Both ladies exclaimed at this duplicity. "But she is, after all, my sister. It's her husband I must blame. That gentleman and I are going to have to have a little talk together, if I'm not much mistaken."

Mrs. Marks nodded her head firmly. "Lining his own pockets, I suppose. Keeping the money, not letting her visit the child—"

"It's not the *food*," Mrs. Morley explained. "It's not the *room*, either, nor the *time*. As far as money goes, it's the *clothes*. But that was *my* problem. I managed. But—you know—what about the *boy?* What about Jimmy? How does it look, everybody has a family and he hasn't got a family. His father is in some far-off foreign country, his mother passed away, his aunt never shows her face. How does it look? How do you suppose he *feels?* No wonder—"

"Now, Lindy, don't get so emotional," Mrs. Marks said. "I always said, the father will turn up some day. Didn't I? Blood is thicker than water. You do a good deed, you don't do it for nothing. Was I right?"

And Mrs. Morley had to admit that her friend and neighbor was right. "Your check was *very* generous, Mr.—Major Thompson," she said. "It more than took care of everything."

But he denied this. Stroking his thin moustache with the tip of a finger, he said that the check could hardly make up for the care and affection which Mrs. Morley, bound by no legal or moral ties, had shown to his motherless little boy.

"Well, I did my best. God knows. I did my *best.* . . ." Her voice got all quavery and she began to cry.

———◦•×•◦———

The ice had begun to break up on the river when they crossed it. Jimmy pressed up close to the window of the car and murmured at the sight. Then he snuggled back in his corner of the seat and smiled shyly at his father.

"Have you ever been to New York before?" asked the Major.

"No. That time . . . one time my aunt *said* we were going to New York. But we went to Mrs. Morley's and I thought *that* was

New York. And she said she was coming back but she never came back. I don't care," he added, after a moment.

"Listen, Jim . . . Your aunt has her own troubles. Don't think hard of her. She left you in a good place, didn't she?"

Their conversation touched on many subjects and Mrs. Gibson, Jimmy's aunt, was soon forgotten. The boy wanted to know all about his father's far-away ranch, but interrupted almost immediately to tell how he had gotten into a fight with three bigger boys who didn't believe about the ranch and he, Jimmy, had beaten them up, all three of them, and they ran home crying and played hookey the next day because they were afraid to come to school and see him. "They thought I would make fun of them and beat them up again," he said.

"Hmm."

"And I *would*. I can beat up anybody."

Major Thompson cleared his throat. "I'm sure you can," he said. "But don't bother. It's not necessary. If *you* know the truth, then it doesn't matter what anybody else thinks. You don't even have to talk to them about it. Why bother?"

Jimmy considered this, then renewed his questions about the ranch. He listened to the stories of the endlessly rolling South American prairies and the snow-capped Sierras, cattle and horses as far as the eye could see, the wide rivers filled with crocodiles and the murderous piranha fish that would reduce a cow to its bones in five minutes—and a man, in two—the grass fires and campfires and bandit attacks—

"Bandits! Were you ever . . . were you ever . . . *shot?*"

No. No, his father had been often shot at. But never shot.

"Were you ever captured by the bandits? And tied up and put in a dungeon?"

Major Thompson smiled, faintly amused. "Something like that," he said.

Jimmy swallowed. "Were you all *alone?*" he asked. The car sped on through snowy fields and lonely farmhouses. The Major looked at the boy's concerned face, shook his head. No, not alone. He had a friend with him who had been captured, too. "What was his name?"

"His name? His name was Captain Pasharooney."

Jimmy's concern left him, and he laughed. "That's a funny name." Then, "No, it isn't. I was only joking. Go on. Tell me . . ."

Early in the afternoon they reached New York, where they had a huge lunch in a restaurant with wood-panelled walls and linen napkins and cut-glass pitchers of water. The Major had a cocktail and his son had lemonade with grenadine in it. They both had grilled steak with french-fried potatoes and onion rings and lots of ketchup and a sauce with a funny name. Afterwards, Major Thompson smoked a thin cigar. He told Jimmy he could keep the big book of matches with the fancy picture on it, and, under the table, slipped him a crisp new bill and told him to tip the waiter.

"Come and see us the next time you're in New York," the waiter said.

"All right. . . . This is for you."

"Thank you very much, sir."

They drove up and down the broad and busy avenues until the major directed the car to stop. Then they went into a very big jewelry store where they picked out a tie-pin and a pair of cufflinks for Jimmy, both with small sapphires set in them; and a brooch for Mrs. Morley. It was a crisp, golden afternoon with a hard blue sky overhead. While they waited on the curb for the car, Jimmy turned his head up and said, "You know what I would like?"

"No, Jim. What?"

"A saddle."

Jarvis opened the door and they got inside. "Is there room at Mrs. Morley's to keep a horse? I doubt it."

"I don't care. I just want—"

"—a saddle. Well, someday you'll have a horse. All right."

The salesman in the store which smelled richly of leather had at first some idea of showing them children's saddles, but Major Thompson, without being told, knew that this wasn't what Jimmy had in mind at all. They bought a real saddle, full-size, with stirrups; and a box of things to take care of keeping the leather in good condition.

They went to the top of the Empire State Building, they

went to the Zoo in Central Park, they picked up some boxes of toy soldiers in old-fashioned uniforms, spent an hour in a theater showing news-reels and short films, and then it was supper time. And for supper, they had hot dogs. Lots of them. With mustard, sauerkraut, and relish.

"Instead of going back the same way we came," Major Thompson said, "how would you like it if we took the ferry across?"

Jimmy licked tentatively at a small blotch of mustard. "Do we have to go back?" he asked.

"I'm afraid so. Yes."

"But you'll come back with me?"

The Major nodded. "But then . . . you know . . . I've explained to you that I'll have to turn around and go away again."

The boy considered, then said, "Let's take the ferryboat, then."

The early night wind was cold despite the crimson shadows still streaking the western horizon. The skyline vanished behind them. "I'd like to look at the water some more," Jimmy said. "But I'm cold."

"Let's go inside to the cabin, then." It was stuffy there, but it was warm. Jimmy pressed close to the window, shading with his hand against the obscuring reflection of the cabin lights, looking out onto the dark river intently. The Major lit another panatella. A man opened the cabin door. Their eyes met. The man vanished, reappeared a second later with another.

"Excuse me, son. There's someone I have to talk to." He flicked his cigar, got up and walked forward. The boy barely turned away, then resumed his watch.

"Well, well, well," said the bigger of the two men. "Billy Rooney. Of all people."

"The old Pasha himself," the other one said. He was thin.

"Gentlemen. Surely you aren't going to Jersey for *pleasure—?*"

"Who's the kid?" the big man said, ignoring the question. The thin man surveyed the astrakhan cap, the well-tailored overcoat, pursed his lips in a silent whistle.

"Who's the kid?"

"Nice-looking boy, isn't he? You'll be surprised when I tell you. Remember Jimmy Thompson?" He flicked his cigar again.

This time the whistle was not silent. "Sure, I remember. *That's* his kid? I didn't know Jimmy had a kid."

The Major's smile was brief. "Jimmy doesn't know it most of the time himself. And when he does, he doesn't care. I thought I'd look him up, seeing that I was at liberty and his father wasn't. I suppose you have a lot of tiresome business you want to bother me about?" The two men nodded. "I thought so. . . . Well, let me say goodbye."

Taking out a cigar which was not a panatella, the big man asked, "How's the kid going to get home? It's a cold night, Rooney."

"I am aware of that. He'll get home all right. There are some people here who have a car, they're driving him home." The two men watched as he walked back.

"Jim." He put his hand on the boy's shoulder. "I'm afraid that I won't be able to come back with you after all. Something has come up. But you can sit up front with Jarvis and the chauffeur, so you'll have plenty of company."

The boy said, "I have to go to the bathroom first." When he came out, the Major and the two men were standing together near the door.

"Jim, here are two old friends of mine who'd like to meet you. Captain Schmitz and Lieutenant Brady, of the United States Foreign Service—James, Junior."

"Pleased to meet you," said Captain Schmitz, of the United States Foreign Service.

"Likewise," said Lieutenant Brady, of the same.

They all walked to the big, black limousine, where it was explained to Jarvis and the chauffeur that Jimmy would be the only passenger on the return trip. "We'd better say goodbye now. There won't be time when the ferry stops. . . . I don't know when I'll see you again, Jimmy. Stay out of fights and be good to Mrs. Morley. She's a good woman. I—"

He stopped, as the boy reached up and clutched him around the neck. The embrace was brief. Jimmy started to get in the car, then turned around. "I won't forget you any more," he said.

94

"I was just a little kid the other time. I was only four years old. Where's the saddle? Oh, there it is." He got in, climbing over Jarvis so that he was between him and the chauffeur. He bounced up and down, said, "Hey, we're coming into the dock!" Then he leaned towards the window and called, "Thank you very much. I had a very nice time. I'll be real bigger when you see me again." Then he turned an eager face towards the quickly approaching ferryslip.

Captain Schmitz said, "Um . . . what's with the car and the driver and the flunkey, Rooney?"

"Hired them from an agency. The receipts are in my pocket."

"You sure do things in style, Pasha," Lieutenant Brady observed.

The boat hit the slip, recoiled, bumped it again, slid along the greased pilings. A bell sounded. A chain rattled. "Well, after all, gentlemen, his father and I were old friends, not to mention our being room-mates at a certain well-known establishment. . . ." His manner changed, abruptly. "Can you imagine that S.O.B., though?" he demanded. "He's got a boy like that and he doesn't even give a damn about it."

The gangway fell into position. People streamed off the boat. Captain Schmitz said, "I suppose you wouldn't know anything about a certain peter job down in the loft district, Rooney?"

"Never heard of it," he answered, once again serene.

"It's got your name written all over it. First thing we said, we said, 'Oh-oh. Pasha Rooney must be out again,' didn't we, Conrad?" asked Lieutenant Brady.

---

But his partner had something else on his mind. "The kid looks like someone I know," he said. "And I don't mean that bum, Jimmy Thompson, either."

Pasha Rooney was watching the cars as they drove off the ferry. "He looks like his mother," he said briefly. "Helen Farrel. She's dead."

Schmitz snapped his fingers. *"That's* who. Yeah. Sure. She was a real good-looker. . . ." He turned to the man in the astrakhan cap. "If I'm not mistaken, you used to like her, didn't you, Rooney? Before she took up with Jimmy Thompson?"

The black car drove down onto the ferry-dock. There was a movement at the window, which might have been that of a small boy waving goodbye. The man in the astrakhan cap waved back. "Yes," he said, after a moment. "I used to like her a lot. . . ."

# THE THIRD SACRED WELL

## OF THE TEMPLE

IN THE EARLY 1960s, Davidson and his wife and young son lived in the small village of Amecameca, Mexico, high on the slopes of the great active volcano, Popocatepetl. The rent for eight rooms in the rear garden patio of Sra. Susanna's pleasant hacienda was $16 per month. How do I know? Because I was Avram's wife back then.

Life in Amecameca was a grand adventure. The town was once named "Ameca." Then it collapsed in an earthquake, and after it was rebuilt it was called "Amecameca." The shy Indians, who came from the surrounding hills to sell their wares at the colorful Sunday market, spoke a language that was closer to Aztec than to Spanish. Very few gringos ever found their way to Amecameca.

"The Third Sacred Well of the Temple" was published in 1965. Avram's story notes said, "Here is the first story I've written in Mexico. What prompted it was all those *Islands in the Sun*–type books. This is what happened to both San Miguel and Puerto Vallarta—people wrote them up all over the place, tourists pour in, and the rents raise."

—*GD*

AVRAM DAVIDSON

- - - · ⊷ · - - -

   **W**hose name, Santo Domingo Alburnosi—note the
**. . .** Moorish influence, if you please: The Man with
the Burnoose!—might give some indication as to just why the
*alcalde* himself was not over-anxious to entertain an official of
the Holy Office. No matter that he was the founder of the
settlement and had built two churches entirely with his
own funds and at least partly with his own hands. No matter that
his religious orthodoxy was locally irreproachable. No matter, no
matter. For the expected Inquisitor was bound to be suspicious
of a man only two generations removed from a *Morisco* an-
cestor.

   "Who could know that no trace of Moslem sentiment still
beat in such a heart?—I am, of course, speculating, conjectur-
ing. What is, however, beyond conjecture or speculation, is that
the Inquisitor—armed with documents of special power, before which the Viceroy trembled and the Captain-General
turned pale, and even the good Archbishop himself was utterly
helpless—the Inquisitor, I say, with his mules and his men and
his moneybags and his documents, left the port of Santa Luisa
and headed for our own beloved Monte del Incarnacion.

   "He never arrived. No trace of him was ever found. Robbery—of those moneybags of which I spoke, for there were no
banks, no traveler's checks in those days—robbery. Thus, the
verdict of history. But I might be bold enough to suggest my
own verdict, based on my personal researches over some period of time. This, however, must wait upon another occasion,
for I see by our hostess's charming old ormolu clock that I must
now cease from boring you further. This lovely timepiece, like
our cherished Mountain itself, often seems to keep its own
time—but it is not to be heeded the less for that, is it? Thank
you for your patience."

   The speaker, Richard Stanley, sat down to applause as
hearty as the other three men and two women present could
make it. A slight flush of pleasure came over his round face and

98

was visible even in the part of his silky white hair. He looked around, still a trifle hesitant, then began to beam.

"Richard, you always make everything sound so fascinating!" exclaimed the hostess, Helen, a slender woman of late middle-age, whose face still testified to the sometime presence of beauty. "What did really happen to that old Inquisitor? Won't you even give us a hint?"

"Richard, old boy, you even had *me* interested," a thickset man with a dark red beard commented, eagerly taking a mug from the tray offered by a smiling, silent servant. "Helen, I say! I thought *I* was the champion local drink-mixer, but this tops anything I've ever concocted!"

A man and a woman, both still young, came up and offered their hands to the white-haired Richard Stanley. Their manner was shy and they were slow to speak, but—patiently and wordlessly—he encouraged them.

"We both enjoyed your talk tonight," the young woman said at last. Her husband nodded, smiling.

"I am so glad. You didn't think my prose a little too purple?"

They shook their heads simultaneously, their faces reproaching the very suggestion. But an older man, big of body though slightly stooped, clapped Richard on the back.

"Purple? Of course it was purple. All the greatest prose ever written is purple. Dr. Johnson, Lafcadio Hearn . . ."

Richard's face became even pinker with pleasure. In the momentary silence, the hostess's soft voice was heard, explaining her success with the mixed drink.

". . . the juice of one quarter. That's all. I have never really been sure, you know, Captain, if they are lemons or limes, or perhaps a hybrid. And if you ask, they just smile and shrug, of course. And of course they are right. What does it really matter?"

The Captain nodded, his slightly rufous eyes peering over the rim of the blue pottery mug as he took another swallow. "I'm glad to hear they're ripe again. The seasons seem to pass so quickly. I wish there were more of them, whatever they are. But maybe this way is best, with just enough to go around. . . ." His voice ebbed, contentedly.

At one end of the room a fire of native cedar burned brightly, a faint odor of its scented flesh perfuming the air. The fireplace was raised, and a rounded hood of stone and plaster blended gently into the wall, tinted with a cream-colored wash. Dark old wooden beams stretched across the ceiling, ochreous leather chairs stood here and there, and in the center was a settee which seemed only the sturdier for its two hundred years.

On the tiled floors were Indian rugs, with a few choicer specimens hanging on the wall. One showed Achichihuatzl, the local myth-hero, in victorious combat with the evil serpent Ixtitihuango—both so highly stylized as to be unrecognizable to the unfamiliar.

And facing them was a long and narrow 18th-century picture of St. George slaying the dragon. It was painted on a single piece of wood, presumably by a local artist, for although the *santo* wore the clothes and armor and ceremonial regalia of a Spanish officer, at the temples of his helmet were the bird-wings of Achichihuatzl, and the dragon had more in him than a hint of Ixtitihuango; the feet of the victor were thrust into stirrups of the sort still to be seen in the equipage of every horseman in Monte del Incarnacion and environs—though nowhere else— and the lance piercing the scaly hide of Evil might have been modeled after the ancient one hanging over the fireplace.

Outside a very gentle rain was falling. The scent of clean wet earth, mingled with that of night flowers and blossoming trees, came through the little triangular window under the eaves, and mingled again, not at all unpleasantly, with the pleasant and savory smells from the kitchen—of bits of meat grilling over embers, and over the sauce into which they would presently be dipped: chili powder and fresh-chopped chili, honey, tart fruit, and the rich juice and dripping of the meat itself.

Somewhere, in a nearby *quinta*, a voice accompanied by a guitar and the Indian *tompillo*, began a song—the high ornate notes of antique Hispanic cantilation; then, suddenly, but somehow appropriately, the deeper and steadier melody of the *oaxixen*.

The guests and hostess listened, silent, pleased. They exchanged looks of deep satisfaction. The servants came in with trays of food, the voice and its accompaniment ended, and a night bird sounded its few sweet notes in the lemon grove. . . .

RICHARD STANLEY HAD for some years taught history at a small college, but found that he was increasingly unable to cope with his work. Some men would have found it bearable, even soothing, to go through the same scheduled subjects year after year; to receive the same answers to the same questions and to issue the same grades; to arise at fixed hours and lecture at fixed hours; to parry semester after semester the unripe rudeness of adolescent students; to engage in the unvarying hypocrisy of rigid and petty small-college faculty politics and socializing.

It was not out of any resolved attitude or principle that Richard Stanley found any or all of this unbearable. Something in his metabolism seemed to be at fault—ceased, so to speak, to secrete the necessary hormones or enzymes. Conscientiously he reported this to his president.

"We can't have any nervous breakdowns on our faculty," the man said helpfully. "Tell you what you better do. Better see Dr. Wombaugh, the students' psychologist—he can help you decide what you're going to do next year."

Thus subtly informed that he need expect no renewal of contract (and, in fact, desiring none), Richard Stanley obediently reported to the office of Dr. Wombaugh. There he found a copy of *The Literary Digest* (predicting the election of Alf M. Landon by a landslide), a copy of a soon-to-be-extinct humor magazine full of He/She jokes, and a copy of *The National Geographic*.

He thumbed listlessly through a pictorial account of the nesting habits of the bulbul of the Hindu Kush, an article on Picturesque Patagonia, another on New Insights to Old Zeeland, and came, finally, to a description of the Republic of Hidalgo—Where the Palm and the Pine Meet.

By the time the doctor's assistant got around to looking into the waiting room, Mr. Richard Stanley was no longer there. His savings were not large, but travel was cheap in those days. The port of Santa Luisa, where the banana boat left him, was full of unshaven customs officials with rude manners, demanding cab drivers with worse, and swarms of street gamins with none at all. In short, a larger, tropical, and equally uncopeable version of a small college.

The fact was obvious: the Palm would not do. Would the Pine? Richard Stanley had to see.

It took him three days, in that not very large country, to get by railroad, riverboat, and narrow-gauge railroad to his destination. He did not know, then, that it was his destination. He knew that he seemed suddenly to come alive one afternoon when the toy train jerked to a stop in front of a toy station. He was no longer hot, no longer torpid. Not only was there not a palm in sight, there—not twenty feet away—was the great-grandfather of all pines.

Richard Stanley seized his bag and got off the train. The sign on the tiny depot read *Monte del Incarnacion*. He could see no mountain. Only one person in sight seemed to be moving, an old Indian lady draped all in black. He followed her.

On the other side of the station, in a tiny plaza flanked by a tiny church, sat a large brown man on the driver's seat of a curious vehicle, half stage-coach, half diligence, with sides bulging out and a pair of folding steps behind. The old woman clambered up the steps. Richard Stanley followed. They were presently joined by a man in a linen suit and a large black mustache.

After a while the train whistled and tooted and chuffed away. The four mules stopped trying to bite off their harness and broke into something vaguely resembling a gallop. The road went up steadily. A stone marker said *Monte del I K 10*. Now and then a gap in the trees lining the road showed a glimpse of the countryside. It was quite beautiful—hills and valleys and forests and lakes and farms, with blue mountains in the distance and green ones near at hand.

"I think this is it," Stanley said, half aloud. "I really do."

Late in the afternoon the mules ambled into the town of which the railroad station was merely . . . the railroad station. "Oh!" Richard exclaimed. "Oh, my!"

Above the town the great Mountain of the Incarnation raised its massy peak, wreathed in but not obscured by fleecy clouds. There was only one automobile in sight, but there were a good many horses. The plaza itself was cobbled, but nothing else was paved. The air was clear and fresh and sparkled in the late afternoon sunlight. A group of Indian men came by, clad in a sort of white kilted costume belted by a sash of red and purple which went over one shoulder. They smiled at him, greeted him in a language which was not Spanish. Richard smiled back.

The town which surrounded him was totally Spanish—or, rather, totally Spanish Colonial. With the solitary exception of a two-story red brick building—evidently a convent and school of the time of Pius IX—there did not seem to be a single structure which had been built in the Republican period.

On one side of the plaza was a building which looked like an inn. Suddenly aware of hunger, Richard went in and sat down at a table. He was served, with grave courtesy, a large clean meal; and after a few long and tranquil hours over coffee, rum, and mild cigars, he was shown to a large clean room. The room had a window at each end, one opening onto the courtyard and the other onto the plaza. The Mountain showed at both.

"I do not believe," Richard Stanley said, shortly after he had wakened and washed, "that I will ever leave."

And he never did.

<hr />

THE MORNING AFTER the gathering at which he had read the latest of his papers on the history of the Monte del Incarnacion region, Richard Stanley was at the side of his room which served as a study, examining an old map lent to him by his friend, the Director of the little-visited library and museum, when the proprietor of the inn entered. Stanley anticipated the familiar questions by praising his recently eaten breakfast: the eggs were exquisitely fresh, the coffee deliciously hot, the fruit perfectly ripe—in short, a rich and succulent meal.

Don Nestor beamed, bowed, and eventually came to the point of his visit. There was in the dining room of the inn a stranger, either an Englisher or a Northamericano, who desired to know if there were any other Englishers or Northamericanos in the community. And, as Don Ricardo was the nearest such, he, Don Nestor had—

"Perfectly," said Stanley. "I will go down to see him in a little moment."

"Ah, you are very genteel. I will tell him. With permission . . ."

"Pass, your mercy."

Stanley took a last fond look at the old map, covered with old-fashioned Spanish calligraphy and Indian symbols or pictographs, and at length walked down the winding stairs to the first floor of the inn.

An informal but decently dressed man of early middle-age was drinking coffee. He looked up and waved.

"You must be the English-speaking fellow the owner was telling me about," he said.

"I am Richard Stanley."

"Bob Pepper. Know how I knew? The complexion. I can tell it every time."

Stanley took the proferred seat. "There are many natives of the area," he said, "who are lighter or ruddier than I am. Let us not forget that the Goths were in Spain, the Celts before them, and as for the Iberians—"

"I can tell it every time. Something about the complexion. Isn't this a great little town? Beautiful, unspoiled, a *lovely* climate—"

Stanley nodded, smiling assent to every point.

"—lovely people—*AND*—*do you know what I paid for breakfast?* I. Paid. One. *Dolar.* One, I tell you, count them, one. For eggs, steak, coffee, toast, *damned* good jelly, some kind of fruit, *very* good fruit—for all this I paid one *dolar!* Isn't that in*cred*ible? All that for only twelve and a half cents, U.S.A. Wow!"

Warming to all this appreciation of his chosen residence, Stanley invited the visitor, Bob Pepper, to take a walk around the town. "If you'd like. That is, if you can spare the time."

"I'd like nothing better. If *you* can spare the time."

A wagon ornamented with pictures illustrative of the history and miracles of St. Fransico, and loaded with corn for one of the small mills in the town, passed by, its horse-bells jingling. The driver, removing his hat, greeted Stanley and his companion.

"Oh, I can always spare time," Stanley said, putting his own hat back on. "That's one reason why I love it so here. I don't suppose you've ever heard of Heeber College in New Wurtemburg, Nebraska. . . . I thought not. I could never spare time there. The local citizens here regard time only as something which is sounded by the church bells. The bells only sound noon, midnight, and the ecclesiastical hours. And those of us who hail from more bustling climes have fallen—happily, I will say—into the local ways of thought."

He showed Bob Pepper the bull ring, with its quaint and unusual carved wooden balconies; the now-disused bear pit—bears had been brought, on occasion, from as far away as California, at great cost; the Little Market, which had once been enlarged so that ever since it had been bigger than the Big Market; the baroque church, *La Parroquia*; and the ancient and original church of the founding father.

"What are those people doing on the steps of those little-bitty churches next to that big wild pink one?" demanded Bob Pepper. And he was so struck by the reply that he hastily pulled a notebook and jotted it down. Chapels dedicated to The Seven Wise Virgins of the Parable! Which the Indians identified with The Seven Sweet Sisters of their own mythology! Said their Christian prayers properly inside! Then came outside and made their pagan offerings on the steps! Incense, cornmeal, rose petals, honey, parrot feathers—and whatnot!

*Wow!*

Bob Pepper was completely enamored of all that Richard Stanley had to say about Monte del Incarnacion.

AFTER LUNCH—A lunch so big with a price so small that Pepper could scarcely eat it all from excitement—the newcomer declared that he had some pictures to take. He invited, he even pressed his guide to come along; but Stanley explained that he paid a call every Friday afternoon on his friend, Captain Stone.

"We have a rather funny, odd custom here, Mr. Pepper—Bob. We visit each other only once a week, and we have a once-a-week get-together where we *all* meet. We—by *we* I mean the other English-speaking people here in town—there are only six of us, so it works out quite well, giving all of us periodic days entirely to ourselves and preventing our getting on each other's nerves—and so we remain very happy and contented here, you see."

Bob Pepper nodded and agreed to meet him later on at Captain Stone's *quinta*. "Gee, this is a peach of a place!" he exclaimed deliriously, arranging his photographic equipment, and starting out into the clean picturesque streets. Then a sudden thought occurred to Stanley, and he called the visitor back.

"Are you—would you be interested perhaps . . ." he said haltingly, rather wistfully, ". . . in old Indian ruins?"

"*Would* I!"

Stanley, in a rush of words, explained to him that the remains of the Temple of Achichihuatzl lay higher up the Mountain, deep in the woods. He could hardly say that he had "discovered" them; they had never been lost, only neglected. . . .

". . . and he said he would very much like to see the Temple, so I promised to take him tomorrow," Stanley finished his account of the newcomer to the red-bearded Captain Stone.

The Captain, who had been nodding and grunting and showing other signs of following the narrative, gave a little start as Stanley finished. He raised his rufous eyebrows. "What? Sun over the yard-arm? Let's see what there is to drink, then I want to show you my scale model of the Battle of Jutland. Gin! Gin! Good old *genebra!* And you, old boy, I suppose you'll want yours fancied up with pomegranate juice and other foo-foo waters."

Stanley nodded delightedly.

The Captain hummed a naughty, nautical song to himself, off-key, as he raised bottle and glass. Then he stopped humming. A puzzled, unhappy look came over his face. For a moment he stood still, then he lowered glass and bottle.

"Richard, forgive me. I'm afraid I was not following all you said with the attention which courtesy requires. But did I hear— *did* you say that this fellow's name was *Pepper?*"

"Why, yes. Why?"

The Captain stared at him, and uttered a groan of deepest misery. Then, swiftly, he poured a tumbler half full of straight gin and drank it down in three swallows. Then he looked at his astonished guest and pronounced a religious phrase in a most profane tone.

"This is the end," he said. "This is the end."

---

ONCE AGAIN THE San Jorge looked down on a gathering of the tiny English-speaking colony of Monte del Incarnacion; but this time the atmosphere was quite different. It was late afternoon; there were no songs, no spicy smells from the kitchen, and no one was smiling. Captain Stone had the floor.

"All right, let's get on with it," the Captain said. "We have a bitter draft to swallow, and what the antidote might be—if there is any—I do not know . . ."

He paused, shifted his eyes to a point where the rafters and ceiling met, and went on in a stiff, painful tone of voice. "Briefly, my story is this: I was commander of one of His Majesty's ships and one night—a night which I should like to forget—I put that ship on the Goodwin Sands. Two tugs were required to get her off. Charges were made against me—charges ranging from incompetence to intoxication. I was spared the disgrace of being cashiered. I was allowed to resign. Naturally, I was expected to remove myself as far from England as I could, and so I did."

He did not suppose, the Captain said, that any of them had ever heard at that time of Olang Batto. He himself had located it with some difficulty. Picture to yourselves (he asked his friends) an island only half a day's journey by sea from Singapore, yet on no regular shipping route and known to hardly anyone in that great city. Clean sea breezes, yellow sands, rents so small as to be almost invisible by civilized standards, ample and inexpensive provisions, competent servants at ridiculously low salaries. Malay fishing villages and a trading town which was a small Chinese city in miniature.

"There I lived," the Captain said, "for twenty years in perfect peace, in perfect contentment. My slender income was not only sufficient, I was even able to save a bit. No one had ever heard of my past, or would have cared about it. And then one day—"

He paused. His throat worked. "One day, as I was walking along the boat landing to see if my copies of *The Times* had come in, a young man stepped ashore from a sampan and hailed me in English. I greeted him courteously, invited him to my place, gave him drinks and tiffin, and escorted him all round the island. There being no hotel, I lodged him and fed him for two days until a trading vessel heading for Kuala Lampur chanced to put in and took him aboard. I heard nothing further from him for some months.

"Further intelligence came like a burst of thunder upon my heretofore peaceful existence. The man, it seemed, was not a mere wanderer as I had thought, not even a mere tripper or beachcomber. He was a *journalist*, I learned to my horror. He had written up his experiences in articles variously describing Olang Batto as The Poor Man's Shanghai or The Tahiti of the Malayan Archipelago. This article was syndicated—I believe that is the term—and consequently appeared in newspapers published in Singapore, Sydney, Melbourne, Bombay, Calcutta, Capetown, London, New York, Los Angeles, and every large city in the Republic of Texas."

The results were catastrophic. Within two years Olang Batto had become a port of call. Tourists thronged its once little-frequented lanes. Hotels were built, restaurants, cabarets. The nights, formerly disturbed only by the booming of the surf and the occasional roar of a bull crocodile, now became hideous with jazz music. Rents went up 1000 and even 2000%. Servants betook themselves to high-paid positions in the expensive villas of newcomers. Tailors who had once been happy to make a suit of pongees for five Straits dollars now demanded fifty—and were insolent and dilatory. Farmers ceased to bring their produce to private dwellings and sold them at inflated prices to the multitude of establishments erected to cater to the needs of tourists.

"I was even recognized on the street by a newspaper photographer from *The Daily Mail*," Captain Stone continued bitterly. "I packed my belongings and fled into the night, obtaining passage on a sea junk engaged in the pearl shell and bêche-de-mer trade." A single tear slipped down into his red beard. He plucked a large handkerchief from his sleeve and blew his rufous nose resoundingly. "Need I say," he concluded, "that the man who had brought all this about was the infamous scribbler and penny-a-line spy, Robert Pepper?"

The somber silence which followed was finally broken by the soft voice of the hostess. "I was born and raised in Canada," she said, "and had an uneventful but rather happy life, particularly with my husband and only child. I lost them both—under tragic and well-publicized circumstances which I cannot bear to describe. You must excuse me.

"Most of my income perished with my husband. I had and have no commercial talents. Not caring much what happened to myself, but being under the necessity of sustaining life and finding some occupation or preoccupation, I went to Newfoundland, and settled in the smallest, most remote community I could find which offered some minimum of amenities.

"The place was called Little York Cove. The people fished for cod, hunted seal, raised potatoes. In the nearby rivers were salmon and trout. It was a rather severe life, but it was simple and clean. I became an amateur fisherwoman of some skill, and I learned to make the most of the brief winter days as well as the long, long ones of summer. I could not afford to buy a house, but I rented one for a moderate sum and gradually fixed it up to my liking. I was happy."

Happy, that is, until a brief but searching visit by a man she did not know. His visit resulted in a series of newspaper and magazine articles describing Little York Cove as a Fisherman's Paradise and a New Low-Priced Vacationland. The village was not adequate to house and supply the swarms of people attracted by the articles. So new buildings were erected, but even so there was an inevitable increase in rents.

Helen's landlady informed her, regretfully, that she could no longer let her have the house for its current price as she had been offered five times that amount by a Montreal Sporting Club. And then a story appeared in the St. John's newspaper (which circulated locally), describing the boom at Little York Cove, and incidentally mentioning that among the residents was a woman who had lost her husband and child under tragic and once well-known circumstances, which it proceeded to recapitulate in gory detail.

Helen left the next week.

The name of the writer whose report had worked these far-reaching changes was Robert Pepper.

---

THE STORY TOLD—slowly, painfully—by Don and Donna Smith was not too dissimilar. All their lives they had suffered from extreme shyness. They had met, in fact, at a party to which they had been dragged by different sets of friends, and found each other huddling diffidently in the same corner.

After their marriage they acted on a mutual resolve to avoid crowds, and believing that in a country of a different language their bashfulness would be less obvious and hence less troublesome, they moved to a town in the Cape Verde Islands. They obtained a lease, at a most moderate sum, on one of the many splendid old houses that dated from the period when the town was an outpost of Portuguese empire. Food was equally inexpensive; they kept several horses and they swam a good deal. Also resident in the town were an Indo-Chinese ex-King and a family of exiled Balkan nobles.

The shy Smiths smiled politely at them in passing and were in turn politely smiled at. They did not so much invite Robert Pepper into their *facienda* as suffer his presumptive presence; they were infinitely relieved when he left.

Pepper thoughtfully sent them clippings in several languages which commended the Smiths for their "hospitality" and spared no detail, however slight, about San Jao—Hideway Home of Princes and Potentates and Sun-kissed Shangri-la.

At first it meant little to the Smiths. Bewildered when the flowering tree-lined streets of the old town began to swarm with visitors, they retreated behind their walls, refusing in terror to answer the repeated calls of the bell, or—when the bell was disconnected—trying not to hear the constant pounding on the gate. Isolation proved impossible when they were informed that their sea-near *facienda* had been sold as a nucleus of a posh residential hotel to be erected by a syndicate of Scotch herring smokers in search of a better climate and a more diversified portfolio.

The last to tell his story was a thin dry grayish man who in a thin dry grayish voice briefly related a like account. Arthur Clay had settled in the neighboring Republic of Santa Anna "before"—as he put it—"any of these countries had signed extradition treaties with the United States." Making botany his new interest, he had classified over 1,800 species of plant life unknown to taxonomical science before the questing eye of R. Pepper had lighted on the pleasant piedmont area called Las Mesas, where Mr. Clay was making his home.

Enlarging on the picturesqueness of the native costumes and festivals, the fertility of the soil, the amiability of the population, and the low tax policy of the Santa Anna government, Pepper's widely syndicated column had brought such an influx of new people to Las Mesas that before long Arthur Clay beheld, vanishing before his eyes, the wild plant life he could no longer afford to study and catalogue. . . .

Captain Stone's deep and angry voice jerked them out of their profound silence.

There was, he declared, a sort of fourfold pattern visible in this whole ironic business. *First* (he counted on a huge hairy finger), a group of people who, for one good reason or another, were unable to live in their original homes and societies. *Second,* this same group of people had the useful talent of being able to locate little-known, remote, and pleasant places in which they *were* able to live. *Third,* this filthy swine, Robert Pepper, seemed to possess a similar talent for nosing out such places, but only after they had originally been discovered by the same group.

"*Fourth,* and most damnable," the Captain trumpeted, "is that every 'discovery' he makes is—for everyone except himself—utterly self-defeating! He writes about places which are little-known; directly they become famous! He writes about places which are cheap; immediately they become expensive! He advertises places which are unspoiled, and in a short time they are spoiled into corruption. He is, in short, a cuckoo laying his cockatrice's eggs in nests which he invariably fouls as a reward for hospitality!"

When the echo of his voice had died away Helen said, hopeless beyond despair, "And there is nothing we can do about it."

"Yes, there is! There is!" cried Captain Stone. "We can at least refuse to help the rogue! We can refuse to assist him in spying out the land! We can—"

He fell into a fit of coughing, toward the subsidence of which Richard Stanley was heard to say, "But I promised."

"Promised what?" Arthur Clay asked.

Promised to show Pepper the ruins of the Temple of Achichihuatzl, Richard Stanley said. The next morning.

In vain it was pointed out to him, in tones most urgent, that this was just the sort of thing on which Pepper doted. Ruins! Temples! Picturesque antiquities! He would lap it up, spread the news far and wide.

"What do you think will happen to all of us when he gets done?" Captain Stone demanded, face redder than his beard.

"What do you suppose will happen to *you?* You told me yourself that you live on the $750 a year you get from two non-amortizing mortgages your sister gave you. Could you live on that anywhere else in the world?

"Do you know how much Coca-Cola a thousand tourists a month can drink? They won't be satisfied to drink it *tempo* as the locals do, they'll want it *frio*—and not from an ice bucket, either, because they'll be afraid of bugs in the ice. No, they'll want it chilled in a refrigerator, and nice old Don Nestor will have to buy one—he'll have to buy a big one—he'll have to borrow money to pay for it—and he won't be able to go on lodging you and feeding you at the bargain-basement rates he's charging now.

"What will you do when he raises your rent, Richard? Where will you go? How will you live?"

They all looked at him—the furious Captain Stone, the hopeless Helen, the grim Arthur Clay, and the terrified Smiths.

He had no answer. All he could say, over and over again, was, "But I promised, I promised . . ."

The next morning he met Bob Pepper, already bubbling over with enthusiasm. "How far are these ruined temples of yours, Dicky-boy? Very far?" He was festooned with cameras and such impedimenta.

"Not really. Not if you don't mind a rather long walk."

"*I* don't mind! I'll take lots of shots on the way. Love that scenery! Hey, see that *muchacha*? What a pair of legs! Hey?"

He did not take many shots after all, for the trail along which Stanley led him was a narrow track between thick growths of trees; so Pepper began to ask questions about the ruins and who built them. Stanley warmed to the subject.

The local Indians (he said), though not comparable in the level of their culture and technology with the Aztecs, Mayas, or Incas, had nevertheless achieved a rather high degree of both. They worked well in stone and metal, had a complex and extremely interesting code of manners, and were opposed to shedding human blood.

"Red-skin Quakers!" Pepper exclaimed, pushing aside an obtrusive branch. "You must have made quite a study of all this, huh?"

"Oh, I have. For years. And I've learned things which—it sounds romantic but it's true—no other living white man knows."

Bob Pepper grinned happily. He'd have to get all this down on paper. No other living white man—great! Simply great! Such as what?

They had come now to the ruins themselves. Stone statues green with moss leaned at crazy angles, and native pines grew in the courtyard, thrusting up great slabs of stone and covering others with a thick layer of pine needles.

"Well," said Stanley, shy and proud at the same time, "legend refers to The Three Sacred Wells of the Temple. But only two of them—the locations of only two of them, I mean—are known."

"Sacred Wells! Great!"

One—Stanley pointed it out—was The Well of Good Wishes. The other was The Well of Secret Sorrows. And the third—

"It took me over ten years of consulting old accounts and very old maps, and gaining the confidence of the Indians. But in the end, Mr. Pepper—Bob—I finally found it."

Past the area of stone floors and statues they went, and finally stopped under a huge and stately old pine. With his feet Stanley scraped and scraped. The pine needles fell away in heaps to reveal a circular stone engraved with petroglyphs.

"Don't try to lift it—you couldn't," said Stanley. "But *I* can."

Deftly Stanley pressed down at a certain point. Smoothly the stone lid swung up on its pivot. The well gaped ancient and black. Bob Pepper rubbed his hands and peered down.

"Won't the schoolteachers from Des Moines go for this!" he exclaimed. "What's this one called?—don't tell me—it's The Well of the Virgins, right?"

"No," said Stanley. "It isn't. It's called The Well of the Messenger of Evil Tidings."

And Stanley put his right foot diagonally behind Pepper's ankles at the Achilles tendons, and pushed. The irrepressible journalist went straight down without touching the sides. There was no outcry, and only after a long time, a muffled, echoing splash.

Richard Stanley scuffed back the heaps of pine needles and

brushed them with a handy fallen branch. Once again the stone cover lay hidden from sight.

He turned and began to walk briskly back to town. If he did not dawdle along the way he would be just in time for lunch. Don Nestor's lunches were as enormous as they were delicious. And, perhaps not least of all, they were so very, very cheap.

# THE LORD OF CENTRAL PARK

———◆◆✕◆◆———

"THE LORD OF CENTRAL PARK" was first published in 1970. It is a playful story that shows Davidson's skill as a prose stylist. In an introduction to an earlier Davidson Collection (*The Redward Edward Papers*, Doubleday, 1978), author Michael Kurland explained:

"Some of you who read this collection are venturing into the arcane, erudite world of Avram Davidson for the first time. Probability theory insists that, despite the acres of trees cut down to provide the wood pulp, the scores of dragons killed and bled to provide the ink, some of you will not have read any of the earlier published works of Don Avram. For that few I issue the following warning: breathe steadily through the nose, if possible, proceed slowly and examine the foliage. Do not search for meanings, as they are scattered like empty oyster shells around the Walrus. I hope that helps. The prose itself will be purely and indisputably Davidson.

"Avram Davidson is the master of the parenthetical phrase. Many's the time I've seen a parenthetical phrase groveling before Avram's stern hand, begging for mercy. But he takes them and twists them to his will. In the spirit of the true explorer, Avram is ever pushing and prodding at the bounds of language."

—*GD*

This all took place a while back. . . .
It was a crisp evening in middle April.

Cornelius Goodeycoonce, the river pirate, headed his plunder-laden boat straight at an apparently solid wall of pilings, steering with the calm of a ferryboat captain nearing a slip, and cut his motor.

Up in Central Park, where he was kipped out in a secluded cave, Arthur Marmaduke Roderick Lodowicke William Rufus de Powisse-Plunkert, 11th Marquess of Grue and Groole in the Peerage of England, 22nd Baron Bogle in the Peerage of Scotland, 6th Earl of Ballypatcoogen in the Peerage of Ireland, Viscount Penhokey in the Peerage of the United Kingdom, Laird of Muckle Greet, Master of Snee, and Hereditary Lord High Keeper of the Queen's Bears, heard a familiar beat of wings in the night and held out a slice of bread just in time to catch a medium-rare charcoal-broiled steak.

Not a mile away the Grand Master of the Mafia, Don Alexander Borjia, admired for the ten-thousandth time the eternally enigmatic smile on the lips of the *original* Mona Lisa, which hung, as it had for 50 years, on the wall of the Chamber of the order's Grand Council.

‘A certain foreign visitor, who called himself Tosci, came down the gangway ladder on the side of the yacht which in daylight flew the flag of the landlocked nation whose citizenship he claimed, and got gingerly into the launch which was to bear him to shore.

Daisy Smith, in her trim and tiny bachelor-girl apartment, prepared herself a tuna-fish sandwich without enthusiasm, and reflected how much more—how very much more—she would rather be preparing, say, roast beef and potatoes for a young man, if only she knew a young man she considered worth preparing roast beef and potatoes for.

And across the North River, on the Jersey shore, a thin line of green still hugged the outline of the cliffs; and over that, a thin line of blue. And then the night rolled all the way down, and the lines of light were lost. . . .

The momentum of Cornelius's boat carried it swiftly toward the bulkhead. A crash seemed inevitable. Then Cornelius picked up an oar and prodded one certain timber well below the waterline. Instantly a section of the pilings swung open, just wide enough and just high enough for the boat to pass through; then it swung shut once more.

The boat proceeded onward in gathering darkness as the light from the river dimmed behind it. Gauging the precise instant when the momentum would cease to propel his boat against the mild current of Coenties' Kill—walled in and walled over these 150 years—the man lowered his oar and began to pole. The eyes of an alligator flashed briefly, then submerged.

Presently a light showed itself some distance off, then vanished, reappeared, vanished once more in the windings of the sluggish creek, and finally revealed itself, hissing whitely, as a Coleman lamp. It sat on the stone lip of what had been a fairly well-frequented landing in the days when De Witt Clinton was Mayor and Jacob Hays was High Constable of the City of New York. Cheap as labor had been in those days—and fill even cheaper—it had been less expensive to vault up rather than bury the Kill when the needs of the growing metropolis demanded the space. Experience had proved that to be the case when other Manhattan "kills" or streams, refusing meekly to submit to burial, had flooded cellars and streets.

The Goodeycoonce-the-river-pirate of that time had noted, marked, mapped, and made the private excavations. They were an old, old family, loath to change what was even then an old family trade.

"Well, now, let's see—" said the present-day Cornelius. He tied up. He unloaded his cargo onto a pushcart, placed the lamp in a bracket, and slowly trundled the cart over the stone paving of the narrow street, which had echoed to no other traffic since it lost the light of the sun so long ago.

At the head of the incline the path passed under an archway of later construction. The Goodeycoonce-of-*that*-time, trusting no alien hand, had learned the mason's trade himself, breaking in onto a lovely, dry, smooth tunnel made and abandoned forever by others—the first, last, and short-lived horse-car subway. The wheels of the push-cart fitted perfectly into the tracks, and the grade was level.

Granny Goodeycoonce was reading her old Dutch family Bible in the snug apartment behind her second-hand store. That is, not exactly *reading* it; it had been generations since any member of the family could actually read Dutch; she was looking at the pictures. Her attention was diverted from a copperplate engraving of the she-bear devouring the striplings who had so uncouthly mocked the Prophet Elisha with the words, *Go up, ballhead* ("Serve them right!" she declared. "Bunch of juvenile delinquents!"), by a thumping from below.

She closed the Book and descended to the cellar, where her only grandchild was hauling his plunder up through the trap door.

"Put out that *lamp*, Neely!" she said sharply. "Gasoline costs *money!*"

"Yes, Granny," the river pirate said obediently.

---

DENNY THE DIP stared in stupefaction at the sudden appearance of a steak sandwich's most important ingredient. Then he stared at the winged visitor which had appeared a second after the steak. The winged visitor stared back—or, perhaps "glared" would be the *mot juste*—out of burning yellow eyes. "Cheest!" said Denny the Dip.

There had been a time when, so skillful was the Dip, that he had picked the pocket of a Police Commissioner while the latter was in the very act of greeting a Queen. (He had returned the wallet later, of course, via the mails, out of courtesy, and, of course, minus the money.) But Time with her wingèd Flight, and all that—age and its concomitant infirmities, much aggravated by a devotion to whatever Celtic demigod presides over the demijohn—had long rendered the Dip unfit for such professional gestures.

For some years now he had been the bane of the Mendicant Squad. His method was to approach lone ladies with the pitch that he was a leper, that they were not to come any nearer, but were to drop some money on the sidewalk for him. This, with squeaks of dismay, they usually did. But on one particular evening—this one, in fact—the lone lady he had approached turned out to be a retired medical missionary; she delivered a lecture on the relative merits of chaulmoogra oil and the sulfonamides in the treatment of Hansen's Disease ("—not contagious in New York, and never was—"), expressed her doubts that the Dip suffered from anything worse than, say, ichthyosis; and the paper she gave him was neither Silver Certificate nor Federal Reserve Note, but the address of a dermatologist.

Her speech had lasted a good quarter of an hour, and was followed by some remarks on Justification Through Faith, the whole experience leaving Denny weak and shaken. He had just managed to totter to one of those benches which a benevolent municipality disposes at intervals along Central Park West, and sink down, when he was espied by the 22nd Baron and 11th Marquess aforesaid, Arthur Marmaduke et cetera, who was walking his dog, Guido.

The dog gave Denny a perfunctory sniff, and growled condescendingly. Denny, semisubliminally, identified it as a whippet, reidentified it as an Italian greyhound, looked up suddenly and whimpered, "Lord *Grey* and Gore?"

"Grue and Groole," the dog's master corrected him. "Who the juice are you?" The dog was small and whipcord-thin and marked with many scars. So was his master. The latter was wearing a threadbare but neat bush-jacket, jodhpurs, veldt-schoen, a monocle, and a quasi-caracul cap of the sort which are sold three-for-two-rupees in the Thieves' Bazaar at Peshawar. He scowled, peered through his monocled eye, which was keen and narrow, the other being wide and glassy.

"Cor flog the flaming crows!" he exclaimed. "Dennis! Haven't seen you since I fingered that fat fool for you aboard the *Leviathan* in '26. Or was it '27? Demned parvenu must have had at least a thousand quid in his wallet, which you were supposed to divide with me fifty-fifty, but didn't; eh?"

"Sixty-forty in my favor was the agreement," Denny said feebly. "Have you got the price of a meal or a drink on yez, perchance?"

"Never spend money on food *or* drink," said the Marquess primly. "Against my principles. Come along, come along," he said, prodding the Dip with his swagger stick, "and I'll supply you with scoff *and* wallop, you miserable swine."

The Dip, noting the direction they were taking, expressed his doubt that he could make it through the Park.

"I don't live *through* the Park, I live *in* the Park, mind your fat head, you bloody fool!" They had left the path and were proceeding—master and hound as smoothly as snakes, Denny rather less so—behind trees, up rocks, between bushes, under low-hanging boughs. And so came at last to the cave. "Liberty Hall!" said the Marquess. "After you, you miserable bog-oaf."

A charcoal fire glowed in a tiny stove made from stones, mud, and three automobile license plates. A kettle hummed on it, a teapot sat beside it, in one corner was a bed of evergreen sprigs covered with a rather good Tientsin rug woven in the archaic two blues and a buff, and a Tibetan butter-lamp burned on a ledge. There was something else in the cave, something which lunged at Denny and made fierce noises.

"Cheest!" he cried. "A baby eagle!" And fell back.

"Don't be a damned fool," his host exclaimed pettishly. "It's a fully grown falcon, by name Sauncepeur . . . There, my precious, there, my lovely. A comfit for you." And he drew from one of his pockets what was either a large mouse or a small rat and offered it to the falcon. Sauncepeur swallowed it whole. "Just enough to whet your appetite, not enough to spoil the hunt. Come, my dearie. Come up, sweetheart, come up."

The Marquess had donned a leather gauntlet and unleashed the bird from the perch. Sauncepeur mounted his wrist. Together they withdrew from the cave; the man muttered, the bird muttered back, a wrist was thrown up and out, there was a beating of wings, and the falconer returned alone, stripping off his gauntlet.

"Now for some whiskey. . . . Hot water? Cold? Pity I've no melted yak butter to go with—one grew rather used to it after a bit in Tibet; cow butter is no good—got no body. What, straight? As you please."

Over the drink the 11th Marquess of Grue and Groole filled in his visitor on his career since '25—or was it '26? "Poached rhino in Kenya, but that's all over now, y'know. What with the Blacks, the Arabs, and the East Injians, white man hasn't got a prayer in that show—poaching, I mean. Ran the biggest fantan game in Macao for a while, but with the price opium's got to, hardly worthwhile.

"Signed a contract to go find the Abominable Snowman, demned Sherpas deserted only thirty days out, said the air was too thin for their lungs that high up, if you please, la-de-da—left me short on supplies, so that when I finally found the blasted *yeti*, I had to eat it. No good without curry, you know, no good a-tall.

"Lost m'right eye about that time, or shortly after. Altercation with a Sikh in Amritsar. Got a glass one. Lid won't close, muscle wonky, y'know. Natives in Portuguese East used to call me Bwana-Who-Sleeps-With-One-Eye-Waking; wouldn't come within a hundred yards after I'd kipped down for the night."

He paused to thrust a Sobranie black-and-gold into a malachite cigarette holder and lit it at the fire. With the dull red glow reflected in his monocle and glass eye, smoke suddenly jutting forth from both nostrils, and the (presumably) monkey skull he held in one hand for an ashtray as he sat cross-legged in the cave, the wicked Marquess looked very devilish indeed to the poor Dip, who shivered a bit, and surreptitiously took another peg of whiskey from the flask.

"No, no," the Marquess went on, "to anyone used to concealing himself in Mau Mau, Pathan, and EOKA country, avoiding the attention of the police in Central Park is child's play. Pity about the poor old Fakir of Ipi, but then, his heart always was a bit dicky. Still, they've let Jomo out of jail. As for Colonel Dighenes—"

And it was brought to the attention of the bewildered Dip that the Marquess had fought *for*, and not against, the Mau Maus, Pathans, EOKAs, et cetera. The nearest he came to explaining this was, "Always admired your Simon Girty chap, y'know. Pity people don't scalp any more—here, give over that flask, you pig, before you drink it all. It's a point of honor with me never to steal more than one day's rations at a time.

"Travel light, live off the country. I was one of only two White men in my graduating class at Ah Chu's College of Thieves in Canton. Took my graduate work at Kaffir Ali's, Cairo. I suppose you little know, miserable fellow that you are, that *I was the last man to be tried by a jury of his peers before the House of Lords!* True, I did take the Dowager's Daimler, and, true, I sold it—lost the money at baccarat—never trust an Azerbaijanian at cards, but—"

He stopped, harkened to some sound in the outer darkness. "I fancy I hear my saucy Sauncepeur returning. 'What gat ye for supper, Lord Randall, my son?'—eh? Chops, steak, Cornish rock hen, what? Curious custom you Americans have—charcoal grills on your balconies. Though, mind, I'm not complaining. Bread ready? *Ahhh*, my pretty!"

The steak was just fine, as far as Denny the Dip was concerned, though Lord Grue and Groole complained there was a shade too much garlic. "Mustn't grumble, however—the taste of the Middle Classes is constantly improving."

---

THE MAN WHO called himself Tosci rose to his feet.

"Don Alexander Borgia, I presume?" he inquired.

"No, no, excuse me—Borjia—with a 'j,' " the Grand Master corrected him. The Grand Master was a tall, dark, handsome man, with a head of silvery-grey hair. "The Grand Council is waiting," he said, "to hear your proposition. This way."

"I had no idea," Tosci murmured, impressed, "that the headquarters of the Mafia were quite so—quite so—" He waved his hand, indicating an inability to find the *mot juste* to fit the high-toned luxury and exquisite good taste of the surroundings.

"This is merely the Chamber of the Grand Council," said Don Alexander. "The actual headquarters, which we are required by our charter to maintain, is in back of a candy store on

Mulberry Street. The dead weight of tradition, huh? Well, pretty soon that time will come of which the political philosophers have predicted, when the State shall wither away. 'No more Tradition's chains will bind us,' yeah? After you." Don Alexander took his seat at the head of the table and gestured the visitor to begin.

The latter gazed at the assembled Masters of the Mafia, who gazed back, unwinking, unblinking, but not—he was quite sure—unthinking.

After a moment he began, *"Signori—"* and paused; then, *"Fratelli—"*

—and was interrupted by Grand Master Borjia.

"Excuse me, Hare Tosci, or Monsoon Tosci, or however you say in your country, but evidently you have fallen victim to the false delusion that the Mafia is a strictly Eyetalian organization, which I have no hesitation in saying it is an erroneous concept and a misinformation disseminated by the conscript press, see? I would like it clearly understood that you should get it through your head we of the sorely misconstrued and much maligned Mafia do not discriminate in any way, shape, or form, against race, creed, color, national or'gin, or, uh, what the hell is the other thing which we don't discriminate against in any way, shape, or form, somebody?"

"Previous kahn-dition of soivitood," said a stocky Grand Councilor, wearing a Brooks Brothers suit, two cauliflower ears, and an eyepatch.

"Yeah. Thanks very much, Don Lefty McGonigle."

"Nat a-tall," said Don Lefty, with a slight blush, as he bent his slightly broken nose toward the orchid in his buttonhole— one of three flown up for him daily from Bahía. " 'Rank is but d'guinea stamp, an' a man's a man for all dat,' " he added. "A quotation from d'poet Boyns; no offensive ettnic connotations intended."

"Exactly," said the Grand Master, a slight scowl vanishing from his distinguished features. "Our Grand Council is a veritable microcosm of American opportunity, as witness, besides myself, Don Lefty McGonigle, Don Shazzam X—formerly Rastus Washington—Don Gesú-María Gomez, Don Leverret

Lowell Cabot, Don Swede Swanson, Don Tex Thompson, Don Morris Caplan, and Don Wong Hua-Fu, which he's the Temporary Member of the Permanent Representation of the Honorable Ten Tongs—in a word, a confraternity of American business and professional men devoted to the study of the Confucian classics, the Buddhist Scriptures, and the art of horticulture as it might be exemplified by the peaceful cultivation of the *ah-peen* poppy."

He paused and drew breath. "The Mafia," he continued, "despite the innumerous slanders and aspersions cast upon it by scoffers, cynics, and the ever-present envious, is no more than a group of humble citizens of the world, determined to provide, besides certain commercial services, a forum wherein or whereby to arbitrate those differences which the lack of communication—alas, all too prevalent in our society—might otherwise terminate untowardly; as to its supposed origins in romantic Sicily, who, indeed, can say? What's on your mind, Tosci?" he concluded abruptly.

Mr. (or Herr, or Monsieur, or whatever way they say in his country) Tosci blinked. Then he smiled a small noncommittal smile, appropriate to the citizen of a neutral nation.

"As you are aware, my country is landlocked," he began. "Despite, or perhaps because of this situation, the question of providing a merchant marine of our own arises from time to time. It has arisen lately. My company, the *Societé Anonyme de la Banque de la Commerce et de l'Industrie et pour les Droites des Oeuvriers et des Paysans,* known popularly and for convenience as *Paybanque,* is currently interested in the possibilities of such a project.

"It is those 'certain commercial services' of the Mafia, of which you spoke, that we propose to engage. Our merchant marine headquarters in the New World would naturally be located in the New York City port area. Although at the present time the North River, or such New Jersey areas as Hoboken or Bayonne are most heavily favored by shipping, it was not always so. It is our opinion that excellent possibilities exist along the East River side of Manhattan, particularly the lower East River.

"It is our desire therefore that you provide us with a land, sea, and air survey, largely but not exclusively photographic in nature, engaging for the duration of the survey more or less centrally located quarters on the waterfront area in this locale. Something in the neighborhood of the Williamsburg Bridge would be ideal. Our representatives would participate with you, though the home office, so to speak, would remain aboard my yacht.

"This portfolio," he went on, placing it on the table and opening it, "contains a more detailed description of our proposal, as well as the eleven million dollars in United States Treasury Notes which your Northern European contact informed us would be your fee for considering the proposal. If you are agreeable to undertake the work, we can discuss further terms."

He ceased to speak. After a moment the Grand Master said, "Okay. We will leave you know." After Tosci had departed, Don Alexander asked, "Well, what do you think?"

"An Albanian Trotskyite posing as a Swiss Stalinist. If you ask me, I think he wants to blow up the Brooklyn Navy Yard," Don Morris Caplan said.

"Of *course* he wants to blow up the Brooklyn Navy Yard," Borjia snapped. "That was obvious right from the beginning— I can spot them Albanian deviationists a mile away. Now the point is: Do we *want* the Brooklyn Navy Yard blown up? It is to this question, my esteemed fellow colleagues, which we must now divert our attention."

＊＊＊

EVENTS WENT THEIR traditional way in the Goodeycoonce household. Granny had dressed herself up as though for a masquerade, the principal articles of costume consisting of a tasseled cap, a linen blouse with wide sleeves, a pair of even wider breeches, and wooden shoes; all these articles were very, very old. She next picked up a pipe of equally antique design, with a long cherrywood stem and a hand-painted porcelain bowl, and this she proceeded to charge with genuine Indian Leaf tobacco which she had shredded herself in her chopping bowl. The tobacco was purchased at regular intervals from the last of the

Manahatta Indians—that is, he was one-eighth Last-of-the-Manahatta-Indians, on his mother's side—who operated the New Orleans Candle and Incense Shop on Lexington Avenue. ("*I* don't know what them crazy White folks want with that stuff," he often said; "they could buy *grass* for the same price.") Granny struck a kitchen match, held it flat across the top of the pipe bowl, and began to puff.

Neely seated himself and took up a spiral notebook and a ballpoint pen. A scowl, or rather a pout, settled on his usually good-natured countenance.

First Granny coughed. Then she gagged. Then she inhaled with a harsh, gasping breath. Then she turned white, then green, then a bright red which might have startled and even alarmed Neely, had he not seen it all happen so often before. Presently she removed the pipe. Her face had taken on an almost masculine appearance. She rolled up one hand into a somewhat loose fist, then the other, then she placed one in alignment with the other and lifted them to her eye and peered through her simulated telescope.

Neely, in a tone of voice obviously intended as mockery, or at least mimicry, said, " 'To arms, to arms! Blow der drums and beat der trumpet! De dumdam Engels ships ben gesailing up de River!' "

The eye which was not looking through the "telescope" now looked at him, and there was something cold and cruel in it. Neely's own eyes fell. After a moment he mumbled, "Sorry, Oude Piet. I mean Oom Piet. I mean, *darn* it, Heer—um—Governor—ah—Your Highness."

The eye glared at him, then the "telescope" shifted. After a while a heavily accented and guttural voice, quite unlike his grandmother's usual tones, came from her throat and announced, in a businesslike drone, "Shloop by der vharf in Communipaw. Beaver pelts—"

Neely clicked his tongue in annoyance. "You're in the wrong century, darn it, now!" he cried. Again, the cold old eye glared at him. But he stood his ground. "Come on, now," he said. "A promise is a promise. What would the *Com*pany say?"

The "telescope" shifted again. The drone recommenced.

"Pier Dvendy-Zeven—Durkish Zigarettes—Zipahi brand—
vhatchman gedding dronk—"

Neely's ballpoint scribbled rapidly. *"That's* the ticket!" he
declared.

———◆◆◆◆◆———

DAISY SMITH FINISHED the tuna-fish sandwich (no mayon-
naise—a girl has to watch those calories every single *min*ute)
and washed the dish. For dessert she had half a pear. Then the
question could no longer be postponed—what was she going to
*do* that evening? It had all seemed so simple, back in Piney
Woods, New Jersey: she would take her own savings, all $80,
plus the $500 or so, most of it in old-fashioned long bills, but in-
cluding the $100 Liberty Bond, which had been found in the
much-mended worsted stocking under Uncle Dynus's mattress
after his funeral (the note found with it—thise is four *Dasi*—
seemed to make traffic with the Surrogate's Court unnecessary),
and come to New York. There she would find, in the order
named, an apartment, a job, and Someone-To-Go-Out-With.

She had found the first two without much trouble, but the
third, which she had thought would proceed from the second,
did not materialize. Her employer, Mr. Katachatourian, was the
nicest old man in the world, but, though a widower, he was *old*;
somehow the importing of St. John's bread—his business—
didn't seem to attract *young* men. And if, from time to time, with
trepidation, he took a flyer on a consignment of sesame seeds,
or pistachio nuts, it helped Daisy's prospects not at all. The jobbing of sesame seeds, or pistachio nuts, attracted exactly the
same sort of gentlemen as did the jobbing of St. John's bread—
either middle-aged and married, or elderly.

Once, to be sure, and once only, Daisy had made a social
contact from her job. Mr. Imamoglu, one of the largest *ex*porters
of St. John's bread on the eastern Aegean littoral, had come to
New York on business, had dropped in to see his good customer,
The Katachatourian Trading Company, and had immediately
fallen in love with Daisy. With true Oriental opulence he took
her out every night for a week. He took her to the opera, to the

St. Regis, to the Horse Show at Madison Square Garden, to Jack Dempsey's restaurant, to a Near Eastern night club on Ninth Avenue, to Hamburger Heaven, to a performance of *Phèdre* in the original French, to the Bowery Follies, and to a triple-feature movie house on 42nd Street which specialized in technicolor Westerns, of which Mr. Imamoglu was inordinately fond.

Then he proposed marriage.

Well, the prospect of living in a strawberry-ice-cream-pink-villa in the fashionable suburb of Karşiyaka across the picturesque Bay from the romantic port of Izmir, where she would be waited on, hand and foot, by multitudes of servants, *did* appeal to Daisy. But although Mr. Imamoglu assured her that both polygamy and the harem were things of the past in Turkey, that, in fact, neither veil nor *yashmak* could be procured for love or money in all his country, still, you know, *after all*. And furthermore, Mr. Imamoglu was somewhat on in years; he must have been in his thirties.

And besides, she didn't love him.

So Daisy said No.

The departure of the semidisconsolate exporter left Daisy's evenings emptier than before. Go to church? Why, bless you, of course she went to church, every single Sunday, sometimes twice, and met a number of young men who played the organ or were in the choir or conducted a Sunday-school class. Most of them lived in the YMCA and were careful to explain to Daisy that it would be many, many years before they could even begin to *think* of marriage; and their ideas of a social evening were quite different from Mr. Imamoglu's; they would arrange to meet her somewhere after supper and then go to a free illustrated lecture on the Greenland missions; followed by a cup of coffee or a Coke, followed by a chaste farewell at the subway kiosk.

Sometimes a girl thought she might just as well be back in Piney Woods, New Jersey.

What, then, to do tonight? Wash her hair? Watch TV? Catch up on her letters? Mending? Solo visit to a movie? She decided to take a walk.

A few blocks from her apartment she saw a familiar trio leaning in familiar stances against a wall. They nudged one another as they saw Daisy coming, as they had the first time and as they did every time. By now she knew there would be no wolf whistles, no rude proposals.

"Good evening, miss."

"G'evening, miss."

"Evening, miss."

"Good evening," Daisy said, pausing. "Oh, look at your new hats!" she exclaimed. "White fedoras. My goodness. Aren't they nice!"

The three men beamed and smirked, and readjusted their brims. "All the big fellows wear white fedoras," said the leader of the trio, whose name was Forrance.

"The big fellows?"

"Sure. Like on that, now, TV show, *The Unthinkables.* Al—Lucky—Baby Face—*you* know."

As Forrance mentioned these people his two associates pursed lips and nodded soberly. One was quite small and suffered from nosebleeds. ("Must be a low pressure rarea comin' down from Canada," he would mumble; "I c'n alwees tell: Omma reggella human brommeter.") He was known, quite simply, as Blood.

His companion, as if in compensation, was obese in the extreme. ("A glanjalla condition," was his explanation; he indignantly denied gluttony. Taxed with overeating, he pleaded a tapeworm. "It's not f' *me,*" was his indignant cry, over a third helping of breaded pork chops and French fries; "*it's f' the woim!*") Not unexpectedly he was called Guts. Now and then he pretended that it was an acknowledgement of personal courage.

"Al?" Daisy repeated. "Lucky? Baby Face? White fedoras? *The Unthinkables?* But *you're* not *gang*sters?" she burst out. "*Are* you?" For, as often as she had seen them, she had never thought to ask their trade.

Forrance drew himself up. Blood slouched. Guts loomed. A look of pleased importance underlay the grim look they assumed at the question. "Listen," Forrance began, out of the side of his mouth, an effect instantly spoiled by his adding, "miss."

"Listen, miss, you ever hear of—" he paused, glanced around, drew nearer—"the Nafia?" He thrust his right hand into his coat pocket. So did his two lieutenants. Daisy said, No, she never did; and at once the three were cast down. Was it, she asked helpfully, anything like the Mafia? Forrance brightened, Blood brightened, Guts brightened.

"*Sump*thing like the Mafia," said Forrance. "Om really very surprised you never—but you're from outatown, aintcha?"

"But what do you *do?*" Daisy demanded, mildly thrilled, but somehow not in the least frightened.

"We control," said Forrance impressively, "*all the gumball and Indian nut machines south of Vesey Street!*"

"My goodness," said Daisy. "Uh—are there many?"

"We are now awaiting delivery of the first of our new fleet of trucks," said Forrance formally.

"*Well,*" said Daisy, "lots of luck. I've got to go now. Good night."

"Good night, miss."

"G'night, miss."

"Night, miss."

The crisp air was so stimulating that Daisy walked a considerable distance past her usual turning-around point, and then decided to come home by a different route, window-shopping on the way. And in one window she noted many good buys in linoleum and tarpaulins, ships' chandlery, bar-and-grill supplies, and various other commodities; but somehow nothing she really *needed* just at the moment.

Then the flowered organdy caught her eye, but the bolt of blue rayon next to it was just as adorable. She looked up at the sign. THE ALMOST ANYTHING SECOND-HAND GOODS AND OUTLET STORE, it said. Wondering slightly, Daisy opened the door and went in. A bell tinkled. After a moment another door opened and a tall vigorous-looking woman, whose brown hair was turning grey, came in from the back. She smiled politely on seeing Daisy.

"I thought I might get some of that organdy in the window, the one with the flowers, enough for a dress."

"Yes, isn't it lovely? I'll get it for you right away. Was there anything else in the window you liked, while I'm there? Leather goods, outboard motors, canned crab-meat?"

"No, just—"

"Seasoned Honduras mahogany, yerba maté, Manila hemp? Turkish cigarettes—Sipahi brand?"

"No, just the organdy, and, oh, maybe that blue rayon?"

"That's lovely, too. You have very good taste."

While the lady was reaching into the window, the door at the back opened again and a voice said, "Granny," and then stopped. Daisy turned around. She saw a well-made young man with a healthy open countenance and light brown hair which needed combing. He wore a peacoat, corduroy trousers, and a woolen cap. He stared at Daisy. Then he smiled. Then he blushed. Then he took off his cap.

Daisy instantly decided to buy, not just enough material for a dress, but both entire bolts, plus so large an amount of leather goods, outboard motors, canned crab-meat, seasoned Honduras mahogany, yerba maté, Manila hemp, and Turkish Sipahi cigarettes as would leave the proprietor no choice but to say, "Well, you can never carry all that by yourself; my grandson will help you take it home,"—or words to that effect.

What actually happened was quite different. The lady emerged from the window with the bolts of cloth and said, "I really don't know which is the lovelier," then noticed the young man and said, "Yes, Neely?"

"I finished the, uh, *you*-know," said the young man. He continued smiling at Daisy, who was now smiling back.

"Then start stacking the Polish hams," his grandmother directed crisply. "Smash up all those old crates, pile the raw rubber up against the north wall, but not too near the Turkish cigarettes because of the smell. Go on, now."

"Uh—" said Neely, still looking at the new young customer.

"And when you're finished with *that*," his grandmother said,

"I want all the cork fenders cleaned, and the copper cable un-wound from the big reel onto the little ones."

"Uh—"

"Now, never mind, *Uh*—you go and do as I say, or we'll be up all night. . . . *Neely!*"

For a moment the young man hesitated. Then his eyes left Daisy and caught his grandmother's glance. He looked down, swallowed, scraped his boots. *"Well?"* Neely threw Daisy a single quick glance of helplessness, wistfulness, and embarrassment. He said, "Yes, Granny," turned and went out the door.

Daisy, her purchase under her arm, walked home full of indignation. "There are no young men any more!" she told herself vexedly. "If they're *men*, they're not *young*, and if they're *young*, they're just not *men*. 'Yes, Granny!' How do you like *that?* Oh, I'd 'Yes, Granny' him!" she declared. "I'd show *him* who was boss!" she thought, somewhat inconsistently.

"Milksop!" she concluded. She was surprised to realize that, in her annoyance, she had bought only the flowered organdy. There was really no help for it; much as she despised the grandmother and grandson, if she wanted that blue rayon she would have to revisit THE ALMOST ANYTHING SECOND-HAND GOODS AND OUTLET STORE a second time. Too bad, but it wasn't really *her* fault, was it?

THE MAN CALLED Tosci stepped from the yacht's launch onto the gangway ladder and was steadied by a stubble-faced man in dungarees. "Thank you, boatswain," he said.

"Did you enjoy your visit ashore, M. Tosci?" the bosun asked.

"Ah, New York is such a stimulating city," said Tosci, going up the ladder. "One simply cannot absorb it on a single visit."

He handed his hat to the man, who followed him to his cabin, where he tossed the hat aside, and turned on a device which not only blanked out the sound of their actual conversation against any electronic eavesdropping, but supplied a taped innocuous conversation to be picked up by such devices instead.

"Well?" the "boatswain" demanded.

Tosci shrugged. "Well, Comrade Project Supervisor," he said, "they took the Treasury Notes and said they would let us know. One really could not expect more at the moment."

"I suppose not," the Project Supervisor said gloomily. "Do you think they will *take the contract,*' as I believe the phrase goes?"

"Why should they not, Comrade Project Supervisor? How could they resist the temptation? We are, after all, prepared to go as high as a *hundred* and eleven million dollars. It would take them a long time to collect a hundred and eleven million dollars from their, how do they call it, 'numbers racket.'"

"About a week and a half; not more. Well, well, we shall see. Meanwhile, I am hungry. You took your time coming back."

"I am sorry, Comrade Project Supervisor, but—"

"No excuses. Bring me my supper now. And see that the cabbage in the borscht is not soggy as it was last night, and that there are no flies in the yogurt. Do you hear?"

"Yes, Comrade Project Supervisor," said Tosci.

<hr>

DON SYLVESTER FITZPATRICK, Second Vice-President of the Mafia (Lower Manhattan Branch) and son-in-law of Don Lefty McGonigle, sat brooding in his tiny office in the wholesale foodstuffs district. Despite his title he was a mere petty don in the hierarchy; well did he know that it was rumored he owed even this to nepotism, and these circumstances rankled (as he put it) in his bosom. "A man of my attainments, which they should put him in the front ranks of enterprise," he muttered, "and what am I doing? I'm in charge of the artichoke rake-off at the Washington Market!" Don Sylvester laughed bitterly; Don Sylvester sulked.

Meanwhile, in the Grand Chamber Council, discussion among the senior dons went on apace.

"Blowing up the Brooklyn Navy Yard," said Don Tex Thompson reflectively, "might be just the thing the national economy is in need of. Unemployment among skilled laborers went up seven point-oh-nine percent in the last fortnightly period, and among unskilled laborers the figure scores an even higher percentile. The Mafia," he said, "cannot remain indifferent to the plight of the workingman."

"Not if it is to retain that position of esteem and preeminence to which it is rightly entitled," said Don Morris Caplan.

"To say nothing of the excellent effect upon our National Defenses of clearing out all that obsolete equipment and replacing it with the newest devices obtainable through modern science," Don Shazzam X (formerly Rastus Washington) declared. "The Congress could scarcely refuse appropriations in such circumstances."

Don Wong Hua-Fu pursed his thin lips and put the tips of his six-inch fingernails together in church-steeple fashion. "The Honorable Ten Tongs do include sound common stocks in the various heavy-metals industries in their portfolio. Still," he said, "we must consider the great burdens already borne by the widows and orphans who constitute the majority of American taxpayers."

And Don Leverret Lowell Cabot pointed out another possible objection. "We cannot neglect our own heavy commitments in the Brooklyn Navy Yard area," he said. "As part of our responsibility to the men who man our country's ships we have, need I remind the Grand Council, leading interests in the bars, restaurants, night clubs, strip-joints, clip-joints, and gambling hells of the area—to say nothing of the hotels used for both permanent and temporary residence by the many charming ladies who lighten the burdens of the sea-weary sailors."

"It's a problem, believe *me*," sighed Don Gesú-María Gomez. "Little does the public know of our problems."

"Decisions, decisions, decisions!" Don Swede Swanson echoed the sigh.

"Gen-tle-men, gen-tle-men," said Don Lefty McGonigle, a note of mild protest in his hoarse voice. "Aren't we being a lit-tul pre-ma-chua? *We* are not being asked to blow up duh Brooklyn Navy Yahd dis minute. *We* are not even being asked to de-*cide* if fit should be blown up dis minute. All we are being asked to do, gen-tle-men, is to decide if we are going to make a soyvey of de Iowa East Trivva estuary from d' point of view of its amen-i-ties as a pos-si-ble headquarters faw moychant marine offices. I yap-peal to you, Grand Master, am I creckt?"

Don Alexander Borjia tore his eyes away from the Mona Lisa on the wall. The lineaments of La Gioconda never ceased to entrance him, and there was the added fillip to his pleasure that the rest of the world naïvely thought the original still hung in the Louvre, little realizing that this last was a mere copy, painted, true, by Leonardo, but by Leonardo in his ancient age. The switcheroo had been arranged by Don Alexander's father, the late Grand Master Don César Borjia, before the First World War. Copies of masterworks of art, stolen at various times from museums and private collectors around the world, adorned the other walls. But Don Alexander Borjia's favorite remained the Mona Lisa.

"Don Lefty McGonigle is correct," he said. "Take the con-tract for the survey, charge them eighty-seven million dollars for it, and when it comes time for a decision on the *big* question, so we'll leave them know further. All in favor say *Aye.* Opposed, *Nay.* The Ayes got it."

There was a silence.

"A foyda question," said Don Lefty finally. He fingered the cabochon emerald which nestled in his watered-silk four-in-hand, and fiddled with his eyepatch.

"Speak."

"Whom is to be ap-poin-ted to take over d' soyvey?"

"Whom did you have in mind?"

"A young man which he oughta be given more responsibil-ity than he's being given, to wit, my son-in-law, the Second Vice-President of the Mafia, Lower Manhattan Branch. Wod-daya say, gen-tle-men?"

The pause which followed this suggestion seemed faintly embarrassed. Then Don Swede Swanson was heard to express the opinion that Don Sylvester FitzPatrick couldn't find the seat of his pants in the dark with both hands.

Don Lefty turned to him and pressed both his hands to his chest. "You wound me!" he exclaimed, his voice deep with suppressed emotion. "Night afta night I come home an' my liddle Philomena is eating huh haht out. 'Daddy, Daddy, Daddy,' she asks, weeping, 'what has everybody got against poor Sylvester? Didn't he soyve his apprenticeship the same as everybody else? Is-int he loyal? Trustwoythy? Coyteous? Kind? So why, afta twelve years, is he still only in chahge of ahtichokes at Wahshington Mahket?'

"An' ya know what? *I* don't know what ta *say* ta huh! *If* fit was a matta of money, so I'd buy him a sand-and-gravel company, or a broory. But it's a matta of tra-*di*-tion, gen-tle-men! All of youse got sons. I ain't got no son! All I got is my liddle Philomena. A bee-uty in thuh Hollywood sense a thuh woid she may not be, but she yiz the yimage of huh sainted mother, rest her soul, an' huh husband is like a son ta me, so when ya spit on *him*, gen-tle-men, it's like ya spitting on *me!*"

Throats were cleared, eyes wiped, noses blown. Don Alexander essayed to speak, but was prevented by emotion. At last the silence was broken by Don Swede Swanson. "So let be Sylvester," he said huskily. There was a chorus of nods.

"OF COURSE, THERE is one hazard of the chase involved in my sweet Sauncepeur's snaffling hot broils off these outdoor grills," Lord Grue and Groole observed. "It—shall I sweeten the air in here a bit? I've a packet of frankincense that my friend, Osman Ali the Somali, sent me not long ago; I wouldn't *buy* incense, of course," he said, sprinkling the pale yellow grains on the glowing embers. A pungent odor filled the cave.

Denny the Dip coughed. The Marquess donned his gauntlet and examined the falcon's talons, particularly about the pads. "It makes the poor creature's petti-toes sore. I've experimented with various nostra and it's my considered opinion that Pinaud's Moustache Wax is above all things the best. Is there anything more left in the flask? Shall we kill it, as you say over here? Ah, good show."

With a gesture he motioned to Denny to take the bed; he himself reclined on a tiger skin which was stored during the day in a dry niche. Thus settled, he grew expansive. "Ah, it's not what I've been accustomed to, me that used to have my own shooting lodge in the grouse season, waited on, hand and foot, by a dozen Baloochi servants; well, and now here I am, like a bloody eremite, living on me wits and the $5.60 I get from home each week."

Denny lifted his head. "You're a remittance man?" he inquired.

"Sort of remittance man, you might say, yes. Me nevew, Piers Plunkert, pays me two quid a week, not so much to stay away as to stay alive. 'Avoid alcohol, Uncle,' he writes, 'and mind you wear your wooly muffler when the north wind blows.' It's not filial piety, mind, or avuncular piety, or anything like it. You see, if I pop off, *he* becomes the twelfth Marquess of Grue and Groole, and all the rest of that clobber—the mere thought of it makes his blood run cold. No, he's not a Labour M.P.; his fix is worse than that. He's one of the *Angry Young Men!*

"Struth! Lives in a filthy little room in South Stepney, and composes very bad, very blank verse damning The Establishment, under the pseudonym of 'Alf Huggins.' Well, now, I ask you—would *you* pay any attention to an Angry Young Man named Lord Grue and Groole? No, of course you wouldn't. And neither would anyone else.

"Once a year I threaten suicide. 'It doesn't matter about me, my boy,' I write. '*You* will carry on the name and title.' My word, what a flap that puts him in! *Always* good for ten quid pronto via cablegram."

A sound, so dim and distant that it failed to reach the ear of Denny the Dip, caused the peerless peer to break off discourse and raise his head. "Bogey," he announced. "Policeman, to you. Weighs about a hundred and sixty and has trouble with his left arch. Neglects his tum, too—hear it rumble!"

Denny strained, could hear nothing but the traffic passing through the park, its sound rising and falling with the wind, like surf. He murmured, "What a talent you got, Grooley! What a team we'd make!"

"A team we certainly will *not* make!" the peer snorted. "But, as to your playing squire to my knight, hmm, well, we'll consider it. I plan to take a brisk walk in the morning, down to the Battery and vicinage. We'll see if you can stand the pace— no sinecure being gunbearer, as it were, to the man who out-walked The Man-Eater of Mysore. And another thing—" He thwacked the Dip across the feet with his swagger stick. "No more of this 'Grooley'! Call me Sahib, Bwana, Kyrios, or M'lord."

---

"HMM," MURMURED LORD Grue and Groole, pausing and look-ing in the shop window. "I find that curious. Don't *you* find that curious, Denny?"

Denny, panting and aching from the long trek down from Central Park, was finding nothing curious but his inability to break away and sink to rest. "Wuzzat, Gr—I mean Bwana?" he moaned. He was bearing, in lieu of gun, the Marquess's swag-ger stick.

"Use your *eyes*, man! There, in the window. What do you see?"

The Dip wiped the sweat out of his eyes. "Leather goods?" he inquired. "Outboard motors? Canned crab-meat?" The Mar-quess clicked his tongue, and swore rapidly in Swahili (Up-Country dialect). "Seasoned Honduras mahogany?" the Dip continued hastily. "Flowered organdy? Blue rayon? Manila hemp?"

"*Ahah!* Just so, a great lovely coil of Manila hempen rope. Notice anything odd about it? *No?* You were pulling the wrong mendicant dodge, you should've used a tin cup. You really don't see that scarlet thread running through it, so cleverly and closely intertwined that it cannot be picked out without spoil-ing the rope? You *do* see it; good. No use to ask if you know what it means; you don't, so I'll tell you. It means that rope was made by and for the Royal Navy. It is *never* sold, so it must have been stolen. No one would dare fence it in Blighty, so they've shipped it over here. Clever, I call that. Must look into this."

He entered the shop, followed by Denny, who sank at once into a chair. The dog Guido, looking as cool and fresh as his master, stood motionless. Mrs. Goodeycoonce emerged from the back.

"Afternoon, ma'am," said Lord Grue and Groole, touching the brim of his quasi-caracul cap, and giving her no chance to speak. "My name is Arthur Powisse, of the Powisse Exterminating Company. Allow me to offer you my card—dear me, I seem to have given the last one away; ah, well, it doesn't signify. This is my chief assistant, Mr. Dennis, and the animal is one of our pack of trained Tyrolean Rat Hounds. We have just finished a rush job at one of the neighborhood warehouses, and, happening to pass by and being entranced by your very attractive window display, thought we would drop in and offer you an estimate on de-ratting your premises."

Mrs. Goodeycoonce opened her mouth, but the Marquess swept on. "I anticipate your next comment, ma'am. You are about to say, 'But I keep a clean house'—and so you do, so you obviously do. But do your *neighbors?* Aye, there's the rub; they don't, alas. Around the corner is an establishment of the type known as, if you will pardon the expression, a common flophouse—the sort of place where they throw fishbones in the corner and never sweep up. Three doors down is the manufactory of Gorman's Glossy Glue Cakes, a purely animal product, on which *Ratus ratus* thrives, ma'am, simply *thrives!*"

Something flickered in Granny Goodeycoonce's eyes which seemed to indicate she had long been aware of the proximity of Gorman's Glossy Glue Cakes, particularly on very warm days, and found in it no refreshment of soul whatsoever.

"How often at night," Lord Grue and Groole waxed almost lyrical, "when all should be quiet, must you not have heard Noises, eh?—and attributed them to the settling of the timbers, the expansion and contraction of the joists and beams. Not a bit of it! *Rats!*" His voice sank to a whisper. "Oh, the horror of it! First one grey shadow, then another—"

He took a step forward, she took one backward, he advanced, she retreated. "Then great grisly waves of them, first in the foundations, then in the cellar, then—does this door lead to the cellar? I had better examine it."

———◆◆◆◆◆———

LATER THAT EVENING found the Marquess and his bearer deep in the shadowy doorway of an empty warehouse. "It was the advent of that offensively wholesome-looking young chap, her grandson, that broke the spell," the Marquess mused. "Said she'd consider it. No matter. I saw the cellar. Those crates and crates of Polish hams! Those bales of raw rubber! Turkish Sipahi cigarettes! That infinite variety of portable, seaborne merchandise!

"It can only mean one thing: the people are pukka river pirates. I know the signs—seen them on the Thames, the Nile, Hoogli, Brahmapootra, Whampoa, Pei-Ho—*eheu fugaces*. Nice set-up she's got there—snug shop, tidy house, fine figger, and a widow woman, I'm sure—no sign of a husband and anyone can see she's not the divorcing type. Hmm, well, question is: How does the lad get the stuff there? How do river pirates *usually* get the stuff there? Just so."

And they had walked along the waterfront, the Marquess examining the water as intently as one of the inhabitants of the Sunda Straits peering for *bêche-de-mer*, the Dip plodding along to the rear of Guido, as sunken beneath the weight of the swagger stick as if it had been an elephant gun. He reflected on the day he might have spent, conning old ladies out of coins, and on a certain bat-cave he knew of, where an ounce and a quarter of Old Cordwainer retailed for the ridiculous sum of 31 cents. But there was that about the Marquess which said *Hither to me, caitiff, and therein fail not, at your peril*; therefore Denny plodded meekly.

"Ho," said His Lordship, stopping, and pointing at the filthy waters of the East River, which, in a happier time, lined with forests and grassy meads, were thick with salmon, shad, cod, alewives, herring, sturgeon, and all fruits of the sea; now the waters were merely thick. "Observe," said His Lordship. "You see how—there—the oil slick, orange peel, bad bananas, and other rubbish floats down with the tide. Whereas the flotsam rides more or less straight out from under us and joins the current at a right angle. The *main* current, that is. Let's have a dekko," he declared, and shinnied down the side of the wharf timbers almost to the water's edge.

His enthusiasm, as he clambered up, almost communicated itself to the Dip. "Whuddaya see, Sahib?" he asked, craning.

"Enough. Tonight, when the eyes of the Blessed Houris in Paradise, yclept 'stars' in our rude Saxon Tongue, shine as clearly as this filthy air will allow them to, we shall follow young Mr. Goodeycoonce. Here are rupees, or whatever the juice they call them—'quarters'? Just so. Go thou and eat, and return within the hour. As for me, a strip of biltong will do, and fortunately I took care to refill the flask. They make good whiskey in Belfast, I must say, cursed Orangemen though they be." He raised his drink and waved it across a trickle in the gutter. "To the King over the water"—and drank. His glass eye glittered defiance to all the House of Hanover.

---

ALL WAS QUIET in the kitchen behind THE ALMOST ANYTHING SECOND-HAND GOODS AND OUTLET STORE. Granny Goodeycoonce was pasting in her scrapbook the latest letter she had received in reply to a message of congratulations sent on the birthday of one of the Princesses of the Netherlands. It read, as did all the others in the scrapbook: *The Queen has read your letter with interest and directs me to thank you for your good wishes.* And it was signed, as nearly as could be made out, Squiggle Van Squiggle, Secretary.

"Gee," said Neely, looking up from a trade journal he was reading, "here's a bait business for sale on Long Island, on the North Shore." There was no answer. He tried again. "And a boat basin in Connecticut. 'Must be sold at once,' the ad says, 'to settle estate.' Gee."

His grandmother capped the tube of library paste. "I suppose Princess Beatrix will be getting engaged pretty soon," she observed. "I wonder who to. How old is the Crown Prince of Greece? No, that wouldn't do, I suppose; he'll be *King* of Greece some day, and she'll be Queen of Holland. Hmm." She knit her brows, deep in the problems of dynasty.

"They could be combined," Neely suggested.

Granny Goodeycoonce looked up, amazed. "What, Greece and *Hol*land?"

"No, I mean a bait business and a boatyard. People," he explained enthusiastically, "would buy *bait* to fish with from their *boats*. And—"

She clicked her tongue. "The idea! A Goodeycoonce becoming a fishmonger!"

"Better than being a river pirate," he mumbled.

"Never let me hear you use that word again!" she snapped. "The very idea! Have you *no* respect for the traditions of the family? Why, it makes my blood boil! And don't you forget for one minute, young man, that I am a Goodeycoonce by descent as well as by marriage; don't you forget *that!*"

"Fat chance," Neely muttered.

His grandmother opened her mouth to release a thunderbolt, but at that moment there came a thud from the cellar, followed by a clatter.

"Oh, my land," Granny whispered, a hand at her throat. "Rats! I should've listened to that Limey. Is the door to the cellar locked?"

Answer was superfluous, for at that moment the door swung open and in stepped the Limey himself, more properly described as Arthur Marmaduke Roderick Lodowicke William Rufus de Powisse-Plunkert, Baron Bogle, Earl of Ballypatcoogan, Viscount Penhokey, Laird of Muckle Greet, Master of Snee, 11th Marquess of Grue and Groole in the Peerage of England, and Hereditary Lord High Keeper of the Queen's Bears. "Good evening, all," he said.

Neely went pale. "I knew it!" he cried. "I knew we couldn't go on getting away with it forever, not after almost three hundred years! That exterminator story was just a dodge—he must be from the Harbor Patrol, or the Coast Guard!"

The Marquess took his swagger stick from the quivering Denny (who had made the underground voyage with his head under his coat, for fear of bats), and smacked it gently into the palm of his hand. "You know, I resent that very much," he said, a touch of petulance in his voice. "I will have you know that I am no copper's nark, common informer, or fink. I—"

"You get out of my house," said Granny Goodeycoonce, "or I'll—"

"Call the police? Oh, I doubt that, my good woman; I doubt that entirely. How would you explain all those cork fenders in the cellar? The copper cable, raw rubber, Turkish Sipahi cigarettes, Polish hams? To say nothing of enough sailcloth to supply a regatta, a ton of tinned caviar, five hundred *oka* of Syrian arrack, twenty canisters of ambergris, several score pods of prime Nepauli musk, and, oh, simply ever so many more goodies—all of which, I have no hesitation in declaring, are the fruits of, I say not 'theft,' but of, shall I say, impermissive acquisition. Eh?"

Granny Goodeycoonce, during the partial inventory, had recovered her aplomb. "Well, you simply couldn't be more wrong," she said, a smile of haughty amusement on her lips. " 'Impermissive'? Poo. We have the best permission anyone could ever want. Neely, show this foreign person our permission."

Still pale, and muttering phrases like *I'll be an old man when I get out*, Neely unlocked an antique cabinet in one corner of the room and removed a flat steel case, which he handed to his grandmother. She opened it with a key of her own, and reverently extracted a parchment document festooned with seals, which she displayed to the Marquess with the words: "Look, but don't touch."

He fixed his monocle firmly in his good eye and bent over. After a while he straightened up. "Mph. Well, I must confess that my knowledge of Seventeenth Century Dutch orthography is rather limited. But I *can* make out the name of Van Goedikoentse, as well as that of Petrus Stuyvesant. Perhaps you would be good enough to explain?"

Nothing could have pleased Granny more. *"This,"* she said

in tones both hushed and haughty, "is a Patent from the Dutch West India Company, granting to my great-great-great-great-great-great-great-grandfather, Nicolaes Jacobus Van Goedikoentse, *and* 'to his heirs forever,' the right of collecting customs in the harbor port of Nieuw Amsterdam. It was granted in return for Myn Heer Van Goedikoentse's valiant help in resisting the insolent British demand for surrender in 1662. Governor Stuyvesant promised he would never forget."

For a moment no word broke the reverent silence. Then, slowly, Lord Grue and Groole removed his cap. "And naturally," he said, "your family has never recognized that surrender. Madam, as an unreconstructed Jacobite, I honor them for it, in your person." He gravely bowed. Equally gravely, Mrs. Goodeycoonce made a slight curtsy. "Under no circumstances," he went on, "would I dream of betraying your confidence. As a small effort to amend for the sins of my country's past I offer you my collaboration—my very, very *experienced* collaboration, if I do say so."

Three hundred years (almost) of going it alone struggled in Mrs. Goodeycoonce's bosom to say No. At the same time she was plainly impressed with Lord Grue and Groole's offer—to say nothing of his manner. It took her a while to reply. "Well," she said finally, "we'll see."

---

DON SYLVESTER FITZPATRICK, Second Vice-President of the Mafia (Lower Manhattan Branch), was nervous. The survey was almost finished, and the Grand Council still hadn't made up its mind about blowing up the Brooklyn Navy Yard. In fact, it was even now debating the project in their Chamber, at the window of the anteroom to which Don Sylvester now sat. Elation at being at long last removed from the artichoke detail had gradually given way to uneasiness. Suppose they *did* decide to blow it up? Would the United States Government take the same broad view of this as the Dons did? Visions of being hanged from the yardarm of, say, the USS *Missouri*, danced like sugar plums in Sylvester's head.

A flutter from the crates at his foot distracted his attention. In one was a black pigeon, in one was a white. Very soon the mysterious Mr. Tosci would appear with $87,000,000 in plain, sealed wrappers, and be told the Grand Council's decision. Even now the Mafiosi bomb squads were standing by at the ready in Brooklyn. Informed only that morning that police had put the traditional, semiannual wire tap on the Mafiosi phones, the Mafiosi had brought out the traditional, semiannual pigeon post.

"Now, remember," Don Lefty McGonigle had instructed his son-in-law, "d' black boid has d' message *Bombs Away* awready in d' cap-sool fastened to its foot. And d' white boid's got d' message *Everyt'ing Off* inscribed on d' paper in d' cap-sool on *its* foot. Ya got dat?"

"Yeah, Papa," said Don Sylvester, wiping his face.

"So when ya get d' woid, *Yes,* ya leddout d' *black* pigeon. But if ya get d' woid, *No,* den ya leddout d' *white* pigeon. An' nats all dere's to it. Okay?"

"Okay, Papa."

"Om depending on you. Philomena is depending on you. So don't chew be noivous."

"No, Papa," said Don Sylvester.

---

WHEN FORRANCE TOLD Daisy that the "Nafia" was awaiting delivery of the first of its new fleet of trucks he was speaking optimistically. The new truck was "new" only in the sense that it was newer than the one it replaced, a 1924 Star, which had to be thawed out with boiling water in cold weather and cranked by hand before it would start, in all weather. The Nafia treasury had suffered a terrible blow when the Cherry Street Mob, in the mid-fifties, took over the distribution of birch beer south of Vesey Street—during the course of which epic struggle Guts had his ears boxed and Blood suffered a sympathetic nasal hemorrhage; as a result, the treasury could only afford to have the single word NAFIA painted on the side panels. Still it was *some*thing.

"Rides like a dream, don't it," Forrance said, as they headed along South Street one bright afternoon.

"No, it don't," said Blood. "It liss."

"Whaddaya mean, 'it liss'?"

"I mean, like it liss ta one side. Look—"

Guts said, "He's right, boss. It *does* liss. Them new gumball machines ain't equally distributed. They all slide to one side."

Forrance halted the truck with a grinding of gears. "All right," he said resignedly; "then let's take'm all out and put'm back in again, but *evenly* this time."

So the smallest criminal organization in New York got out of its fleet of trucks to unload and reload its gumball machines.

———

TOSCI PAUSED ON the deck of the yacht to receive his superior's final instructions. "I have counted the money," he said. "Eighty-six million in negotiable bearer bonds, and one million in cash."

"Very well. Perhaps they will have time to spend it all before we Take Over; perhaps not. I have instructed the Chief Engineer to test the engines in order that we can leave as soon as the decision is made. They *say* the bombs are set for four hours, but who knows if we can believe them?"

As if to confirm his fears, the Chief Engineer at this moment rushed on deck, grease and dismay, in equal parts, showing on his face.

"The engines won't start!" he cried.

"They *must* start!" snapped the Project Supervisor. "Go below and see to it!" The Chief, with a shrug, obeyed. The Project Supervisor scowled. "An odd coincidence—if it is a coincidence," he said. "Personally, I have never trusted sailors since the Kronstadt Mutiny." To conceal his nervousness he lifted his binoculars to his eyes, ordering Tosci not to leave the ship for the time being. Scarcely had he looked through the glasses when an exclamation broke through his clenched lips.

"There is a truck on the waterfront," he cried, "with the Mafia's name on it! And three men are lifting something from it. Here—" he thrust the glasses at Tosci—"see what you can make of it."

Tosci gazed in bewilderment. "Those machines," he said. "I've never seen anything like them. I don't understand—why should the Mafia be unloading such strange devices so near our ship?"

Suspicion, never far below the surface of the Project Supervisor's mind, and usually right on top of it, burst into flames. "They must be electronic devices to keep our engines from functioning!" he cried. "They think to leave us stuck here in the direct path of the explosions, thus destroying alien witnesses! Clever, even admirable—but we cannot allow it. Come—" he seized Tosci by the arm holding the portfolio in which the bonds and money were— "to the launch! We must see about this!" Together they rushed down the gangway ladder into the boat.

---

"WHITE PIGEON IF it's No," Don Sylvester mumbled. "Black pigeon if it's Yes. White, No. Black, Yes. I got it." But he was still nervous. Suppose he fumbled his responsibilities at the crucial moment—*suppose he bungled the job?* For the hundredth time his fingers examined the catches on the cage, lifted one up a fraction of an inch, closed it, then lifted the other—and there was a sudden sound from the cage.

Don Sylvester's startled fingers flew to his mouth. The catch snapped up. The black pigeon hopped out, fluttered to the window sill, cooed again, and—as Sylvester made a frantic lunge for it—spread its wings and flew out. It soared up, up, up, circled once, circled twice, then flew off toward Brooklyn.

Sylvester stared at the air in wordless horror. Then he stared at the door of the Grand Council Chamber. Any moment now, it might open. He tiptoed over and listened.

"I say *no!*" a voice declared.

"And I say *yes!*" declared a second voice.

Helplessly, his eyes roamed the anteroom, fell at length on the telephone. Regardless of possible wiretaps, he quickly and fearfully dialed a number. "Hello?" he whispered hoarsely. "Hello, Philomena? Listen, Philomena—"

149

———◆◆◆———

THE BLACK PIGEON flapped its way toward Brooklyn with leisurely strokes, thinking deep pigeonic thoughts. Now and then it caught an updraft and coasted effortlessly. It was in no hurry. But, of course, it really was not very far to Brooklyn, as a pigeon flies. . . .

———◆◆◆———

"EASY DOES IT—watch my toes, ya dope—down, down."

"Good afternoon, boys," said Daisy. "I just came out to mail a letter to Turkey. Did you know that airmail is ten cents cheaper to the west bank of the Hellespont, because it's in Europe? Oooh—gumballs! Let me see if I have a penny—"

"No, let me see if *I* got one, Miss—"

"No, lem*me* see, Forry—"

"Aa, c'*mon,* I gotta have one—"

While the three Nafiosi were plunging in their pockets, the yacht's launch drew up to the pier. Out of it came Tosci, the Project Supervisor, and three crewmen. "What are you up to?" Tosci shouted.

"What's it to you?" Forrance countered.

"I order you to remove those machines from this area at once!"

Instantly truculent, Forrance thrust out his jaw. "Nobody orders the Nafia what to do with its machines," he said. "Anyways, not south of Vesey Street," he amended.

"Put them on the truck and see that they are driven away," Tosci instructed a crewman, who began to obey, but was prevented by Blood. The crewman swung, Blood's nose, ever sensitive, began to bleed, and Daisy, aroused, cried, "You let him alone!" and wielded her pocketbook with a will. The crewman staggered. Guts, gauging his distance to a nicety, swung his ponderous belly around and knocked him down.

"Take the girl," shouted the Project Supervisor, in his own language. "She is undoubtedly their 'moll.' We will keep her aboard as a hostage." And while he, Tosci, and one of their men engaged the tiny syndicate in combat, the other two sailors hustled Daisy into the launch, muffling her cries for help.

---

MRS. GOODEYCOONCE, NEELY, Denny, Guido, and Lord Grue and Groole were out for a walk. No decision had yet been made on the noble lord's proposal, but nevertheless everyone seemed to be growing somewhat closer. The Marquess was telling about the time that he rescued the Dowager Begum of Oont from the horrid captivity in which she had been placed by her dissolute nephew, the Oonti Ghook. All listened in fascination, except the dog Guido, who had heard the story before.

So taken up in his account was the Marquess that he absentmindedly abstracted from his pocket a particularly foul pipe (which respect for the lady had normally prevented his smoking in her presence), and proceeded to charge it with the notoriously rank tobacco swept up for sale to the inhabitants of the lower-income quarters of Quetta; and struck a match to it. At the first unconsidered whiff Mrs. Goodeycoonce coughed. Then she gagged, then she inhaled with a harsh, gasping breath. And next she turned white, green, and bright red.

Neely was the first to notice. "Granny!" he said. "Granny?" Then, "It must be your pipe—"

The Marquess was overcome with confusion and remorse. "Terribly sorry," he declared. "I'd knock the dottle out, except that's all it *is,* you know—dottle, I mean. I say, Mrs. Goodeycoonce—oh, I *say.*"

But Mrs. Goodeycoonce's face had taken on an almost masculine appearance. She rolled up first one fist, loosely, and then the other, placed them in alignment, lifted them to her eyes, and peered out upon the River. And in a gutturally accented and heavy voice quite unlike her usual tones she declared, "Zound der alarm! Beat to qvarters! *Zo, zo, wat den duyvel!*"

The Marquess's eagle-keen eyes followed her glance and immediately observed something very much amiss upon the waters.

"Stap my vitals, if I don't believe a gel is being forced aboard that vessel over there," he said. "Bad show, that. What?"

Instantly the possessing spirit of Peter Stuyvesant vanished and was replaced by that of Mrs. Goodeycoonce. She uttered a cry. "White slavery, that's what it must be! And in broad daylight, too. Oh, the brazen things! What should we *do?*"

Neely hauled an old-fashioned but quite authentic and brass-bound telescope from his pocket and swung it around. As he focused in and recognized Daisy, struggling desperately while being taken up the gangway, he uttered a hoarse shout of rage.

" 'Do'?" he yelled. "We've got to save her! Come on! My boat! Let's *go!*"

---

THE BLACK PIGEON passed over City Hall, dallied for a few moments in the currents around the Woolworth Building, and then pressed on in the general direction of Sand Street. . . .

---

As NEELY'S BOAT zoomed under the bow of the yacht, the Marquess kicked off his shoes, seized the anchor chain, and swarmed up like a monkey. Neely and Denny were met at the foot of the gangway ladder by two crewmen, who shouted, gesticulated, and menaced them with boathooks. But in a moment the boatmen's attention was diverted by a tumult from above. Part of this was caused by Lord Grue and Groole who, darting from one place of concealment to another, called out (in different voices) battle cries in Pathan, Kikuyu, and Demotic Greek; and part of it was caused by the alarm of the crew at being boarded—so they thought—by a host of foes.

While their opponents' attention was thus distracted, Denny and Neely gained the deck where Neely at once knocked down the first sailor he saw. Denny's contribution was more circumspect. Noting an oily rag in a corner he took out a match. In a moment clouds of black smoke arose.

"Fire!" cried the Dip. "Fire! *Fire!*"

Part of the crew promptly swarmed down the ladder into Neely's boat and cast off. The rest jumped over the side and commenced swimming briskly toward the nearer shore.

"Hello!" Neely shouted, stumbling along the passageways, opening doors. "Hello, hello! Where are you?"

A muffled voice called, he burst in, and there was Daisy, gagged and bound, struggling in a chair. Neely cut her loose, removed the gag, and—after only a very slight hesitation, perhaps natural in a shy young man of good family—kissed her repeatedly.

"*Well,*" said Daisy tremulously, as he paused for breath, and then to herself, "I guess he's not such a milksop after all."

On deck Denny the Dip and the Marquess stomped out the smoldering rag, though not, however, in time to avoid having attracted two police boats, a Coast Guard cutter, the Governor's Island ferry, a Hudson River Dayliner, and the New York City Fireboat, *Zophar Mills,* all of which converged on the yacht.

"Thank you, thank you," called out the Marquess, between cupped hands. "We don't require any assistance, the fire is out. You will observe, however, that officers and crew have abandoned the ship, which means that she is now, under maritime law, by right of salvage, the property of myself and my associates, both *in personam* and *in rem.*"

The failure of the engines to start, it was ascertained after a careful scrutiny, was owing to the intrusion of a large waterbug into one of the oil lines; this was soon set right. An attempt of a floating delegate of the Masters, Mates, and Pilots Union to question the Marquess's right to take the helm of the salvaged vessel was quickly terminated by the revelation that he possessed a first-class navigation certificate in the Siamese Merchant Marine. The delegate addressed him henceforth as "Captain," and, on departing, offered him the use of all the amenities of the Union Hall.

It was while seeing this personage off that Lord Grue and Groole observed a familiar shadow on the deck of the yacht, and, taking off his quasi-caracul and waving it, lured Sauncepeur down from what the poet Pope once so prettily described as "the azure Realms of Air."

"She has clutched a quarry," he observed. "Well-footed, my pretty, well-trussed. Let me have pelt, dearie—nay, don't mantle it—there. Good. You shall have new bewits, with bells, and silver varvels to your jesses, with my crest upon them. Hel-lo, *hel*-lo, what have you *done*, you demned vulture? You've taken a carrier pigeon!" He opened the message capsule. *"Bombs Away,"* he read. "Rum, very rum. Doubtless the name of a horse, and some poor booby of a bookmaker has taken this means of evading the puritanical Yankee laws dealing with the dissemination of racing intelligence. Hmm, well, not my pidjin. Haw, haw!" he chuckled at the pun. "Denny!" he called.

"Yes, M'Lord?"

The Marquess tossed him the bird. "A pigeon for the pot. See that Sauncepeur gets the head and the humbles; afterwards she's to have a nice little piece of beefsteak, and a bone to break."

———

THAT, IN A way, concludes the story. The epilogue is brief. Don Lefty McGonigle, though heartbroken at the abrupt and (to him mysterious) disappearance of his son-in-law and daughter, takes some comfort in the frequent picture postcards that Philomena sends him from such places as Tahiti, Puntas Arenas, Bulawayo, and other locales where the Mafia's writ (fearsomely hard on deserters) runneth not. The Nafia (originally organized in 1880 under the full name of the National Federation of Independent Artisans, a "Wide Awake" or Chowder and Marching Society, as part of the presidential campaign of General Winfield Scott Hancock, whose famous declaration that "the tariff is a local issue" insured his defeat by General J. Abram Garfield)—the Nafia still controls all the gumball and Indian nut machines south of Vesey Street; and revels in the publicity resultant from its members' brief incarceration, along with Tosci, the Project Supervisor, and the three crewmen. The Cherry Street Mob would now not *dream* of muscling in on a syndicate whose pictures were in all the papers in connection with a portfolio containing $87,000,000; it is the Mob's belief that the fight was caused by the Nafia's attempting to hijack this sum.

Cornelius ("Neely") and Daisy Goodeycoonce have purchased, out of their share of the salvage money, one of the most up-and-coming bait-and-boatyard businesses on Long Island Sound. Granny Goodeycoonce at first was reluctant, but on learning that Daisy's mother was a Van Dyne, of the (originally) Bergen-op-Zoom, Holland, Van Dynes, she extended her blessings. It remains her view, however, that the family profession of nocturnal customs collecting is merely in abeyance, and will be kept in trust, as it were, for the children.

Granny is, in fact, for the first time in her life, no longer a Goodeycoonce, but Mistress of Snee, Lady of Muckle Greet, Baroness Bogle, Countess Ballypatcoogen, Viscountess Penhokey, Marchioness of Grue and Groole—and, presumably, Lord High Keeperess of the Queen's Bears—although on this last point Debrett's is inclined to be dubious. The fact that the older couple has chosen to go on a prolonged honeymoon with their yacht to the general vicinage of the Sulu Sea where, those in the know report, the opportunities for untaxed commerce (coarsely called "smuggling" by some) between the Philippines, Indonesia, and British North Borneo are simply splendid, is doubtless purely coincidental.

One thread (or at most two) in the gorgeous tapestry we have woven for the instruction of our readers remains as yet untied. This is the question of what happened to Tosci and his Project Supervisor after their release from brief confinement on unpressed charges of assault.

It is unquestionably true that their pictures were in all the papers. It is equally true, and equally unquestionable, that the Mafia frowns on publicity for those connected with its far-flung operations. Rumors that the two men were fitted for concrete spaceshoes and subsequently invited to participate in skindiving operations south of Ambrose Light, no matter how persistent, cannot be confirmed.

A Mr. Alexander Borjia, businessman and art connoisseur,

questioned by a Congressional investigating committee, said (or at any rate, read from a prepared statement): "My only information about the so-called Mafia comes from having heard that it is sometimes mentioned in the Sunday supplements of sensation-seeking newspapers. I do not read these myself, being unable to approve of the desecration of the Lord's Day which their publication and distribution necessarily involve. Nor can I subscribe to the emphasis such journals place upon crime and similar sordid subjects, which cannot but have an unfortunate effect upon our basically clean-living American youth."

It was at or about this point that Senator S. Robert E. Lee ("Sourbelly Sam") Sorby (D., Old Catawba) chose to light up his famous double-bowl corncob pipe, of which it has been said that the voters of his native state sent him to Washington because they could not stand the smell of it at home. Mr. Borjia (evidently as unimpressed as the Old Catawba voters by Senator Sorby's statement that the mixture was made according to a formula invented by the Indians after whom the State was named)—Mr. Borjia coughed, gagged, gasped, turned white, green, red; and after leveling an imaginary telescope consisting of his own loosely rolled fists, proceeded (in a strange, guttural, and heavily accented voice quite unlike his own) to describe what was even then going on in the secret chambers of the Mafia in such wealth of detail as to make it abundantly clear to the Executive, the Judicial, and the Legislative branches of the Government (as well as to himself, when with bulging eyes he subsequently read the transcripts of his own "confession") that he must never be allowed outside any of the several Federal caravanserais in which he has subsequently and successively been entertained.

And there let us leave him.

### AFTERWORD FOR THE LORD OF CENTRAL PARK

I HAVE BEEN told (by whom?—who knows by whom?—you think I have time to ask the ID of every nut who comes down the pike?) (ans.: No.)—I have been told that Plato, somewhere, says in effect that when a carpenter makes a table he is merely copying, in wood, a table (a prototable?) which already exists in his mind. Which already exists in his mind as a sort of mental reflection of a sort of celestial table. As it were. If Plato did not call this latter an archetype of a table, it was because Plato had not read Jung. Although of course, if Plato *did* call it an archetype, does this mean that Plato *had* read Jung? If history is, as some Greek philosophers said it is, cyclical, perhaps Plato had indeed read Jung. (This, by the way is called "metaphysics." If you had a brother, would he love noodles?) What is all this leading up to? Why are you so suspicious? The archetype or it may be the prototype of this story is a book by Robert Nathan. Chap who had lost his home during the Depression, and all his goods save for a four-poster bed, had moved the bed to a cave in Central Park. What's the matter? Shakespeare didn't steal from Holinshed? I wrote this story a long time ago, and on reading the as-yet-untitled ms., Lorna Moore, then wife to Ward Moore, said, "I know just the title for it: *The Lord of Central Park*." And I thought she was right. And I still think so. But somewhere along the line came an editor who thought he had a better one. And so it goes. (It *does* go so.)

Now. Was there an actual prototype for the Lord of Central Park himself? Well . . . In a way it is a composite; of all the magnificent loonies which used to flourish in the days of the Ever-victorious British Raj. And in a way it is based slightly upon an actual (nonroyal) duke who *was* actually the last man to be tried by the House of Lords as "a jury of his peers." The House of Lords has relinquished this right. And is Britain visibly better off? However. Not my pidgin. The duke is dead now. So never mind which one. *Fe dux* does not, after all, imply the duke was gay.

And as for the Manhattan exemplified in this tale of things odd and curious, there are those who say that it is not the real Manhattan. To which *I* say, It is *a* real Manhattan: I have walked its streets. And if much has been destroyed in the Manhattan of others, none of it has been destroyed in the Manhattan of my mind. The archetype remains, for archetypes do not suffer themselves to be destroyed.

(*Note:* Augustus Van Horne Stuyvesant has died, at a great age, after this story was written. He was the last living male descendant of Peter Stuyvesant, last Dutch Governor of New York, then New Amsterdam, New Netherlands.)

# MURDER IS MURDER

❖

"MURDER IS MURDER" is a very short story with a very striking title and the conflicts of a Russian crime novel. The story was published in 1973, and spins variations on the familiar theme of murder for inheritance.

Avram was a master of idiosyncratic variations. When a publisher asked him for biographical information he responded,. "For the benefit of those interested in astrology, my rising sign is attached to a Goodyear blimp, and my moon is in Omaha."

Michael Kurland, in his introduction to *The Redward Edward Papers*, described the quirky Davidson persona: "Avram has a whim of iron. He holds a ninth-degree black belt in idiosyncrasy, being the originator of several of the more complex modern moves. He is not antagonistic toward all mechanical devices; he is quite fond of the water wheel and maintains a strict neutrality toward the spinning jenny."

*—GD*

❖

Guy Benson used to tell himself that if Cousin May had never borrowed the book from the library he would never have got the idea. But all the same he rather thought it would have come to him anyway. The need was constant, the solution so easy—and so near.

"So, Guy," Cousin May had said, in that deep voice to which authority, amusement, and scorn seemed to come quite naturally; "so, Guy, you agree with that wretched fellow in the book, do you?"

Guy passed a hand through grey-blond hair, thinning fast now. "In the theoretical discussion, yes—but not in the brutal murder of the old miser, no."

May boomed at him: "But what is the difference?" She waved the library copy of *Crime and Punishment.* In the chair by the marble-topped fireplace Cousin Jenny pouted. She never liked conversations to grow loud and excited. It disturbed her. Even now, in fact, her soft little hands fluttered nervously toward the tray on the tiny table next to her.

"What is the difference between them?" Cousin May demanded. "The theoretical question—if you could press a button and kill a man whom you have never seen, but whose death would make you rich—"

Cousin Jenny quavered, "Oh, please! *Don't* talk about such things." The coal fire in the grate cast glints of ruddy light on the small but richly furnished room.

"—presents no moral issue at all different from bludgeoning to death an old miser for the money hidden in a trunk," Cousin May trumpeted, ignoring Cousin Jenny. "Murder is murder."

Guy disagreed. "Murder is as murder feels," was how he put it. "Violent killing would *feel* like murder. But pressing a button would *not* feel like it. And besides, all men must die. My man dies painlessly. Think what later agonies my simply pressing a button may well have saved him."

In her fluty voice Cousin Jenny said, "Oh, *such* a morbid conversation. May, dear, *would* you mind?—some fresh water, please. This in the jug is stale and tepid. Little bubbles, you know . . ." Her voice died away.

Cousin May shifted her heavy face to where Cousin Jenny sat, a little vial in one thin hand, an empty glass in the other.

"Another one of your capsules," she snorted.

"I *need* it," said Jenny staunchly.

"Capsules, pills, powders, injections, diathermy; every doctor in the city has gone to Florida at least twice on what he's gotten from you." May's voice dwindled away into the kitchen, from which a sound of running water came, then grew louder as she returned with a wet-glistening tumbler. "Your heart, your head, your nerves, your enzymes—oh, well. Here you are. Drink it down. No use *my* doing any more talking."

But she continued to talk as capsule and water rippled their way down Cousin Jenny's throat, now beginning to grow thin as the years went on—and on—and on.

Guy thought of all those years, and all the money spent on doctors by Cousin Jenny in those years, and then one single sentence of Cousin May's broke through his bubble-thoughts.

"These sickly fancies of yours will be the death of you yet," said Cousin May.

---

THAT WAS FIVE years ago. Five years in which Guy's position in the world (which had never been too good) had got steadily worse. The three-room apartment had given way to one room, without bath, in a decayed lodginghouse. The truth was that Guy gambled. And his luck was bad. Someday, he assured himself, his cards would turn, his number would come up at the wheel, his stock, his horses—but in the meanwhile he lived in a cheap little room and six days a week ate scanty meals.

But Sunday night he dined at Cousin Jenny's.

The candlelight, the embroidered linen, the savory soup, the rich brown-glazed fowl, the roast, the multitude of smaller (though by no means small) dishes moving round the table—curried this, candied that, stewed something, buttered something else. Dessert. Delicious pastries. Coffee with rum in it. Then, in the small front room there were brandy and Turkish cigarettes, while the coal fire glimmered on the polished furniture, golden picture frames, and leatherbound books.

Once at such a moment there had come to Guy's mind a phrase from the Bible—he supposed it must be from the

Bible—perhaps he had heard it in church in those dim, far-off days when he had still gone to church: *Hast thou slain and also taken possession?*

The money had all been made by their common grandfather, but Guy's father had lost much of his share, and Guy had lost the rest. Cousin May's income, though small, was sufficient, since she lived with Cousin Jenny, whose own father had not only retained all he inherited, but actually had increased it.

About money Cousin Jenny seldom spoke, but Guy knew that she had two fixed ideas on the subject: one, money should not be given to young people (young people!—he was five years her junior) because "it was bad for their character and better for them to stand on their own feet"; two, family money should be "left in the family."

Aside from a few small charitable bequests all Cousin Jenny's estate would go to Guy and May. That is, when she died. But year succeeded year and she continued to ail, to consume capsules, pills, powders, before meals, after meals, on retiring at night, and on awakening in the morning. She made the rounds from one expensive doctor to another and she never—so far as Guy could see—grew any iller, or feebler, or looked any worse. *If you could press a button and kill . . . whose death would make you rich, would you do it?*

And Guy's heart cried out, "Yes, yes, I would!"

---

HE HAD HAD the "button" for two years now. Soon after he had moved to his present room, a medical student, expelled for drunkenness, had killed himself in the dingy lodginghouse. Guy, summoned by the worried landlady into the dark hall smelling eternally of boiled cabbage and cheap bacon, broke down the door. The body was on the bed, the box was on the table by the bed, and in the box were two tiny white tablets.

When the police arrived there was only one tablet in the box. The other was in Guy's shirt pocket. For two long years, wrapped in a screw of paper tucked into an old sock, it had lain in a corner of a drawer in his rickety bureau.

Guy had approached Cousin Jenny's house from the rear, to avoid any possibility of being seen on the street. He was now at the back door, key in hand. He had the key lawfully: it had been given him to come and check the house during the ladies' annual vacation ("Just to see that everything was in order"), and he had retained it at their request ("Just in case you ever need it").

There was no chance of his being heard as he walked stealthily into the darkened house, for Cousin May slept so soundly by nature that firebells could not awaken her, and Cousin Jenny always (naturally) "took something" to make her sleep. And if by one chance in 10,000 someone *did* awaken and ask why he was there—"I felt a presentiment. I had to see if everything was all right."

Jenny would marvel and accept, and May would snort, but no more than usually.

It was all so easy, as easy as pressing a button: alongside Cousin Jenny's bed stood her night table with its tray of medical supplies; on the tray was a small saucer in which she put the large capsule she would take on waking up in the morning. Guy knew the capsules were not sealed, for once he had heard her complain that one had opened and spilled. It would be necessary for him only to pull off the top cap, insert the tiny tablet, close the capsule, and replace it; then—as silently as he had entered—leave.

I should have done this years ago, he thought, entering the hall. Somehow he did not feel so calm, so cool, now that he was inside. His breath came harder, his heart beat faster, and there seemed to be not enough air. To his surprise he found his legs trembling.

This will never do, he thought. In the hall, his eyes made out the shape of a chair. I will sit down for a moment, and rest, he said to himself, just for a moment, until I feel better—

---

NEXT MORNING AT nine o'clock a canary-colored taxi-cab stopped in front of the house and let out Cousin May and Cousin Jenny, each with a suitcase.

"Oh, I *knew* he'd be late," said Cousin Jenny petulantly. "Well, I won't enter the house until he comes."

"Now, you have only yourself to blame," said Cousin May. "*I* never heard anything, never saw anything. Such a nuisance, staying in that hotel. I hope you'll have no more notions like this one, Jenny."

Jenny moved from one grievance to the other. "But I *did* hear them, May," she protested, wide-eyed and pouting. "I really did—rustling noises at night, in the walls, in the woodwork, in the hall. Insects, mice—why, perhaps even rats!" She shuddered.

May shrugged, looked at her watch.

"Where *is* that man from Wilson's?" she asked. "He's five minutes late." She walked down the steps to peer both ways along the street, Jenny following.

"Curb your imagination, Jenny," May's voice ran on. "Beware of these sickly fancies or they will be the death of you yet."

Behind them, on the front door, was a sign with large red letters. In each of its four corners was a skull and crossbones.

*Danger,* the sign read. *Do Not Enter. Poison Gas. Rats. Wilson Pest Control Service.*

Inside the house all was silent.

# THE DEED OF THE
# DEFT-FOOTED DRAGON

---

"THE DEED OF THE Deft-Footed Dragon" was published in 1986.

The Chinese laundryman, On Lung, is drawn from David-son's sojourn in China at the close of World War II. Avram was in Peking during the Japanese surrender, and he took the opportunity to escape the confines of military life and explore the ancient culture of China. Avram's fascination with Asia lasted all of his life. His last novel published during his lifetime (which I co-authored due to his ill health) concerns Marco Polo's travels through China and Asia (*Marco Polo and the Sleeping Beauty*, Baen Books, 1988).

Michael Kurland, in his introduction to *The Redward Edward Papers*, described Avram's sojourn in China: "Davidson served with the Marines in the South Pacific. He ventured as far into northern China as Peiping, whereupon the Chinese immediately changed the name to Peking, and closed the country to all foreigners for twenty-five years."

—*GD*

---

It was frightfully hot in the streets. Most of the shops were cooler, particularly since the day was fairly young, but some of the shops were even hotter, and behind the beaded curtain in one of them a man was taking advantage of the concealment thus offered to work stripped to the waist; and even so the sweat poured off his torso and onto his thin cotton trousers. He did not think of complaining about the weather, sent as it was by the inscrutable decree of Heaven. Still, it was necessary to admit that it did slow his work down. Not that he toiled one hour the less at the washtubs, not that he toiled one hour the less at the ironing-board. Man was born to toil, and—brutal though the savages were among whom he toiled—it was almost inevitable that eventually he would have saved one thousand dollars: then he might retire to his native country and live at ease. However, the heat. And the sweat. What slowed his work down was that from time to time he was obliged to wipe his hands dry and carefully fold the garments he had ironed; in order to avoid staining them with his perspiration he was obliged to stand far away as he folded: *this* slowed the work down. *Mei-yo fah-dze*, there was nothing to be done about it; he filled his mouth with water and carefully sprayed a small amount onto the garment on the ironing-board; then he picked up a hot iron from the stove and made it hiss upon the cloth.

"It is unfortunate about the girl-child's absence," one of his countrymen then present observed.

"So." The water had evaporated. Another mouthful. Another spray. Another hiss.

"She justified her rice by folding the garments while you ironed."

"So."

This countryman was called Wong Cigar Fellow. He rolled the cigars themselves, then he peddled them to others. Sometimes he carried other things for sale from his basket—these varied—but always the cigars; hence his name. "It is said that once you pursued a far more honored craft than this one, far away in the Golden Mountain City." The man said nothing. The pedlar said, "All men know this is so, despite your great modesty. Do you not regret the change?"

"*Mei-yo fah-dze.*"

He puffed his cheeks with water, sprayed, ironed.

Wong Cigar Fellow made as though to rise, settled again. "It is too bad about Large Pale Savage Female."

The name on the shop was On Lung. Sometimes this caused the savage natives to laugh their terrible laugh. "Hey, One Lung," they would say, in their voices like the barking dogs. "Hey, One Lung, which Lung is it? Hey? No savvy? No tickee, no shirtee, hey?" And, baring huge yellow teeth, would laugh, making a sound like *hop, hop, hop.*

The wash-man dried his hands, dried his body, quickly packed up the shirt, and, holding it at arms' length before he could begin to sweat heavily again, deftly folded it around a piece of cardboard.

"Ah, how swiftly the girl-child folded shirts."

"*Mei-yo fah-dze.*" He took another shirt and spread it on the ironing board; then asked, indifferently, "What large pale savage female do you refer to?"

"Large Pale Savage Female, so we all call her. Eyes the ugly color of a sky on a bright day."

"Do not all the savages, male and female, have such ugly eyes?"

Wong Cigar Fellow was inclined to be argumentative. "No, not at all, all. Some have eyes the color of smoke. Some have eyes of mixed colors. And some even have eyes the colors of human beings' eyes. Ha! Now I know how you will remember! Did she not, as they say, 'teach a class'? On the morning of the first day of their week, in one of their temple-buildings which they erect with no thought to *feng-shui,* wind and water and other influences as revealed by geomancy—Yes. The one who taught fairy tales and savage songs to the children of our laundrymen, and did not the girl-child attend?—as why not? it may be that their strange god or gods have authority here in savage territory, so far from the Kingdom in the Middle of the World—besides: girls . . . one gives them away, merely; after eating one's rice for many years, they go off and live in another human's house. . . ."

On Lung uttered an exclamation. Yes! *Now* he recognized Large Pale Savage Female. Not in the least pausing or even slowing his pace, he listened while Wong Cigar Fellow spoke on.

The father of Large Pale Savage Female had formerly been, it was said, a merchant. Next, by cleverly putting his money out at usury, he had gotten a great fortune and owned estates and houses and documents called stocks and bonds which also gained him money. His wife having died, he had taken a concubine. "They call her a wife, but she has had no children, how can she be a wife?" and between concubine and daughter there had grown enmity. . . .

"Even in our own country one hears similar stories," chattered Wong Cigar Fellow. "Still—why does the Old Father not adopt, say, a cousin's son? Marry off the daughter to—"

On Lung said, "Who would marry her? She has such big feet."

"True. That is true. And even while it is true that the savages never bind the feet of their girl-children and even prevent us from doing so, still, even for a savage, Large Pale Savage Female has big feet. Well!" This time he really got up and grasped the pole of his carrying-basket. "It is said that the second wife so-called is gradually obtaining all the old man's property and that, not content with this, has made plans to—as they say— make a will in her favor. He is old and when he dies, what will become of Large Pale Savage Female? She must either go and play for trade in a sing-song house, or stay at home at the second wife's (or concubine's) beck and call, toiling like a servant. It is to drink bitter tea.—Farewell, Deft-Footed Dragon. It may be cooler by evening."

On Lung worked on in his steamy back-room. "One Lung," indeed! The savages had no knowledge that *Lung*, besides being one of the Hundred Names, also meant *Dragon*. It was his success as a warrior which had gained him that full name. Ah, the war! Then came a day when the high military council had summoned him to their chamber. "A treaty of peace has been signed," said the spokesman, "and one of the terms of the treaty—the others of course need not concern you—is that all such warriors are at once to leave the Golden Mountain City and depart for distant places. These august personages would not leave you without means of earning rice money in savage parts, of course. Here is your passage-ticket on the fire-wagon. It is to a town called Stream-by-a-Cataract, in a distant province whose name means nothing and the syllables of which no human mouth can pronounce. Here are fifty silver dollars. The savages are so filthy that they are obliged to make constant changes of clothing, so you will never lack employment in the laundry which it has been arranged for you to assume. Therefore lay down your heart, Deft-Footed Dragon, and never worry about your rice-bowl."

The girl-child (her mother, being weak, had taken a fever and died quickly) was indeed of great use in folding shirts; the savages called her Lily Long. Indeed, after a while, he had found comfort in the child's company: perhaps it was not his destiny to have sons. Because she was needed to fold shirts, because she was rather shy, because there were anyway no children nearby to play with, "Lily" (it was, for a marvel, easy to say; often he said it) spent much of her time in the shop. Also she was useful in chattering with the savages, none of whom, of course, could speak, when they came with shirts and other garments. The farthest away she ever went, in fact, was to the so-called "school" held in the worship place in the morning of the first day of their week . . . as though it were in any way essential to divide the lunar months into smaller quantities. . . . Sometimes she told him something of the strange tales and stranger songs learned there. Now and then he laughed. She was sometimes very droll. It was a pity she was so weak; her mother, of course, had also been so.

Almost as she entered he had recognized Large Pale Savage Female from the descriptions he had heard. "Lily was not at Sunday School today. Is she ill?" From the rear of the shop came the call of *Miss— Miss—* In the woman went. "Why, Lily, you are burning up. Let me put my lips to your brow . . . you have a terrible fever. Wait . . . wait . . ." Well did On Lung know a fever. Had the pills from the savages' apothecary helped? No they had not: therefore he was brewing an infusion of dried pomegranate rind, very good for restoring the proper balance of yin and yang, hot and cold.—In another moment, out rushed

Large Pale Savage Female, swinging her mantle over her fleshy shoulders: it seemed but a second before she was back again, and this time she held the mantle in her arms as though she were swaddling a child; curious, he followed her behind the beaded curtain.

Curiosity gave way almost to alarm: Large Pale Savage Female at once set the mantle on a table and, picking up a cold iron, proceeded to strike it repeatedly upon the garment and its contents. Very nearly, it sounded as though bones were being cracked.

"Desist, *'Miss-Miss,'* " he exclaimed. "That is clearly a costly garment as befits the daughter of a respected usurer and rack-rent landlord, and I fear it may be damaged, and the blame laid on me; desist!"

Smack! Smack! *Smack!*

In a moment the mantle was flung open, inside lay a mass of crushed ice, quicker than he could move to prevent it she had snatched from the pile first one clean wrinkled shirt and then another, tumbled the crushed ice into each and wrapped it up like a sausage; then she set one on each side of the small, feverish body.

"Doesn't that feel better now?"

The female child murmured something very low, but she smiled as she reached up and took the large pale paw in her tiny golden hand.

Large Pale Savage Female came often, came quite often, came several times a day; Large Pale Savage Female brought more ice and more ice; she bathed the wasted little frame in cooled water many times, she brought a savage witch-doctor with the devil-thing one end of which goes in the ears and the other end upon the breast; also he administered more pills. Large Pale Savage Female fed broth to the sick child—in short, she could not have done more if she were caring for a husband's grandfather.

Afterward, Wong Cigar Fellow commented, "Needless to say that I would have gone had it been a boy; although Buddhists have said that even the death of a son is no more than the passage of a bird across the empty sky, who can go quite that far?

Forget the matter in much toil and eventually you will have accumulated the thousand dollars which will enable you to return to the Kingdom in the Middle of the World and live at ease forever."

Only On Lung himself had been present at the burial of the girl-child. He, that is, and Large Pale Savage Female whose much care had not prevailed, plus the priest-savage she had brought along. It was a wet, chill autumn day; the bitter wind had scattered rain and leaves . . . golden leaves . . . henceforth the tiny ghost would sip in solitude of the Yellow Springs beneath the earth. It was astonishing how very painful the absence of the small person was found. One would not indeed have thought it possible.

The heat had become intolerable; he thought of that sudden illness which was compared to the tightening of a red-hot band about the head: nonsense: he was still upright; merely the place seemed very odd, suddenly. Seemed without meaning, suddenly. Its shapes seemed to shift. It had no purpose. No wonder he was no longer there, was outside, was moving silently from one silent alley to another, on his shoulder the carrying pole of the two laundry-baskets, one at each end. No one was about, and, if anyone were, no one would have noted his presence: merely a Chinaman, which is to say a laundryman, picking up and leaving off shirts. No one. Everything was very sudden, now. He had hidden pole and baskets behind a bush. He had slipped through a space where a board was missing from a fence. He was in a place where wood was stored and split. He had a glimpse of someone whom he knew. He must avoid such a one—indeed all others. Silently his slippered feet flew up the stairs. A voice droned in a room. Droned on and on. And on. ". . . come when I call you, hey, miss? Miss, Miss Elizabeth? Beneath you, is it? We'll see if you'll come when I call you pretty soon," the voice droned on. "I say, 'We'll see if you'll come when I call you pretty soon, miss.' Wun't call me, 'Mother,' hey, miss? Well, even if I be Mr. Borden's second wife, I be his lawful-wedded wife, him and me has got some business at the bank and the lawyer's pretty soon today, you may lay to that, yes, miss, you may lay to that; we'll see if you ain't a-going to come when I call you after that, and come at my very beck and call and do as I tell you must do, for if you don't you may go somewheres else and you may git your vittles somewheres else, too, though darned if I know where that may be, I have got your father wrapped around my little finger, miss, miss, yes, I say yes, I shall lower your proud head, miss," the hateful, nasal voice droned on.

So! This was she: the childless concubine of the father of Large Pale Savage Female! *She*, the one who planned to assume the rule of family property and cast out the daughter of the first wife? In this heat-stricken, insane, and savage world only the practice of fidelity and the preservation of virtue could keep a man's heart from being crushed by pain. He who had been known (and rightfully known) as The Deft-Footed Dragon, the once-renowned and most-renowned hatchet-man of the great Ten Tongs, hefted his weapon and slipped silently into the room. . . .

# A QUIET ROOM WITH A VIEW

"A QUIET ROOM WITH A VIEW" was published in 1964. It takes place in a retirement home. I remember reading this story as it poured out of Avram's typewriter, and loving it. There is a wonderful description of a chicken thigh as the tastiest part of the chicken, and lovely descriptions of buttery mashed potatoes and hot apple turnovers, too. How we laughed when we read the story aloud—it must have been just before dinner. In 1964, the grim reality of living in a retirement institution seemed very far away. The years passed, and Avram's health declined, until he too was confined temporarily in a retirement facility. Then the laughter faded, and the dark side of this warm yet chilling story became very real.

*—GD*

Precisely at midnight, as always, in a predestined order and immutable sequence, Mr. Stanley C. Richards was awakened to the tortures.

Midnight. The bells in the Cathedral began to toll—twelve strokes. At *one*, Mr. Richards awoke and was reminded of where he was (which meant he was also reminded of where he was not), sighed, gripped the covers.

At *three*, Mr. Nelson Stucker awoke, quite obviously *not* reminded of where he was or was not, and began to call the name of his dead wife.

At *seven*, Mr. Thomas Bigelow, snatched from slumber by the uncertain cries of Mr. Stucker, began to cough. He coughed whenever he was awake—long, slow, deep, ropy, phlegmy, chest-rattling coughs; during the day, as if ashamed, he preferred to keep out of earshot—at the far end of the garden, in the nearby park, in an unfrequented chapel in the Cathedral, even (in bad weather) in the basement; but at night, poor man, where could he go?

And at the stroke of *ten*, Mr. Amadeo Palumbo, jolted from dreams of the dank little fruit and vegetable store where he had been busy and happy for forty years, jolted into remembrance that not only the store but the very building had been torn down to make room for a housing project which had no need for fruit and vegetable stores—Mr. Palumbo moaned out his woes and grief and loneliness in the language of his childhood. "Oh, Gesu-Mari'!" he keened. "Oh, San' Giussep', San' Giacom'!"

And so, by *twelve*, by the last stroke of the chimes, a stroke echoing infinitely in the clamoring darkness, the tortured pattern of the night was established forever.

The nights seemed to last forever, there in that room under the eaves of the old building full—overfull, in plain fact—of old men and old women.

Bedtime was at half-past ten, and at half-past ten the four old men in the attic room overlooking the airshaft sank quickly enough into slumber, tired out by the fatigue of having lived through another day. But by midnight they were all near the surface again.

It wasn't, really, that the chimes were noisy or unpleasant. On the contrary, they were soft melodious chimes, world-famous, as was the Cathedral itself—to which the Alexandra Home for Aged Couples and Elderly Men was attached by some loose denominational ties. It wasn't, really, the chimes so much that awakened Mr. Stanley Richards, who had lived within sound of church bells before and could easily have slept through them. It was the sure awareness of what was yet to come that killed his slumbers at the sound of the first stroke.

It was Mr. Stucker who was unused to the sound of chimes. Mr. Stucker was very old indeed, and while he knew well enough in the daytime that he was a widower and had been one for many years, he forgot it in the night-time—forgot it again and again and again. Shallow sleep vexed by slight cause, he knew only that he was awakened to find himself not in the double bed in which most of the nights of his life had been passed. He found himself in a strange bed now, without the proper presence of his wife from whom he had not been parted for a single day or single night until parted by her death—death which he could not, or would not, remember in the darkness.

So—

*Dong. Dong. Dong.*

And—

"Henny?" called old Stucker. "Henny? Hen-ny?" And, finally frightened, louder and louder, "Henny, Henny!"

Thus awakening Mr. Bigelow, in the next bed, to his ungovernable and shameful coughing—coughing which only grew worse as he tried to stop it. Poor, coughing Mr. Bigelow! Where could he go and hide his cough in the cold and hostile night?

So, in a matter of seconds, Mr. Bigelow woke up old Amadeo—who knew on the instant exactly where *he* was, and where he was *not*, and why, and that he could never return— never!—to the nice cool basement store, with a coolness so good for the beautiful fruit, the lovely vegetables, and the sweet familiar smell of them, and the familiar customers whom he had served for more than a generation in the old neighborhood (faults and all) which had been—ah, fatal change of tense!— more than a home. His life—gone, gone forever—urbanly renewed into a giant complex of giant boxhouses, with no crowded streets, no saloons, no restaurants, no little candy stores, no pushcarts—and no basement fruit and vegetable store for Amadeo Palumbo.

"Oh, Gesu," he wept. "Oh, Santa Mari' . . ."

And so the cycle would go throughout the whole night. Mr.

Richards was not bothered by chimes, he missed no wife, he had no cough, he mourned for no lost occupation or familiar home or place. He wanted only to sleep, and he could not sleep because his roommates could not let him.

---

"WAKE UP! WAKE up there, Richards. You getting senile or something, falling asleep while people are talking to you?" Mr. Hammond shook him into wakefulness.

Mr. Richards snapped his head up. Smiled. "Sorry for that," he said.

"Not very polite, in my opinion," grumbled Mr. Hammond.

"Now, Harry—" his wife said.

"Don't you *Now, Harry* me, Alice!"

They were all in the sun parlor at the front of the first floor. Mrs. Hammond smiled over her knitting. Mr. and Mrs. Darling looked distressed. "Senile" was not a nice word at the Alexandra Home. Mr. Hammond grunted, creased his newspaper.

"That's a habit I got into many, many years ago," Mr. Richards began.

"What, falling asleep when people are talking to you?" Hammond wouldn't let go.

"No, taking cat naps. Many times we'd have to march all night through the jungle, and then, in the daytime, set one man on guard, and the rest of us would just fall down and curl up, sleep for oh not more than five or six minutes, then jump up and start marching again."

Mr. and Mrs. Darling stopped looking distressed and started looking interested. Mrs. Hammond paused in her knitting. Her husband unfolded his paper again and said, "Man writes here— as I was saying, Richards, before you fell *asleep* on me—man writes here—"

But Mr. Darling was evidently not interested in what a man wrote there. His eyes wider than before, he leaned forward and asked, "Was this when you were fighting the Bolivians in that Grand Shako War, Mr. Richards?"

Once again, firmly and loudly, rattling his paper, Mr. Hammond said, "Man writes here that—"

But Mr. Darling, even louder, said, "Hey, Mr. Richards? Fighting the Bolivians?"

With an apologetic smile to Mr. Hammond, who scowled, Mr. Richards said, "Well, point of order, Mr. Darling. In the Gran Chaco War I was fighting *with* the Bolivians. Against the Paraguayans. By that time the cat nap habit had been established for many years, far as I was concerned, and I taught it to my men. Nicaragua, fighting the bandit Sandino—Venezuela, trying to overthrow the tyrant Lopez—" He chuckled, as if reminded of something.

Mr. Darling, his face now bright with vicarious enjoyment, said, "Hey, Mr. Richards? What—?"

Asking the pardon of the ladies for telling a slightly improper story (the ladies at once assumed an expression both surprised and insistent), but reminding them that the Latin race had different customs from our own, Mr. Richards proceeded to inform them that Lopez, though never married, had had many children.

"Oh, for goodness sake!" said Mrs. Hammond.

"Well, I never!" said Mrs. Darling, a featureless, dumpy woman, though inoffensive enough; but Mrs. Hammond was a very good-looking person, her skin still firm and pink and her snow-white hair neatly set.

Tyrant though he was, Lopez was nevertheless in his own way a sort of what-you-might-call a gentleman, and he had legally acknowledged all his natural children (as the expression goes), and had them legitimatized. One day Colonel Lindbergh flew down to Venezuela and was met at the airport by President Lopez and a number of his children, who presented Colonel Lindbergh with a bouquet of flowers.

Lindbergh took the bouquet and asked, "Are they natural?"

And Lopez had replied, "Yes—but legitimate!"

Mr. Hammond snorted, amused despite himself. Mrs. Hammond laughed softly. Mrs. Darling sat absolutely impassive, while her husband smiled and awaited more, obviously not realizing that the anecdote was completed. So Mr. Richards explained, "Lindbergh meant, were the flowers natural flowers or artificial flowers. But Lopez, when he heard him say, 'Are they natural,' thought he was talking about the children; so . . ." Finally getting the point, Mr. Darling laughed and laughed and wiped his eyes.

"Well, well, you certainly have led an interesting life," he said. "How many wars you been *in*, anyway, might I ask?"

Mr. Richards smiled, shook his head. "I really couldn't say. Some of them weren't big enough to count as *wars*, I suppose—"

Mr. Darling started counting on his fingers. "You were in the *First* Balkan War, I believe you said? Yes; and the *Second* Balkan War, too, right? Against those Turks—terrible people they must have been in those days. And the First World War, and the Chinese Revolution, and helping the Polish fight for the independence from the Russians and—" He lost track and began to renumber his fingers.

Giving his newspaper one final slap before thrusting it into his pocket, Mr. Hammond said, "I suppose you call yourself a Soldier of Fortune?"

"Well, I—"

"Well, it seems to *me*—it seems to *me*, Richards—you were nothing more than just a plain hired killer!"

Mr. Darling's mouth went round. Mrs. Hammond cried, "*Harry.*"

"A mercenary, a killer, that's all!"

"Harry, shame on you!"

Mr. Richards hesitated, but before he could speak, Mrs. Darling did. Her mind moved slowly, very slowly, and when a word or reference entered, it often took several minutes for the effect to become visible. "Mr. Richards," she said now, oblivious of her husband's shock, his friend's embarrassment, Mr. Hammond's anger, or Mrs. Hammond's indignation, "I want to ask you something: did those Turkish men really have all those wives locked up in a harmen, like they say, or is that only a story? I would like to know."

His face clearing, Mr. Richards was ready to answer, but he was forestalled by the canny Mr. Hammond who said, "Chicken for dinner today."

Instantly forgetting all about every Turk who ever lived, about wives, harmens, and all, Mrs. Darling said, "Chicken for dinner?"

Pursing his lips and nodding deeply, Mr. Hammond said, "Yup. Chicken for dinner. A nice chicken thigh, hmm, Mrs. Darling?"

Eagerly and with animation she said, "Oh, yes, I always say that there is nothing like a chicken thigh because the back is too bony and the breast is too rich and the leg has all those grizzles on it and as for the wing—well, it has hardly anything on it; but the thigh—I always say the thigh is just right."

"Well, now, look here, Mr. Hammond," Mr. Richards began; but Mr. Hammond, who had been through this battle before, wasn't ready to retreat.

"Yes, you're absolutely right, Mrs. Darling," he said. "A nice chicken thigh with a brown crust on it and maybe some mashed potatoes on the side, eh? Wouldn't that just touch the spot?"

She had been listening and nodding and smiling; now she exclaimed, "Why, that's just what I always say, yes. A brown crust on it and mashed potatoes, why—Edgar always used to love the way I made my mashed potatoes, didn't you, Edgar? Edgar?"

Edgar Darling reluctantly shifted his attention from Mr. Richards. Wars! Revolutions! Soldiers of Fortune! Latin Dictators with natural children! And then—right here and now—an insult! Still looking eagerly at his adventurous friend, he began to swivel around to face his wife. "Hey, Mabel? What—?"

"Didn't you used to love the way I made my mashed potatoes? Mr. Hammond was just saying, oh, a nice chicken thigh with a brown crust and some nice mashed potatoes would just touch the spot right now, and I was telling him how you used to love the way I made my mashed potatoes. The way I made them was," she explained to the smiling, interested Mr. Hammond, "after I mashed them I used to put in a little milk and a little *butter*milk, too, and salt and pepper and a nice big lump of butter. Edgar used to say, You sure don't stint or skimp on the butter, do you, Mabel, and I'd say, No, I don't believe in it and meanwhile I'd be frying a nice onion chopped up fine and then I'd mix it all together and, oh, Edgar, he just *loved* it! Didn't you, Edgar? We had such a *nice* home," she added, her mood suddenly destroyed.

"The Turks—"

"An apple turnover is very nice," Mr. Hammond observed. Old Mrs. Darling's mouth, which had begun to quiver, slowly began to smile. "Yes," she said. "I always say that a nice apple turnover is *very* nice, provided the *crust*," she said earnestly, "the *crust* is *flaky*, and the way to make a nice flaky crust is that you take—"

---

LATER IN THE afternoon the sun was overcast and many of the residents who had been on the sun porch went into the lobby to sit near the coal fire or went into the music room to watch television. A number of people were taking naps in their rooms, among them Mr. Harry Hammond.

Mrs. Alice Hammond came into the lobby from the elevator and looked around. Stanley C. Richards was sitting at one end of a sofa, gazing at the play of colors among the glowing coals in the grate. He seemed depressed. She sat down next to him, and he looked up. He smiled, but only for an instant.

"Oh, hello, Mrs. Hammond. Good afternoon."

"Good afternoon, Mr. Richards. It's gotten quite misty out, I see."

"Yes. Yes. Quite misty," he agreed absently.

"Of course, now it's just making everything dark and dull outside, but this morning—were you up early this morning? Did you notice from your window how enchanting it was—the view of the Cathedral and the Park, with that very nice light mist over everything?"

He smiled, rather wryly, but again his smile did not last.

"Afraid not, Mrs. Hammond. My window doesn't have a view of anything except the airshaft."

"Oh, that's a pity. We have such a lovely view, and it's so nice and quiet, too. Well . . . And I *am* sorry that I never got to hear your answer to Mrs. Darling's question about the Turkish women, either."

"In the harmen?"

"In the harmen."

Their eyes met, sharing the joke for a moment. Then she looked down, fumbled for her knitting, and said, "I'm afraid Harry wasn't very nice to you this morning. We had quite a quarrel about it—the biggest one we've had since the one we had about the cemetery. Do you know about that one?"

She was surprised he didn't—she thought everyone in the Home knew about it. Many members of Mrs. Hammond's family and many of her friends were buried in Greenlawn Cemetery. It was quite a ride by public transportation, true, but there was a nice clean coffee shop only a block from the grounds, where you could stop and have a cup of tea and a piece of cake.

And Greenlawn was so beautiful. . . . Not that she wouldn't want to go if it weren't; that made no difference. Family was family, and friends were friends, and you didn't stop caring for them just because they were gone, did you? What harm was there in going once a month—or even once a week—to pay your respects? To take a few flowers, to find comfort in how nicely everything was kept, to say a little prayer from the heart—was there anything wrong in that?

"None that I can see, Mrs. Hammond."

"Nor I. But—Harry. He won't go, he just will not go, and he won't let *me* go, either. Oh, not that he ever says, 'I forbid you to go' or anything like that. But he gets so nasty, so unpleasant, and he carries on so whenever I so much as mention it that—well, much as I want to, I don't go. Not any more. And it's the same way about funerals. He won't go. Last month a very old and dear friend of ours passed on. We were indebted to her for many kindnesses. And she had asked me to take charge of the funeral arrangements—that is, everything was paid for—things like the flowers and the hymns and the guest list and things like that.

"I don't mind saying that in the past I did take care of such arrangements for the funerals of various friends and relatives— I liked to see that everything was carried out nicely. It's the last thing, almost, that you *can* do, you know. But Harry wouldn't let me. 'Jenny asked me to, Harry,' I said. 'She was your friend, too. Who else helped you with those Liberty Bonds, and took such a loss, too, if not Jenny?' I asked him. But he said she wouldn't know the difference and he got so angry he worked himself into one of his attacks and so of course I couldn't take care of any arrangements and so it was all left to strangers. . . . I hope you don't mind my telling you all this?"

It was not often that Mr. Richards had occasion to talk to Mrs. Hammond alone, and he found that he enjoyed her company. Perhaps her current conversation was not the most cheerful imaginable, but it was appropriate for a person of a respectable age to think about. And certainly it was preferable to listening to endless monologues about gall bladders and mashed potatoes and the ingratitude of children or how old Mr. X had (supposedly) cheated old Mr. Y at checkers or what a fine woman the late Mrs. A, B, or C had been. No, Mr. Richards didn't mind.

And then she absolutely astonished him.

"Harry is so resentful about you," she said, "because your life is so much richer than his."

"What?" He was dumbfounded.

"Oh, yes." Her clear blue eyes looked at him candidly. "You've been everywhere and you've done everything and he hasn't been anywhere and he hasn't done anything. He wouldn't have known what an adventure looked like. Harry spent all his life working for various linen importers. There is nothing duller in this world, believe me. So he has nothing to look back on and nothing to look forward to. That's why he is so angry when people would rather listen to you tell about your different military experiences fighting for Liberty in foreign countries than to hear him talk about what he read in the paper about the tariff. And I hope you'll forgive him for that terrible thing he said to you this morning."

*No better than a killer . . .*

———◆•❉•◆———

AFTER MRS. HAMMOND had left, reluctantly, to visit ancient Mrs. Hannivan, the Home's only centenarian, who was in her room and feeling poorly and had asked especially for Mrs. Hammond—after she had left, a thought occurred to Mr. Richards which was very attractive to him: namely, that Mr. Harry Hammond wasn't the only one who could take a nap. Stanley C. Richards could take one, too, if he liked, and at the moment he liked to very much. He got up and went to the elevator.

He felt very tired. Last night his roommates had been even noisier than usual; tonight might be no better. There was no possibility of finding another room—there simply were no vacancies (as Mrs. Fisher, the Home's director, pointed out when he spoke to her). And as for any of the single men in the other rooms changing with him—why should any of them be so foolish? They knew very well why he wanted to swap. The only possibility was if one of them should die. Old Tom Scorby had a bad heart. Mr. Kingsley could barely shuffle one foot ahead of the other. Mr. Manning—

Stanley C. Richards reproached himself for such a gruesome notion. The elevator got to the top floor (hottest in summer, coldest in winter) and he went to his room. He almost smiled in anticipation of his waiting bed as he opened the door.

But someone was sitting on his bed.

Mr. Harry Hammond.

———◆•❉•◆———

MR. HAMMOND STARTED, jumped a little bit, on seeing him. His expression had been pensive, but now he smiled.

"This is an unexpected pleasure," said Mr. Richards.

"You think so? Glad you think so." Hammond chuckled. "Just my little joke. Don't mind me."

Mr. Richards said he wouldn't, only—"I was planning to take a nap, and you're sitting on my bed."

Elaborately, his guest rose, walked over to the nearest chair, waved Richards to the vacated bed. "But before you go to sleep," he said, "I have an apology to make. Yes, sir," he said contentedly, "I did you wrong this morning. What I called you, I mean. I take it back. I take it all back, Richards, every bit of it."

Mr. Richards sat down slowly on his bed and looked at his tormentor. After a moment he said, "Thank you."

Mr. Hammond waved his hand, widened his smile. "I would like to get some information. I'm sure you can tell me. You tell everybody a lot of—well, a lot of things. You've been telling it to us for—oh, eight years now, isn't it? That you've been here? Yes, eight years. I admire the way you talk—your command of the language. It just flows out of you, you're so eloquent. You're a regular Old Man Eloquent, aren't you?"

Mr. Richards was puzzled, not so much by his guest's manner which was plainly hostile, but by his purpose. "I didn't get much sleep last night," he said. "What was the information you wanted?"

"Which side were you on," Mr. Hammond asked carefully, "in the First Balkan War, if I might inquire?"

"The Greek side. Why?"

"When was this? The First Balkan War, I mean?"

Mr. Richards frowned. "Oh . . . 1912, 1913. Shortly before the First World War. Why do—"

"And you were in the Second Balkan War, and the First World War, and the Polish-Russian War, *and* various Chinese Revolutions, *and* all those different Latin American Revolutions, and—*oh*, yes!—let us not forget that Gran Chaco War between Bolivia and Uruguay in—"

"Paraguay—"

"Paraguay, sorry. In—?"

"The Thirties sometime. Frankly, I don't remember exactly any more. I could look it up for you. What's all this about, Mr. Hammond?"

In a low, intense voice, as filled with hate and venom as was his face, Mr. Hammond said, "You're a liar."

Richards got up. "I don't know what you want out of me," he said. "I think you're a pretty lucky fellow. You've got a lovely, intelligent wife. You've got a nice big room all to yourselves, a quiet room with a view, where it's peaceful at night. I've got nobody. What—"

"You don't deserve to have anybody. You're a liar. Spent twenty-five years as a Soldier of Fortune all over the world, did you? Did you? Why, you—"

"Get out of here, Mr. Hammond."

Scrambling to his feet, Mr. Hammond headed for the door, his face scowling. He turned around and said, "But I'll fix you! I'll show you up for the bluffer and the four-flusher you are!" He took something from his pocket, held it up. It was a watch. "You left this in the downstairs Men's Room when you washed your hands for lunch. And I found it!" He dangled it triumphantly.

It was too far away to be seen clearly in the dwindling light. But its owner did not have to see it clearly to know what was engraved on the back. . . .

Mr. Hammond had left, was punching the elevator button in the hall, but his parting words still rang in Mr. Richards's ears: "Wait till they see this! Wait—"

Another voice came faintly up the shaft. "Can't take you now, we've got the food carts to take care of." The sick and bedridden were being served their suppers earlier than the other residents, as usual.

Mr. Hammond's feet went slap-slap-slapping toward the stairs. Suddenly Mr. Richards ran out, ran after him. Hammond turned around, his face becoming defiant.

Richards grabbed for the watch, but Hammond quickly pulled away his hand. For a few seconds they stood there, face to face. Many thoughts ran through Mr. Richards's mind. Then he came to a decision. With one abrupt and utterly effective movement, he pushed Mr. Hammond down the stairs.

Mr. Hammond fell down, fell forward, his mouth open on a

long, long sound which never became a word. He landed with a dull noise, and continued falling, limbs quite loose, stair after stair, until he rolled to a stop at the bottom of the landing.

Mr. Richards was right after him. The watch was still ticking. As Mr. Richards looked almost incuriously at the dead man's face, he had time for a brief reflection.

Naturally, it would be a shock to Mrs. Hammond. But her bereavement would not be without compensations. She would not have to put up with Harry Hammond's selfishness and vile temper any longer. There would be a funeral, and she could make all the arrangements to her heart's content—flowers, hymns, guest lists, everything.

And henceforth she could visit Greenlawn Cemetery as often as she liked. There would be one more grave to which she could bring flowers and see that everything was nicely cared for, one more well-kept grave over which she could say a little prayer. And then, afterward, have a cup of tea in the nice clean coffee shop nearby.

Of course, there was bound to be a certain amount of loneliness at first. She would feel it, she was bound to, particularly when she was by herself in the Hammond double room—the one with the lovely view. The nice quiet one, where no old men cried out, no old men coughed forever, no old men moaned aloud the whole sleepless night through.

Moving very quickly, Mr. Richards swept up the watch and put it in his pocket. Later, he would have the back replaced. It would not do—it would never, never do—to have anyone else see the words engraved there, words he knew by heart.

*Half a Century of Faithful Service*
*1900–1950*
*Stanley Carl Richards*
*Accounting Dep't, Walton & Co.*

Mr. Richards lifted his head. "Help!" he shouted. "Help! Somebody get a doctor, quick! Mr. Hammond fell down the stairs!"

Feet came running, voices were loud, but Mr. Richards

scarcely heard them. What would a proper interval of time be? Three months? Six? He would let events take their course.

Now that he was sure, he could be patient. It would not be long. She would be lonely all by herself in that pleasant double room, that quiet room with a view. He knew, already, what his opening words would be. "Mrs. Hammond—Alice." That was a nice name. It fitted her. "Alice—do you think you could bring yourself to marry a killer?"

# MR. FOLSOM FEELS FINE

———◆◆◆◆———

"MR. FOLSOM FEELS FINE" was published in 1986, during the period in Avram Davidson's life when he wrestled with the Veterans Administration to secure his meager pension.

What is the secret of a successful retirement? Some point to sound health and good medical care, others point to a solid portfolio of investments and pension benefits. But Mr. Folsom found another direction. He followed the trail to Gunk Up High, and the notorious illegal bush-wax trade. Beware.

*—GD*

———◆◆◆◆———

Some people can handle foreign travel, whereas others simply can't. Some can go live in a Himalayan satrapy so remote that it is not perceived on maps more than once in a century (and even that once it appears sketchily in some learned journal showing the distribution of its thirty-seven species of venomous earwigs)—can go live in it and do just fine, riding the small fur-bearing ponies as though they'd been hired for twenty minutes at a fun park and eating the roast slugs as though they were Mighty Max Burgers, whereas there are those who get ptomaine or its latest equivalent from a tortilla chip three feet south by southeast from the border of the U.S.A. Who can say why some people can travel by scooter through bandidi-infested crags and never encounter one single bandido and yet other people manage to alienate the usually imperturbable Royal Horsemen of Bothnia by dropping chewing-gum wrappers in front of their royal horses for a fine of seven *boboes.*

Mr. Edgar Folsom, who retained the same faith in the advertisements that he had had in his twenties, had for a long while planned to "Retire on Two Hundred and Twenty Dollars a Month," and had lavished his savings upon the Good Old Days Retirement Company. Often he and Mamie (Mrs. Edgar) had been almost obliged to chuckle when they considered how they—and other subscribers to the GODRC—were going to beat the system, even if nobody else was—except maybe a handful of intractable Indians in the Wild Rice Country, who could, of course, always live on wild rice. And baskets. Lots and *lots* of edible baskets, woven from succulent shoots.

"Oh, I got to hand it to *you* two," often said unmarried sister (and sister-in-law) Etta Folsom. (Their grandfather had not been originally named Folsom, he had originally been named something harsh and Nordish, a fact which only a distant cousin still claimed to remember. Mamie Folsom had long ago lost this man's address and made little attempt to find it.) *"You* two know what you're doing."

Did Mamie know what she was doing when she passed away, quite suddenly and quite silently, two weeks before his effective (compulsory) retirement date? Perhaps she did. Edgar's slightly delayed letter of notice to the GODRC was answered, eventually, by a firm of attorneys of which Edgar had never heard. It informed him that the Good Old Days Retirement Company (whose ads had not appeared in magazines for quite some time) no longer existed, as, under the laws of a not very well-known and distant state, it had wound up its affairs. Its assets now belonged to a giant conglomerate specializing in, among other things, the manufacture of waxes and wines and the management of ski lodges. This organization had somehow, certainly quite legally, acquired the assets of the Good Old Days

Retirement Company without acquiring any of its liabilities. Anyway, the letter pointed out, you couldn't retire on two hundred and twenty dollars a month any more. Not their fault, but as a matter of policy, if not benevolence—being a bunch of real good guys who know how it is—the conglomerate was going to make Mr. Folsom (in his own right and as sole heir and legatee of Mamie P. Folsom, Deceased) a lump sum, that's-*it* payment of eleven hundred dollars.

"Well, you were always a very stubborn boy, Edgar, and no one could ever tell you what to do. Now, *these* quilts I am going to take with me, *those* quilts I am letting the Historical Society have, and *this* quilt I am letting you take with you," said Etta.

"Take with me *where?* Where are we *going?*" her brother asked. He was slightly bewildered. If Mamie hadn't always told him what to do, Etta had always told him what to do.

"*I* am going to the Sons and Daughters of Bothnia Residence in Calico Falls. Women are admitted at sixty, men at eighty. In the meanwhile, where *you* are going I'm sure I couldn't say. Don't you have a pension? Hand me that wrap of tissue paper, please."

Mr. Folsom smote his brow. "*A pension!*" he cried. "*Of course!*"

———◆◆◆———

IN THE PENSIONS Office of the Civil Functionaries Administration, Mr. Roswell P. Sawell addressed his assistant, Mr. Merton Rush. "Anything new today, Mert?"

"I've just opened a new file," said Mr. Rush. "Application for pension from a Mr.—" he consulted the file "—Edgar Folsom. From Wampanoack."

"Don't matter where from," said his superior. "What's his timeage?"

"Timeage is seventeen years, seven days."

"*He* doesn't qualify for full payment, Rush."

"*I* know that."

"Minimum pension of, hm, let me calculate a second, um, two hundred and twenty dollars a month. Write him. Application denied. Subject named above may appeal. *You* know the routine."

"*I* know the routine."

"Then we'll hold up the appeal for five years, and of course he draws no interest."

"Of *course.*"

But Mr. Merton Rush did not move back into his own office and Ros Sawell asked, in some surprise, "What are you waiting for, then?"

Mert reminded his boss that it was CFA policy to grant three such applications without delay monthly, that so far they had granted only two, and that it was the last day of the month.

"Oh. Um. Yes, so it is. Shoot. Oh, well, *grant* it. He'll soon enough try to collect the pension in a foreign country with a subversively lower cost of living. *Then* we'll jump him."

Mert said, "Oh, *boy,* yes! Estopped. Suspended pending investigation. That's *right!*"

"We got to think of the taxpayers."

<hr />

ETTA HAD A very nice room with her own foyer facing the granite statue of The Intrepid Bothnian on the lawn. Constant hot tap water for making instant coffee. "Well, have you made up your *mind* yet, Edgar, what you're going to do? Your lease runs out this month and your rent will be raised."

Mr. Folsom straightened his bowtie. (He always had a little trouble with it.) "Well, I certainly hope and trust the President will do something about it."

Etta was very patriotic, *but.* "Why should he do something about it?" she asked, for once a bit surprised.

"Well, I wrote and asked him to."

"Oh, *you*—Edgar. What's that sticking out of your pocket instead of a nice clean hankie? A letter. What would you do if I weren't here to remind you." Deftly, she opened and read. "Well, I never. You are going to get a Civil Functionary Partial

Pension of two hundred and twenty dollars a month. Oh, for goodness sake."

Edgar, however, wasn't surprised. Not at all. "There, you *see*. I guess an American citizen can write to his President if he wants results. Guess that Good Old Days Retirement Company, he fixed their little red wagon sure enough."

For once Etta had not much to say, but she said it. "*You* can't retire on two hundred and twenty dollars a month. Have you *seen* the prices lately? Where do you *shop?*"

"Tut," said Edgar. "I'll go live in some country with a lower cost of living. Few can't lick 'em, join 'em. Huh?"

———————

THE YOUNG PERSON in the travel agency repeated his question. "Where can you go for eleven hundred dollars? Well, the pitcheresque Republic of La Banana has just been opened for tourism and foreign migration. We got this bunch of *lit*erature in just today. 'The picturesque Republic of La Banana, which gave its name to the familiar succulent yellow fruit, contains one hundred and fifty-two species of edible wild slugs, also many colorful parrots.' Here, you can read it while I make out your package."

In the newly opened consulate and travel office of the Republic of La Banana, Bombo Duzbuz Jambatch looked at Mr. Folsom listlessly. "You wish to go to our country? Fine. So go. One moment. Health precaution. Stick out tongue, please. Thirty-seven dollar, you pay *me*. Okay, now I make out your Permission."

Mr. Folsom had never traveled very much. "You're put?" Mamie used to ask. "*Stay* put."

He now inquired, "Permission for *what?*"

Bombo Duzbuz Jambatch looked up, surprised. "*Every*thing," he replied. "Enter. Exit. Transit. Operate steamroller. Even, you may to run for elective office. Save that no more we have elections. *Kay.* All finish. Here."

Mr. Folsom took the large and colorful paper, folded it. "When does it have to be renewed?"

The bombo suddenly seemed bored. "How *I* know? *I* am not prophet. Do not push fates. Perhaps never. You think we are tyranty? Go."

Edgar went.

---

IN THE CAPITAL hamlet of Gunk Up High, several gorges away from the non-capital hamlet of Gunk Not So High, Mr. Folsom found there was something of a housing shortage. The best he could obtain for himself was an eight-room *poppick* at a rental of one dollar per room per month, the landlord insisting on renting the *poppick* as a single unit. The other natives rolled their eyes at such cupidity and murmured a local proverb loosely translated as, "Foreigners and their welcome money often make the rich richer." It was, of course, far more room than Edgar needed, but he found that the space gradually filled with the picturesque native furniture, artwork, and bric-a-brac which he found it amusing to buy at the Weeny Bazaar (the Great Big Bazaar dealt mostly in milch-sheep and rhinoceros legs). Sometimes he spent as much as two or three dollars a month on such items.

*Goro-goro luntch-potch*, as they say in the pawkey idiom of La Banana. Meaning, So the time does pass, even so.

---

"WELL, WHAT DID I tell you?" said Mr. Roswell Sawell. "Didn't he run true to form? Here's a change of address for his Civil Functionary Partial Pension check, just as I predicted."

"You certainly can pick 'em, Chief."

"Now, theoretically—" Ros pushed the compliment aside "—any American citizen may elect to receive his pension anywhere in the world—Andorra, Oz, Borrioboola-gha, *any*where. But we don't *like* um to! *We* know that nobody can live on that kind of money! Where's the cost of his *car?* Where's his *gas* money? You know what a *TV set* costs in some a these countries with subversively low standards of living? *Dish*washers? As for, say, the price of *beef*, well, you just price it yourself! If *we* can't make it, *they* can't make it! No, Mert: less a fellow's getting a full career pension of, well, say at least two thousand dollars a month, there's no way he can live on his pension. Which means—well, *you* know what it means!"

Merton nodded his birdy head. "Il-lic-it en-ter-prise." He rolled out the syllables with relish. Relish, and unction.

"Absolutely. Smuggling Scotch whiskey. Promoting ox-races. And, increasingly, the notorious bush-wax trade."

His assistant agreed with him. "That's terrible stuff, that bush-wax."

Terrible? said his superior. Terrible was hardly the word for it. It was diuretic, euphoric, and non-addictive! No wonder the Pensions Office of the Civil Functionaries Administration worked hand in glove with the Illegal Ear Substances Division of the Crack-Down Department. "So let's put a Stop on his pension, and he can swim back, if he likes, and file an appeal. *There's* a good ten years he won't be robbing the taxpayers.— Why are you just *stand*ing there, Mert?"

Merton said because they had already put Stops on eight hundred and thirty-five pensions that month already, which was tops according to policy, and so they'd better wait till next month.

"Don't rock the boat, in other words?"

"You said it, Chief!"

"Well, you may be right. I have a sort of nose for these things. But, *next* month we drop the Himalayan Mountains on him!"

He and his assistant laughed soundlessly.

---

MR. EDGAR FOLSOM never drank Scotch whiskey, thought the ox-races were smelly, and would have been bored by TV had there been any. (The mountain ranges made it impracticable. As for washing his dishes, he threw them all into the gorge behind his house and got new ones.) He was spending so little money he was obliged to buy quite a number of boxes to store the money he didn't spend. He was by now probably the richest man in Gunk Up High, and the lower caste of natives never came near his house at night lest the gods, who obviously *love* rich men (else why are they rich—answer *that* one, would you?), eat their kidney-fat. They may not know much, those innocent, childlike, very dirty natives, but they know that without kidney-fat you just ain't got it.

One day Mr. Edgar Folsom was strolling along a road (path, the very particular might call it) which had yet to receive the biannual attentions of the steamroller. (The fact is that the dictator was very fond of operating it himself and paid no attention to any of the schedules the Department of Public Works submitted to him—very, very occasionally.) Rather incuriously, he observed someone he rather thought was a foreigner. In fact, this one admitted as much to him, saying, "I am a foreigner."

"What brings you here? Not that it isn't a nice little place."

The man said he was allowing vortices of energy to carry him along as he observed the Way and the Eternal Snows.

"Oh."

The foreigner took him by the arm and slightly turned him. He gestured. "Just cast your gaze through the, like, mists of illusion and tell me if there are three energy-forms in uniform standing at the crossroads."

Mr. Folsom slightly squinted. "Well," he said, "usually there are two policemen standing there, I don't know why—I mean, there's never *that* much traffic—but today I guess there *are* three."

The foreigner said that that which was not an enigma was an illusion. "Just point out your house—I mean the compass-point where the non-real you is dwelling, as it were, man. There? Good. Now, would you do me one big favor? My arm hurts today—a mere illusion to be sure, but would you just let me put this in your case and I'll meet you later. Right now it's my, um, time of withdrawal and meditation."

---

OF THE THREE at the crossroads, only one spoke sufficient English to be more than merely amusing. This was Bombo

Yimyam Hutchkutch. "Ah, Meestair Edgar Folsom, you are out to ramble, as often, eh?"

Mr. Folsom acknowledged it. "I was taking some snapshots with my little old Kodak brownie camera and the people there started yelling, so I stopped and gave 'em some pennies—anyway *I* call 'em pennies. So then they all kissed my coat lapels and gave me what they said is the stuffed head of a yeti. I put it in my briefcase. No, that's not it. I dunno what *this* is—some other foreigner asked me to take it down the hill for him, I guess because it will help his hurt arm." And he gazed round the mountain-circled universe with his candid eyes.

From the policemen meanwhile had come noises of suspicion, irritation, and something which another might have taken for dismay. Said the bombo, "*We* will take it down the hill for you, Meestair. *We* will take care to find him and alleviate his hurt arm. What, to think he can move about with this stash and pay us *nothing?* Proceed upon your ramble, Meestair Folsom, and may you live in our nation for a hundred thousand eons."

--------

"*Well*, Chief," said Merton, "guess what just came in?"

"Some more appeals against estoppment of pensions, I suppose," suggested Mr. Sawell indifferently. The Pacific Ocean and the entirety of the Indoo Sea might have been filled with swimming appellants, much cared *he*.

Nay, not so, Merton told him. "It's the monthly exchange list from the Illegal Ear Substances Division of the Crack-Down Department, and guess what? Folsom, Edgar, in La Banana has been instrumental in catching a cache of illegal bush-wax!"

They gazed at each other with a wild surmise. Then, slowly but with admiration, Mr. Sawell said, "I guess he is one of the IED's men. This pension thing, it's just his cover. Of *course* he doesn't have to live on it. Get the big red rubber stamp and stamp his file NTBTW. Get going, now, Mert." And Merton, bowing his head respectfully, proceeded to affix the indication that Edgar Folsom's pension was Never To Be Tampered With.

A civil functionary has many, many duties. The public scarcely knows.

———◆•••◆———

As FOR MR. Edgar Folsom, he has grown tired of hoarding his money. For one thing, he sends contributions to the worthy causes he finds mentioned in the worn, worn copies of *Reader's Digest* that come his distant way as padding in the ox-caravans. And for another, he has bought a choice and select herd of jet-black milch-sheep, plus three dancing bears.

He feels just fine.

# THE IMPORTANCE OF TRIFLES

WHEN "THE IMPORTANCE OF TRIFLES" appeared in *Ellery Queen's Mystery Magazine* (January 1969) the editors diverged from their normal policy of "blurbing" each story with a brief paragraph. Instead, they published a full page of comments, setting the tale in its historical context and praising it and its author. This unusual attention was well justified.

As early as December of 1958 Avram Davidson had written to Frederic Dannay (one half of "Ellery Queen") about a proposed series of stories and asking for advice on his research. The series was to be "set in the days when Mordecai Manuel Noah was Sherrif (or Sheriff) of New York and Jacob Hays was High Constable." The stories would involve "the New York criminal scene, @ 1830, give or take a decade or so." Later in the same letter Avram added, "I am fond of the Jacksonian Era and rather believe that I can do some good stories on the Noah/Hays teeter-totter; certainly I shall enjoy doing them."

It was a decade before "The Importance of Trifles" saw print, and it seems to have been the only story actually written in the planned series. It is a splendid piece of work, a fine police procedural complete with crime, clues, suspects, deduction, and action. It deals also with the social issues of its day—which are not so different from the social issues of ours—and with the seemingly perpetual struggle (Avram's "teeter-totter") between political appointees and law-enforcement professionals. It is that rare story that truly merits the too-often awarded designation of *tour de force*.

—*RAL*

---

Jacob Hays, high constable of the City of New-York, had eaten his usual breakfast of fried eggs and beefsteak, broiled fish (shad, this time), a heap of pan-cakes, a pair of chickens' wings, hot buttered rolls, and tea. More and more people were drinking coffee, as the nineteenth century rolled into its fourth decade, but Jacob Hays still imbibed hyson rather than java.

"Promise me, Mr. Hays," his wife demanded, as he rose to leave, "that if it commences rain you'll take the Broad-way caravan."

"Mrs. Hays, good morning," said her husband briefly. And walked out of the house with brisk strides.

The day was dark, but it would be darker than it had ever been before he would spend eight cents to ride a mile. Many a mickle makes a muckle, his mother used to say; and his father's advice had been: Take care of the pennies and the pounds will take care of you. Besides, did it befit the holder of his office to cram into a crowded caravan like a commission-merchant or a law-clerk? Would the people not think he was doddering if they saw him in an omnibus? He, who patrolled the city afoot by day and by night? Just so.

Presumably, it had been a quiet night, for no message had come to pull him out from his featherbed. No riots or major fires—a mercy.

It had been twenty-six years since old Governor De Witt Clinton, then Mayor of New-York, had appointed him High Constable, and in all that time the City had never ceased to grow—nor had crime ever ceased to keep pace with commerce and culture. Jacob Hays had come to relish quiet nights, though scarcely even one of these passed in which he did not awaken, straining his ears for some sound—near or far—betokening a conflagration in South-street or a murderous "hooley" in the Five-Points. And yet there were citizens who still expected him to undertake the functions of a hog-warden! The very thought of it made him snort. He looked around challengingly—then smiled. There was no trouble in the Broad-way at this time of morning, or, indeed, at any other time of day. The wide, clean street, lined with fashionable hotels and shops and busy office buildings, stretched along for almost three miles, the wonder of the country—proud New-Yorkers said, of the world. And all along it, from the Battery to Twentieth-street, looked upon from wooden shacks and towering five-storey brick buildings alike, a press of carts, drays, wagons, carriages, cabs, and omnibuses filled the eighty-foot width of the road with a ceaseless rumbling.

"Good-morning, High Constable," said a dry-goods merchant, setting out open boxes of new percales and nankeens for passers-by to examine at pleasure. "Good-morning, Mr. Hays," said an admiralty-lawyer, on his way to visit the forest of masts along the lower East-River. "Good-morning, Jacob," said old Alderman Ter Williger.

And two young bloods, of the sort which had begun to infest the Bowery-road, hats cocked as sharply over carefully-soaped locks of hair as gravity would allow, nudged one the other sharply, and hissed, "Old Hays!"

Their expression, as they met his cold, knowledgeable eye, changed from one of studied insolence to a mixture of uneasiness and would-be defiance. He gave his high-constabular staff, which he always carried with him, a slight shake in their direction, and they lowered their gaze and slunk by. No, they were just strutting, and would make no trouble in the Broad-way.

The unpaven, narrow, pig-ridden, and stinking side-streets of the lower city, ill-lit and under-patrolled (but try to obtain additional money for more constables from the Board of Aldermen!)—these were the places they would choose for crime. And it was in the Bowery, with its popular theatres and pleasure gardens, that they would seek their amusement: jostling citizens, insulting ladies, and causing commotions in general.

Once in his office Hays ignored the view of the City Hall

Park, and dealt rapidly with that portion of the day's new business which responded to rapid treatment. Then he looked over his correspondence—runaway daughters and fugitive sons; complaints of bogus lotteries and similar frauds which seemed to go on forever—like "The Spanish Prisoner" swindle, the "English-Estate-in-Chancery-to-which-you-are-heir" swindle. "Any new 'cards'?" he asked his assistant. There were—there always were. Bank robbery in Portland, green-goods merchant hastily departed from Philadelphia, murder in Albany, funds embezzled from London, cargo of rum stolen in Boston, shipment of cotton made off with in Georgia, eleven absconded apprentices, two fugitive slaves, piracy in the Gulph of Mexico. "Post those with descriptions," he directed. "What's next?"

"Next" was a young Colored man whose bright red shirt, wide-bottomed trousers, and glazed hat—the last held respectfully in his hands—told Hays of the man's profession before he even looked at the paper held out to him.

WHEREAS, an ACT of the CONGRESS of the Year 1818, intituled *AN ACT TO DEFINE AND PROTECT THE STATUS OF SEAMEN* [Hays read], does not mention the Status of Seamen who are Persons of Color, and WHEREAS, the *Legislature* of the *STATE OF NEW-YORK* in the Year 1820 has authorized the Certification of Seamen domiciled or denizened in the State of New-York who are Free Persons of Color, now, THERE-FORE, be it known that I, *Jefferson Van Der Wett*, a Clerk of the CITY OF NEW-YORK, do hereby certify that the bearer, *Lucas Oaks*, a Seaman of this City, and a Man of Color, is known to me on good evidence to be a FREE MAN, and I do further Enjoin all Men of whatsoever Cities, States, Territories, and Nations, to recognize him in such Status and not to Hold, Use, nor Dispose of him, the aforesaid *Lucas Oaks*, a FREE MAN of Color, as if he were not in Fact *FREE*.

"Anything against him?" Hays asked. The Constable shook his head. Hays dipped his quill, wrote *No Criminal Record. J.*

*Hays. High Constable, C. of N-Y.*, scattered sand, and handed it to the Negro who departed with thanks.

And so the day proceeded. The Five-Points—that foul and teeming human rookery where Cross, Anthony, Littlewater, Orange, and Mulberry meet—had had its usual murder. The usual sailor had been found dead by violence. This time the almost nightly occurrence was not the same, though often enough it was a sailor found dead in the Five-Points; often in its black and filthy heart—the swarming, putrefying tenement called the Old Brewery.

There was little chance of discovering the killers at the moment, if ever. The night had witnessed their deeds, and as little as the night would testify, so little would the furtive inhabitants of the criminal world testify. Until and unless, of course, the cut-throats had a falling out. In which case there might be a dirty, illiterate note some morning on Hays's desk— a whisper in the ear of the Watch (as the Constabulary was also called)—notes and whispers which might lead to arrest or conviction. Or might not.

It sometimes seemed to Jacob Hays that the work-houses, paupers' wards, and felon-cells of all the world, European as well as American, were pouring their wretched contents into New-York; although he knew well enough that most of the ever-increasing stream of immigrants were good people. It would ill behoove him to rail against "foreigners," as some were doing. Had not his own mother been born abroad? And his father's parents? When you came down to it, whose stock *was* entirely "Native American"?—except for the Indians. And there were those who claimed (Hays recalled a recent sermon at Scotch Presbyterian Church) that the Indians themselves were none other than the Lost Tribes of Israel!

It was Hays's custom, if the affairs of the morning permitted, to take some light refreshment about ten o'clock, and then to read through all the newspapers. That is, not to read every word, but to have a look at the items marked for him by his assistant, Constable Moore, who had standing instructions to check off any bit of news referring to crime or the police. It was always amusing—sometimes instructive—to observe the way in which the same incident was treated in different newspapers, and to see how they agreed (or, more often, disagreed) with the official report of the same incident.

In the staid *Commercial Gazette* of this morning, for example, there was the single line: *The body of a man, as yet unidentified, was found yesterday in Dunstan-Slip.* That was all. *A man.* Not, Hays noted, *a gentleman.* In the lives or deaths of the lower orders of society the *Commercial Gazette* was supremely uninterested.

The *News-Letter* had this to say:

*Yesterday afternoon the body of a man was discerned floating in the River at Dunstan-Slip by a woman of the neighborhood. The dead person, who, by his dress, was evidently a member of the sea-faring class, had not long been exposed to the briny element, and appeared to be in his middle years. It is opined that he came to his death by natural causes. His name has not yet been learned.*

The recently-established *True Citizen and Temperance Advocate*, however, had learned—or said it had learned—his name.

*An intelligent and respectable female identified the remains to this journal as that of one Gorman or Gormby, a sailingman, much given to the prevalent vice of his class (though not only of his class) vide licet, imbibing large quantities of alcoholic liquors—we do not denominate them 'beverages.' Whilst in a condition of intoxication, the dead man, we adduce, fell into the Slip and drowned. Within four blocks of the fatal scene our reporter counted no less than thirty-nine dram-stores, grogshops, gin-mills, brandy-houses, and so-called "grocery" establishments, these last entirely devoted to purveying raw spirits to the ignorant. When will a supine administration awaken to the menace, et cetera, et cetera.*

And the *Register* devoted a full column to what it called a

*dastardly crime, undoubtedly committed by a gang of crimps, bent on conveying the innocent seaman against his will to the cruel mercies of a conscienceless master-mariner bound for foreign ports where the writ of the American Republic runs not. It was doubtless owing to his reluctance to be forced into a berth he did not desire that the unfortunate Jack-Tar resisted so vigorously that his kidnappers decided on his Death. He was tossed into the brackish waters of Dunstan-Slip where, being like the generality of sea-farers, unable to swim, he expired by drowning.*

Old Hays snorted. "Catch any crimps tossing twenty dollars worth of two-footed merchandise away! Those they don't dope, they bash—but, one way or another, they get them aboard alive. Any wounds on him, Neddy?"

"Few bruises, Mr. High—but no wounds," said Constable Edward Moore. "Course he wasn't no Gorman nor Gormby, any more than he was crimped." His tone of voice indicated that he realized he was not telling his superior anything the latter didn't know.

Hays nodded, picked up the official constabulary report, mumbled the words to himself, adding his own comments. "Bruises on breast, abdomen, and face; also, back of neck. Couldn't have gotten them all by falling down: been fighting. Clothes worn and dirty—been on shore a long time. Not known to the Watch or any of our water-front friends—didn't ship out of the port of New-York. Shoes show signs of recent hard use— walked from his last port."

"Wasn't killed for his fortune, we may be sure," said Moore. "The Coroner's inquisition?"

"Dead before he hit the water, seems like. Neck broke. Lungs dry. Hardly swollen, scarcely a mark on him from fish or crabs." Hays thought about his breakfast shad, but he had a strong stomach (twenty-six years as High Constable!) and didn't think about it long. "He was found in mid-afternoon, and conjecture is that he'd been dead since the night before. Woman emptying a slop-bucket spied him."

The two men mused on this unusual fastidiousness in a district where slops were emptied, usually, out the nearest window. Then Moore continued: "Noteworthy features? Had a great swelling of the left ear-lobe. Forget what you call it. Key-something."

But Hays remembered. "A keloid. Scarred over and swelled when he had it pierced for an earring, I expect. Sometimes happens so. We'd know he was a sailor from that alone. Potter's Field?" Constable Moore nodded.

Hays started to put the report down, then sensed, rather than saw, that his assistant had something else to tell him; and waited.

"He had this in his mouth." The Constable held out a screw of paper, unwrapped it. Inside lay a piece of fibre, yellowish-brown in color. "Cotton—raw cotton. A trifle, but I thought I'd save it for you. What do you think?"

Hays shook his head. "No idea. But glad you kept it. File it with the report. What's next?"

"Lady robbed of a diamond heirloom ring wants to see you about it, personal. Englishman with letter of introduction from Lord Mayor of London. Three candidates for the Watch. Man from Eagle Hotel with information about the gang of baggage-thieves. A—"

The High Constable raised his hand. "That'll do for the while. Lady first . . ."

---

Two nights later there was a wild fight involving the crews of three ships moored in South-street. The Night Constable-in-charge was new to the post and, not trusting to his own ability to discriminate between riots major and minor, sent for Hays. He came quickly enough, though the brawl was over by then; most of the men had either stumbled aboard their vessels or staggered away for further entertainment. The few who insisted upon continuing the affair had been hauled off to the Watch-house to meditate on their sins. And several of the spectators vanished the instant they saw the High Constable's well-known figure come in sight.

But by that time something else had developed.

"Hold up your lanterns," Hays directed his men. "The gas-light from the street is so dim I—that's better. Ah, me. More sailors must die ashore than at sea, I think."

The alley was wide enough to accommodate only two men, and one of these was dead. Hays patted the pockets of the pea-coat, was rewarded with a jingle, and thrust a hand inside. "Thirty cents."

For thirty cents a man could eat well and drink himself into a stupor and still have enough left for a night's lodging if he was sober enough to want more than the floor of the city to sleep on. Men were killed for much less than thirty cents. Therefore—

Word had gotten around, and a knot of night-crawlers, still excited from the fight, crowded into the alley, pressing and cran-ing for a glimpse. Hays rose and looked at them; at once several caps were pulled low and faces sunk into collars. He held out his staff. "Clear the alley, citizens. Just so. Constables, take the body out. Has a cart been summoned? Lay him down here. No, don't cover his face. I want him identified, if possible."

It proved easily possible. The dead man was identified be-fore his coat touched the sidewalk. "Tim Scott. Everyone knew Tim Scott. Poor Tim. Poor Tim's a-cold." (This last from a gen-tleman later identified as a play-actor at the Park Theatre.) "Spent his money like a gentleman. Who saw him last alive? Well . . ." A reluctance to be identified in this capacity was at once apparent.

But other information continued to come forth. "Not so long ago Tim bought wine for everyone at Niblo's Gardens. And segars. Yes, segars, too, for all the gentlemen. Did this more than once a night, and for more than a few nights, too. . . . En-emies? Not a one in the world."

"I suppose his friends killed him, then?" Silence again. Cart-wheels rattled, and the crowd, gathered from all the dram-cellars whose yellow lights beckoned dimly through dirty window-panes, parted. As the body was lifted into the cart Hays removed his hat, and—one by one—reluctance evidently springing not so much from contumacy as from ignorance that this little gesture was customary or expected—one by one the greasy hats and dirty caps came off. Then the cart clattered away again. The crowd, still eager for excitement, stirred restlessly.

"All good citizens," said Hays, "will now go home." He did not expect the suggestion to be taken literally. If "home" was a lumpy, dirty pallet on a filthy floor it naturally had no appeal to match that of a brandy-shop or an oyster-stall, where some of the "good citizens" were even now heading to satisfy newly-awakened or previously-ungratified appetites; even if "home" was the streets, the mud, filth, and dim lights were no deterrents—there was nothing better at home. In the streets there were at least company and excitement. But the crowd dissolved, and this was all Hays had hoped for.

The next day Hays paid a further visit to Tim Scott, now naked on scrubbed pine-boards. Constables Breakstone and Onderdonk accompanied him. Both young Watch-officers had taken to heart Hays's almost constant insistence on the importance of "trifles," which was more than could be said for most of the Watch, to whom a crime was insolvable if not accompanied by a knife with the knifer's name burned in the hilt.

"How much would it take to treat the house at Niblo's to wine and segars several times a night, several nights running?" Hays asked, looking at the dead man's face. The death pallor could not dispel entirely the tokens of sun and wind.

"More than a sailingman would be likely to make on a coasting voyage," Constable Breakstone said. He was the son of a ship-chandler, had grown up along the water-front, and knew its ways. At Hays's look of inquiry he continued, "Tim had said his last trip was on a coaster, but he didn't say where to. Besides, he hadn't been gone long enough for an overseas voyage. But that money in his pocket, sir, it wasn't the last of what he'd had."

"You mean there's more somewheres?"

"No, sir. I mean that he'd spent it all some time ago. He'd been cadging off the lads since then. Then the other day he said he was going to get some more. He turned up at Barney Boots's gin-parlor last night with a dollar, and the thirty cents was the last of that. And he was heard to say that this was just the beginning—that he was going to get more very soon. I

asked did he have a particular friend, and it seems he did—
Billy Walters. Some think they'd sailed together on this last trip.
But no one has seen Billy lately. And that's all I know, sir."

Hays nodded. "That's a good bit to go on. Meanwhile—"
He lowered the sheet. "Just so. I thought these would show up
better today." On the dead man's muscular throat were two sets
of small and ugly marks. "Strangled, you see. And strangled
from behind, too. Either someone crept up on him unbe-
knownst, or he knew the man behind him and wasn't expecting
violence. Mr. Breakstone, hold the body up. Now you, Mr. Onderdonk, stand behind him. Let's have your hands. Big ones, a
wide spread—just like these. Let your fingers rest where I
place them."

One by one he placed the young man's fingers so that each
rested on one of the finger marks, or as near to it as possible.
Leaving them so, he peered at the skin of the dead man's back.
"Just so. Jabbed up his knee, used it as a lever, grabbed the
throat, and squeezed. Tim Scott was a strong man. This fellow
was stronger. Had finicking ways, though. All right, let him
down."

Breakstone covered the face. " 'Finicking ways,' Mr. High?"

"Yes," said Hays thoughtfully. "Let the little finger of his
left hand stick out whilst he was doing his evil work. Like he
was drinking a dish of tea. Mr. Breakstone—"

"Sir?"

"You might see that the word is passed among those who
enjoyed the late Tim Scott's hospitality at Niblo's—and those
who enjoyed his business anywhere else, like Barney Boots, for
instance—that it would be the mark of a good citizen and a
good Christian to contribute for funeral expenses."

"I'll do that."

"Let it be known," said Jacob Hays reflectively, "that I particularly favor such contributions. Yes. Just so."

---

CRIME NEVER SLEEPS, but it is no coincidence that in warmer
weather it is more restless than commonly. As the shad run

dropped off and Spring, on its way into Summer, continued to crowd the trees with green, the residents of those districts in which few trees grew seemed more and more to fall into those lawless ways from which they had taken a partial vacation during the Winter months. Which often proved unfortunate for visitors to those districts. Mrs. Jacob Hays, however, was unsympathetic.

"Do not tell me, Mr. Hays," she said, "that you intend to spend the greater part of yet another night on patrol." Her husband, as if obedience itself, did not tell her that, nor anything else—but addressed himself to his supper. "I cannot believe," she continued presently, "that these people who get themselves into trouble are truly innocent of improper intention. What is a respectable person *doing* in the Five-Points? Tell me *that*, if you please, Mr. Hays."

Evidently he did not please, for he said, "Mrs. Hays, good-evening," rose, and departed. He had doubled the patrol in the Five-Points these nights, and that meant taking men away from other places. Wall-street and South-street would howl; well, let them. Or, rather, let them come out in favor of higher taxes to pay for the extra protection the city needed. Let them pave the streets, too, while they were at it; and put up more gas-lamps. Let them—

He stopped. There was some one very near at hand, some one who did not wish to be seen, some one in the pool of darkness which was the space between two buildings at his left. "I know you are there," said Jacob Hays.

And from the darkness a low voice said, "There is a body in the Old Brewery."

"There usually is. What floor?"

"Second."

"Just so. What else?" But there was nothing else. His ears had heard no sound of departure, but he knew that whoever it was had gone. And he walked faster.

On Anthony-street he found Constables Breakstone and Onderdonk, gestured them with his staff to follow him. As he approached the looming hulk of the Old Brewery, the neighborhood was in its usual uproar—screams, shouts, obscenities, drunken songs, the raucous cries which would go on almost till dawn, and then begin again almost at once. Then—from somewhere—not in a shout or scream, not in any tone of hate, but with a sharp note of warning—"Old Hays!"—and silence fell. That is, comparative silence: quiet enough to hear his own and his men's feet on the muddy sidewalk and then, as they entered the building, on the rotten wood of the floor, or, rather, on the accumulated filth of years which lay inches thick over the rotten wood except where the flooring had given way and left ugly, dangerous holes.

"Turn up your lamps," he directed. It was small enough light they gave at best, though enough to keep them from breaking a leg. It was a wonder that the tiny lamps burned at all in here, the air was so foul. There was no railing on the sloping stairs, but still the three men gave the walls a wide enough berth, alive and rippling with vermin as they were.

And all the time there was a murmuring, a muttering, a whispering, a hissing from the darkness. Doors were ajar and dim lights shone and bodies slunk past, but no faces were seen. Rats' claws scrabbled. The stench grew more fearful, more noisome. Doors closed softly as they approached, opened after they passed. But the door at the end of the first corridor did not move, and behind it Hays found what he had come for.

The dead man was sprawled in a chair at the table, head backwards and upwards. A bottle had been spilled recently— the sharp odor of "brandy" (as the raw, white whiskey was called) filled the room and the liquor itself was still damp; but of the bottle there was no trace. Gift horses were seldom looked long in the mouth at the Old Brewery. The dead man's face was bruised, and blood welled from his nose and from a cut over one eye, an eye which stared in fierce amazement at the shadowy ceiling.

In his ribs on the left side a knife had been driven. It was still there.

They examined the floor carefully, but nothing was there except blood and dirt. In one corner was a foul-looking bed whose greasy rags yielded nothing. A cracked water-jug. An empty ditty-bag. And that was all.

As Hays ended his scrutiny of the room he saw that young

Breakstone was intently looking at the dead man's face. The Constable caught his eye, and nodded. "I've seen him before, sir. He came into my father's place a few times, on and off, when his ships were in port, to sell his adventures. But I can't put my mind on his name or his ships! Maybe they will come to me, by and by."

"Any big adventures?"

Breakstone shook his head. "I don't think so. A chest of tea. A few sacks of coffee or wool. A barrel of sugar or molasses. That sort of thing. Once, I think, he had a bale of cotton—that was the biggest."

"Ah, well. Let me hold the lanterns while you get a grip on him. I'll go ahead and light your way. Mind your—" He stopped and bent over just as they passed through the door. Something was on the floor. He picked it up, stuffed it in his pocket, and straightened. "Mind your step. Careful, now."

Slowly and gingerly they made their way down the corridor, down the stairs, and out to the street. And all the while, moved by invisible hands, doors closed as they approached and opened after they passed; and all the while there was a murmuring, a muttering, a whispering, a hissing from the fetid darkness, and the scrabbling of rats in the walls.

---

OF COURSE HAYS found out nothing when, the body having been carted away, he returned to question the inhabitants—particularly those in rooms adjoining the one in which the dead man was found. No one had seen any thing, heard any thing; no one knew any thing, or suspected any thing. By the time he had finished, his head was reeling from the foul air, and the street seemed deliciously cool and fresh in comparison.

As Hays and his men left the Five-Points they heard the unexpected quiet broken by what seemed like a howl from hundreds of throats—a howl of defiance, execration, an utterly evil triumph.

Breakstone half-turned, but his superior's hand kept him steady. "The water-front is no sabbath-school," Breakstone said.

"But it was never like that. At least you have the clean winds from the harbor, and the people give you a smile and a laugh and mostly folks try to keep themselves a bit decent in some ways, anyway. But those in the Old Brewery now—what makes them like that?"

They walked on in silence. Then Hays said, "I don't know, Mr. Breakstone. There's a whole green continent before them, wide-open under the sweet air of Heaven. But they choose to dwell in the dark and the mire. Why are they like that? As well ask the mole and the mudfish, I suppose."

———

IT WAS PAST mid-night when he reached home. And next day there was no time for speculation on social philosophy. The baggage-gang had extended their depredations; and complaints of thefts poured in from the docks around Jay-street, where Hudson-River boats put in, and from the Battery, whence the ferries plied to Jersey, Staten-Island, Brooklyn, and from the great packet-ships in the Upper Harbor. From mere sneak-thieves the ring had advanced to a pretense of being regular baggage-porters and hotel-runners. A genuine rustic, parted from his old cow-hide trunk, was apt to set up an immediate clamor—in which case there was a chance, though a slim one, of its recovery. But a visitor from a small town, with just enough polish to desire not to be known for what he was, would delay out of embarrassment; in which case there was usually no hope for his luggage.

The problems of taking men from elsewhere to patrol the docks, of uncovering information about who was "fencing" (and where), in addition to routine duties of a sort which could nei-ther be postponed nor delegated, kept Hays from seeing Con-stable Breakstone until late in the afternoon.

———

"TRY AS I would," the young man said, "I couldn't remember that sailor's name. So I looked up old Poppie Vanderclooster,

213

who used to help Father in the shop at one time, and took him along to the dead-house. And he knew the face at once. Henry Roberts. They called him Roaring Roberts; he had a big, booming voice. I've asked around, and it seems he'd turned to the bad of late years. Some of the adventures he sold weren't his to sell. He had a lot of money not so long ago, and was throwing it around like a drunken sailor—which, of course, is just what he was. I guess he must have spent it all, or else what would he have been doing in that hole of the Old Brewery?"

The two of them were on their way back to the dead-house. Hays gave an exclamation, and began patting his pockets. "Ah, here it is," he said. "I found it just outside the door of the room, last night, there in the Five-Points. What do you make of it? Not the sort of thing generally worn in the Old Brewery, is it?"

"A gentleman's glove? No—and not the sort of thing Roaring Roberts would've worn, generally, either. Though he might, when he was spending all that money, have bought himself a pair."

"Just so. Well, we'll see."

White-haired old Whitby, the dead-house keeper, surveyed them reproachfully through red-rimmed eyes as they came over to Roberts's body. "You're late," he said. "The inquisition's been over for hours. We're about set to coffin him. Coroner's jury reached the verdict that Deceased had come to his death through haemorrhage caused by forcible entry of a knife, length of the blade four and one-half inches, between the fourth and fifth ribs, thus occasioning the severance of veins and arteries—"

"All right, Whit, we know that—hold up your left hand, Constable." The glove slipped on easily enough; if anything, it was a size too large. "It might be his," said Hays reflectively. "Then again, it might not have anything to do with the matter. I did find it outside the room."

As he slipped the glove off, something fell to the floor. Old Whitby bent down and picked it up.

"Flax? Wool?" he asked, rolling the fibre between his fingers.

"Give it here, Whit," Hays said shortly. At the door he

stopped, handed the glove to Breakstone. "Check all the haberdashers," he said. "See what you can find."

•◦═◦•

ALDERMAN NICHOLAS TER Williger had his counting-house in the same building as his ware-house. Once, when business was smaller and Ter Williger (not yet an alderman) younger, he and his family had lived up stairs. But that old Knickerbocker fashion was going out of style nowadays. Besides, his children—and some of his grand-children—had their own establishments, and Mrs. Ter Williger was dead.

The clerks looked at Hays from their high stools with unabashed astonishment, but his cold grey eyes stared them back to their ledgers. He stalked through the counting-house to the office in the back where, as expected, he found the proprietor.

"Hello, Jacob," said Ter Williger. "It's been too long. I meant to stop and say a few words the other morning, but you seemed preoccupied with deep thoughts. Mrs. Hays is well, I trust?"

"Quite well."

"Capital. Convey my respects. And now. I have a piece of nice, clean Saugerties ice here and I was about to compound a sherry-cobbler. I shall compound two."

" 'Take a little wine for thy stomach's sake, and for thine often infirmities,' eh, Nick?"

The old gentleman cut lemons, broke off pieces of sugar-loaf. "Exactly. You may worship Scotch Presbyterian instead of Dutch Reformed, but you're a fellow-Calvinist and know that 'Man born of woman is born to sorrow as the sparks fly upwards,' and hence predestined to a multitude of 'often infirmities,' for some of which—my long years have taught me—sherry-cobbler is a sovereign remedy." He nodded, pounded ice.

The drink was cool and gratifying. It was quiet in the office, with its dark walls, from which engravings of President and Lady Washington looked down with stern benignancy. After a long moment Nicholas Ter Williger sighed. "I know you and

215

your Caledonian conscience too well, Jacob," he said, "to believe it would allow you to pay a purely social call in the daytime. What aspect of rogue-catching brings you to the office of a respectable, if almost super-annuated, cotton-broker?"

"Cotton brings me here," said Hays. He produced two tiny paper packets, unfolded them, pushed them across the desk. At once Ter Williger's hooded eyes grew sharp. "Nankeen," he said instantly. Then he took up the pieces, pulled the fibres, compared them. "Same crop, too, I'd say. Good quality Nankeen. . . . Where does it grow? Well, China, originally. Nankeen or Nanking, that's a city over there. But we grow it here in our own South nowadays, more than enough for own uses. 'Slave cotton,' they call it, too, sometimes."

Hays considered. Then, "What do you mean, 'slave cotton'? Isn't most cotton grown by slaves?"

Ter Williger nodded. "Yes, but—well, here's how it works, Jacob. Some of the plantations allow their people to grow a little cotton on their own, after quitting time in the big fields, and when this cotton is sold the people get to keep the money. They use it, oh, say, to buy some relish to add to their victuals—saltfish, maybe, as a change from pork and corn-meal—or perhaps a piece of bright cloth for a shirt or a dress. Maybe some trumpery jewelry. Well, just to keep temptation out of their way, because, being property himself, the slave doesn't have much sense of property—here, let me show you."

From the shelf behind him Ter Williger took some sample lengths of fibre. "This is what we call Sea-Island. And this is Uplands. See how much different they are in color from Nankeen? How much lighter, whiter? No slave would be foolish enough to steal some of his master's cotton and try and mix it with his own yellow Nankeen. I don't deal in it myself. Jenkins does, but he's not here now."

Something stirred in Hays's mind. "I had a card not so long ago—large quantity of cotton stolen from Georgia, somewheres."

Ter Williger nodded rapidly. "Yes, I know about that. But that was Sea-Island, not Nankeen. Planter named Remington was holding back quite some bales, hoping for a rise in the market. St. Simon's-Island. Cotton was already baled and in a shed by the wharf. Came morning they found the Negro watchman dead and the bales gone. Sea-Island, you know, fetches top price. Not Nankeen, though." He took up his glass, but it was empty, and he set it down again, regretfully.

Hays rose. "Then Nankeen doesn't grow in any one particular locality?"

The older man pursed his mouth. Then he said, "I tell you what. Why not ask Jenkins? He'd be able to give you better answers. . . . Who's he? Well, not exactly a partner. An associate. We have an understanding, and he uses my premises, too. An up-and-coming young man. Pushes a bit more than I care to. When you get old—matter of fact, Jacob, why don't you come along with me and talk to him? I'm going to his boarding-house now. A dicty place near Greenwich-Village."

Ter Williger reached for his hat, chuckled. "Matter of fact, I live there myself. Jeremiah Gale keeps it, with his wife. She orders the help around and he plays whist with the guests. A well-spread table, and a brightly-furnished house. Just the thing for old moss-backs like me—*and* for young couples like the Jenkinses. House property is high, and so are house-rents and servants' wages. Time enough for them to set up for themselves when they have a few children."

In a few minutes they were sitting in a cab and old Ter Williger rambled on about the fashion for boarding-house living, the prices of butcher's meat, game, fish, wine, clothing; and how much cheaper every thing had been twenty, thirty-five, and fifty years ago.

"Nicholas, I need more men," Hays said presently. "I can't even keep up with crime with my present force, let alone keep ahead of it. I need more men, and the Board of Aldermen has got to give me the money to pay for them."

The City had cooled off as late afternoon faded into early evening. The cab rolled along between rows of neat brick houses, freshly-painted red, with trim white lines drawn to simulate mortar. Green-clad tree branches arched over the street. There was not a pig in sight. It was quite a change from the hustle of the Broad-way, or the squalor of the Five-Points.

Nicholas Ter Williger sighed. "What can *I* do, Jacob? I'm just an old Federalist who's hung on past his time, and they all know it down at City Hall. I shall not run again, and they all know that, too. It's a Tammany-man you should be talking to about this. Am I right?"

He tipped his hat to a passing lady, and Hays followed suit. "Yes," the High Constable agreed, "but if I talk to a Tammany-man about needing more men, he'll smile like a bucketful of chips, say he agrees with me completely, and knows just the men. Two of them will be his nephews, three of them will be his cousins, and the rest of them will be broken-down oyster-men or some thing of that sort, unfit for any sort of work, but all from his ward, and all deserving Democrats. Damnation, Nick, I like to hire my own men! I—oh, are we here now? Just so."

Jeremiah Gale's establishment for paying guests was undistinguishable, with its scrubbed-white stoop and its bright green shutters, from any of the other houses in the row. A neatly-dressed Irish maid opened the door to them. Her manner was staid and respectful, but there was a look in her eye which convinced Hays that she would not always be content to take gentlemen's hats, to say, "Yes, sir," and "Yes, ma'am," to haul firewood, coal, and hot water up three and four flights of stairs, and to toil fourteen hours a day for the $5 a month which was the most she could hope for. Servants did not stay servants long—at least, not in New-York.

The house of Jeremiah Gale was richly, almost sumptuously furnished. Silken draperies, satin-upholstered furniture, mahogany, rosewood, marble, and gilt were everywhere. Jeremiah Gale himself came forward to greet them, a short and rosy gentleman of full habit, in claret-colored coat, pepper-and-salt trousers, and white silk stockings contrasting with the black sheen of his highly-polished shoes. There was a hum of conversation from inside, in which female voices predominated, and some one was playing on the pianoforte.

"Mr. Alderman Ter Williger!" One might have thought it had been last year instead of this morning that they had parted. "I trust I see you well, and not overly fatigued from the duties of the day?" A genteel bow, and then another genteel bow. "Mr.

High Constable Hays! Delighted to meet you again!" (To the best of Hays's recollection they had never met before.) "How very happy I am that Mr. Alderman Ter Williger has honored us by bringing you to dinner. You will do us the pleasure of taking dinner, sir? My cook has dressed a pair of turkey-hens with bread-sauce—"

But Hays pleaded his wife's discomfiture, were he to spoil the edge of his appetite for her supper by partaking of Mr. Gale's cook's pair of turkey-hens; and Mr. Gale was obliged to smile ruefully, and express a hope amounting to certainty that the High Constable would honor them on another occasion. Then he led them into the parlor.

The pianoforte had ceased, but the lady seated at it was talking busily to another, who had evidently been turning the music for her. She raked the new-comers with a swift glance, but kept on talking.

"Ah, *mais non, mais non!*" she exclaimed. "Two months in England and two weeks in France? *Incroyable! Au contraire*—that is to say, on the contrary; you must revise your plans and spend two months in France and only two weeks in England. Do you not agree with me, Mr. Jenkins?"

"Perfectly, my dear."

"If, indeed, it is absolutely necessary to visit England at all! The land of our fathers it may be, call it the Old Home, but—oh, my dear, so cold, so coarse! That fat old king and his ugly wife! And so unwelcoming to Americans, are they not, Mr. Jenkins?"

"Alas, my dear, we found it so."

"*Mais, ooh, la belle France!* There you have civilization—fashion—*ton.* We will give you the names of dear friends we visited, Mr. James Jenkins and I, two years ago—people of the finest quality, the most exquisite manners, the epitome of elegance, *mais oui*; and here I see dear Alderman Ter Williger with a distinguished-looking guest. Who can it be?"

And at this point the lady (presumably Mrs. Jenkins) arose from the pianoforte and took what Hays was absolutely certain was her first breath since she had begun speaking.

Mrs. Jenkins was as expensively dressed as it was morally

possible for a lady to be, and quite handsome, too. Mr. James Jenkins was a large-framed man with a red, smooth-shaven, and smiling face. Mrs. Van Dam (the unwise, would-be spender of two months in England) was thin and sallow. Mr. Van Dam—a whale-oil commission-merchant—was thinner and sallower. Miss Cadwallader was a boney lady of a certain age and of over-poweringly aristocratic family. Mr. O'Donovan made it known at once that he was from *Northern* Ireland and a Protestant as well. Mr. Blessington was superintendent of an assurance agency and evidently had nothing to say when away from the premises of that essential if unromantic business. And Mrs. Bladen was a widow-woman with a lap-dog and two fat, unmarried daughters.

Such, with the addition of Alderman Ter Williger, were Mr. Jeremiah Gale's paying guests.

In the small sitting-room to which Mr. Gale showed them, Mr. Jenkins listened with the greatest good-nature to Hays's questions. "Nankeen grows over a wide area," he said, "and while there *are* people who'll insist—particularly down South—that they can tell from what location a given staple comes, even from which plantation or field, I must regard a claim to such close knowledge as rather—well, pretentious. . . . Have I been in the South? Frequently."

The Alderman, who had been listening with some small signs of impatience for the dinner-bell, said now, "Mr. Jenkins made a trip South not long ago to buy Nankeen." The High Constable asked where it had been stored in New-York, and Jenkins said it had not been stored there at all, but had been trans-shipped immediately.

The Liverpool packet-boat was about to sail, he explained, it being the first of the month, the traditional sailing date for packets; and he had heard that the Captain not only had cargo space aboard but was looking for an adventure—the private cargo which all ships' personnel were entitled to take aboard in amounts varying according to rank. The Captain had bought Mr. Jenkins's entire shipment.

The dinner-bell rang, and all three rose. "So there is not,

then," Hays inquired, "any way to trace a small amount of this cotton?"

"None that I know of. It comes in to the City all the time, lays on the wharves, and anyone can draw a handful from a bale; samples are pulled in the Exchange and discarded—why, sir, the wind blows it about the streets. Can we trace the wind?"

———•◦•◦•———

So MUCH FOR that, Hays thought, as the cab rolled its way downtown. The two murdered men had been sailors and probably had access to baled cotton, at sea or on shore, a hundred times a year—though why one would put it in his mouth and another in his glove was a question which baffled him completely. Perhaps Breakstone had discovered some thing about the glove itself.

But the Constable hadn't. It was an ordinary gentleman's glove, the haberdashers all said, sold by the dozens and the gross.

Hays sighed, tossed the glove to his desk, and looked at it discontentedly. "I can't believe," he said at last, "that it isn't a clew. Gentleman's gloves in the Old Brewery? No, my boy, it *has* to signify. Of course some one might have stolen a pair—no one would steal just one—but he'd not have carried them all the way back home with him; he'd have sold them for a half-dime to the first fence he came across—yes, and drunk up the half-dime directly, too. I am convinced that this glove was dropped by the man who killed Roberts. In which case it does have some thing to tell me. Perhaps I've not been listening. Hmm."

He picked up the glove and began to examine it carefully, inch by inch, holding it close to his eyes. Suddenly his frown vanished, gave way to a look in which astonishment vied with self-reproach.

"Ahh!" he exclaimed. "Here's something I hadn't noticed before—and shame upon me, too. Do *you* see it, Mr. Breakstone? No? Fie upon you! Look here."

Hays began to turn the glove inside-out, poking at the fingers with the small end of a pen-holder until they were all reversed. "See it now? Eh?"

Breakstone said, "I see these few wisps of cotton here, sir. But we knew there was cotton in the glove. I still don't see why. Do you?"

But Hays did not answer the question directly. "I want you to set to work on a riddle: What connection is there between Roaring Roberts and Tim Scott? And what connection between those two and the man found dead in Dunstan-Slip? What connections in life?—and in death?"

It was at this moment that the steam-tug *Unicorn* happened to ram the ferry-boat *Governor Tompkins* half-way between New-York and Brooklyn. Twenty passengers were thrown overboard, and only nine picked up from the water alive. Hays was no better with a boat-hook than any one else, but his presence on the river served to discourage the presence of those "volunteers" who were more interested in the contents of water-soaked pockets than in seeing the dead brought ashore for Christian burial.

Five of the missing eleven were found, by and by; and Hays retired from the scene. Experience told him that the rest wouldn't show up for some time.

As Breakstone, himself rather wet about the sleeves and shirt-front, made his way along South-street early that evening, he overheard this point discussed. Some thought the full moon would "draw" the dead to the surface, while others insisted that only the concussion of water-borne cannonry could dislodge them.

Meanwhile, the life of the city roared along. Cargo was laden aboard many of the vessels whose bow-sprits pointed toward the top storeys of the South-street buildings, and cargo was taken ashore from many others. Men with blackened clothes and faces poured coal into the holds of new-fangled steamers. "Cream! Cream! D'licious ice-cream!" shouted the peddlers, not even ceasing their hoarse cries when setting down their wooden pails to serve a clerk or apprentice, safely out of employer's sight.

Wine by the pipe, sugar and tobacco by the hogshead, potash by the barrel, rum by the puncheon, nails by the keg, tea by the chest, cotton by the bale, and wool by the bag; shouting supercargoes, cursing carters, hoarse auctioneers, brokers scurrying between ship and shore and sale; grave old merchants and hard young sea-captains, red-faced dray- and barrow-men, pale-faced clerks and fresh faced 'prentice-boys; the reek of salt-fish, the cloying odor of molasses, the spicy scent of cinnamon-bark, the healthy smell of horses, and the sharp tang of new leather—all this was South-street, the city's premier water-front and the focal point of all New-York's commerce.

"Leatherhead! Leatherhead!" yelled a barefooted, dirty-legged boy, passing on the run. Breakstone paid no attention. The leather helmet he wore may not have been pretty, and it was often hot and heavy in the summertime, but—besides the protection it offered from brick-bars, stones, and clubs—it was the only article of uniform the New-York City Watch wore, and he was proud of it.

Otterburne's West-India Coffee-House was where Hays had said he would meet him, and there, in an upstairs room overlooking the East-River and Upper Harbor, was the High Constable himself, dipping his mahogany-colored face, for a change, into a mug of Mocha and milk.

"Have you got the answer to my riddle?" Hays asked, wiping his mouth on the back of one huge hand.

"Parts of it—I think." Then Breakstone abandoned his reserve and leaned forward eagerly. "I found out quite a bit when I was out in the boats. Do you know a Captain Lemuel Pierce, who has the *Sarah* coasting-sloop?" Hays considered for a second, then nodded. "Well, here's what it comes to: Roaring Roberts, who we found dead in the Old Brewery, had been seen more than once in company with Tim Scott—who we found in the alley three streets up from here. I'd mentioned to you that Scott had spoken of a mate named Billy Walters? Yes, and Billy Walters—who hasn't been seen of late!—had a great keloid on his left ear-lobe—"

Hays blew out his cheeks. "So *he* was the man they pulled out of Dunstan-Slip! This ties all three together with a second cord. And Lem Pierce—?" Billy Walters was said to have sailed with Captain Lem on their last voyage; Pierce's sloop was a coaster, and Tim Scott's last voyage was also on a coaster. "Lem has a wicked reputation," Hays said thoughtfully. "Coercion, crimping, blackmail, barratry, usurpation . . . I dare say he's turned his hand to a touch of piracy in his time, too. Where does the *Sarah* lie now, Constable? You've done well," he added, before Breakstone could answer. "Many a mickle makes a muckle—go on, you were saying?"

Breakstone said that the *Sarah* sloop had been down in Perth-Amboy, being over-hauled. Report was that she was on her way to the City, with only the Captain and a man from the ship-yard handling her, and should arrive just before sundown at Bayard's Wharf.

"Over-hauling costs money," Hays observed. "Scott and Roberts had been spending a lot of money, too. Bound together with a third cord, you see. And 'a three-fold cord is not easily broken,' says the Proverbs of King Solomon. Come to think of it, there's another king mentioned in the Book of Proverbs. Yes. Just so. King Lemuel! Well, late to-night, about ten or so, we'll go down and visit this Lemuel and discuss Scripture—and other things!"

But when they visited that Lemuel they found him dead.

<hr />

THEY HAD PICKED their way along the wharf through heaps of firewood the sawyers had prepared and left for galley-stoves. It was well past the farthest zone of gas-light, and neither the dim ships'-lamps nor the tiny Watch-lanterns that Hays's men had did much more than make the ambient darkness seem darker.

"Ahoy, there!" Hays hailed a dim figure enjoying a pipe in the cool of above-decks. "Where's the *Sarah*? A sloop, just came in early this evening?"

Afterwards, he was to regret that hail. Then—"*Sarah*? Don't know the name, but a sloop made fast a few hours back, to the forward end of the wharf."

Her lamp was trim and bright, her paint fresh, her name bold and red. Captain Lemuel Pierce had clearly not been trying to hide. But no one answered the call and they boarded the vessel in silence. The cabin-door swung open and inside, on the deck, with his scabbard empty at his belt and his knife deep into his throat, lay the sloop's Captain.

"He's still bleeding!" Breakstone exclaimed.

"Search the ship," said Hays tersely. And then they heard it—a scrabble, a clatter, a thump, and the sound of running feet. They rushed top-side in time to see a man on the next wharf vanish into the darkness. Pursuit proved vain.

"He must have hopped over onto the ship behind this one," Hays said as they returned, winded and chagrined, "when he heard me hail and ask for the *Sarah*. Ah, well, let's do as we were about to do, anyway—search the ship."

But aside from water-ballast and a very small amount of stores, there was nothing to be found in the hold. Captain Pierce had bought a deal of new clothes, and in one coat-pocket there was a handful of gold eagles.

"A hundred dollars," Hays said, slipping the ten coins back. "A fortune for a sailor, but not so for a master. Did we scare off a robber before he could find it? Or was he a robber at all? The log—"

The log, however, listed nothing between the voyage from Perth-Amboy and one of six months previously to Wilmington, with a mixed cargo of linen, wine, rice, and flour: which was much too early for *the* voyage.

"Not an honest man at all, you see," said Hays, almost sorrowfully. "Didn't keep a proper log. Even so—to murder a master of craft under my very nose, as it were! There's insolence for you! Ahum. What is that behind your feet, Mr. Breakstone?"

The Constable tried to move forward and look backward at the same time, and before he had even completed the movement he answered that it was "Just a scrap of paper." He blinked at Hays's steady gaze and air of still waiting, then he blushed. He stooped and picked it up, looked at it, handed it over. Hays gave it a quick glance.

"*Just* a scrap of paper? Look again—Leatherhead!"

The scrap was straight on one edge and jagged on the other, and it had a few words or parts of words on one side.

a
known to
do further
es, Territor
Status and

"It seems to be part of some kind of legal paper," Breakstone said, after a moment.

"Just so." Hays's tone was almost grudging. "You ought to have seen it at once and handed it to me to find out *what* kind of legal paper. Trifles, trifles—but it's trifles that count! I sign this kind of legal paper by the dozen. Had I a quarter-of-a-dollar fee for each one—which I don't!—I could have bought a summer-cottage up at Spikin-Duyvil by now. Well, listen: I'll emphasize the words you see here:

" '. . . *a* Seaman of this city, and a Man of Color, is *known to* me on good evidence to be a FREE MAN, and I *do further* Enjoin all Men of whatsoever Cities, States, Territories, and Nations, to recognize him in such *Status and*—,' and so forth. We give these to the Black seamen in case they put in to a port of a slave state or a slave-holding colony or country, to keep them from being seized and sold. Now, what does it tell you?"

"That the man who killed the Captain was a Black seaman?"

"Not necessarily—but it hints at that, very powerfully, yes. Some one who wanted the papers of a free Negro sailor was here to see Pierce—he grabbed for it—but Pierce held on tight—it tore. Let's follow the obvious trail first. We know that Captain Lem had come into money lately. We know the same of Tim Scott and Roaring Roberts. Pierce spent his on the sloop. The other two poured it out like wine. Now. Do you know of any Colored sailors who've been known to spend lavishly of late?"

The wake of a passing vessel rocked the sloop. The cabin-lamp stayed level in its gimbals, but its light trembled a bit just the same, sending shadows across the High Constable's craggy face.

"No, not lavishly—that's to say, not foolishly. But now that I think about it," Breakstone mused aloud, "Cudjo Washington used to sail, on and off. And just a little while ago he opened an oyster-cellar in lower Collect-street, not far south of Anthony. A dicty place, as I think of it now—dicty for an oyster-cellar in Collect-street, that is. It must have cost him something."

Hays summoned the two Night Constables who had been standing guard at the foot of Bayard's Wharf and the one next to it, told one to rattle at the Coroner's shutters, and the other one to stand by the body—a task he plainly had no fancy for, but plainly he had even less fancy to refuse Old Hays.

"And now," said Old Hays, "we'll call on Cudjo Washington. I could relish a basin of little-necks or cherry-stones, I believe. But I'd relish information even more."

THERE WERE MORE men about that night than was usual for the hour, and presently some one called out from a little group which was gathered under a lamp-post.

"Jacob! Hello, there! Stop a bit." Hays crossed over and recognized Alderman Ter Williger, Mr. Jenkins, Mr. Jonathan Goodhue the fancy dry-goods importer, and his partner, Mr. Perit.

"These are late hours, gentlemen," Hays commented, "for merchants who must be up early tomorrow."

"Ah, it's to-morrow that keeps us up so late to-night," said Ter Williger genially. "To-morrow is the first of the month— that means tonight is packet-night—we've all been staying late at our counting-houses getting everything in order against the packet-vessels' sailing in the morning. Come and take a glass of lager-beer with us, Jacob: join us in a well-earned quarter-hour of ease." And, with a *Yes, yes,* and a *Do, sir,* Messrs. Goodhue and Perit seconded the invitation.

But Hays shook his head. "I'm off to Collect-street on business. And while lager is available there, I'll not invite you to join me. An ugly business and an ugly neighborhood."

Ter Williger, Goodhue, and Perit pursed their lips and raised their eyebrows. Jenkins drew out a segar, a match, and a piece of glassed paper, struck fire and lit up.

"Is that one of the new Congreve matches?" Mr. Perit asked. Jenkins, his mouth occupied with drawing smoke, didn't answer.

"Yes, it is," said Goodhue. "A great improvement over the old acid bottle. Well, well, then, Mr. Hays, we daren't detain you. Another time, perhaps."

"To be sure. Yes, we must go now. A good-night, gentlemen."

Collect-street, below Anthony-street, while not offering the amenities of, say, Washington-square, was still a cut or two above the Five-Points. A stranger might be lured into a room here, and beaten and robbed, and he might die of it; but he was not likely to be murdered in the open street for fun.

Several fences operated almost openly, ready to buy anything from a dead man's dirty shirt for a penny to a nob's gold watch for a dollar. There were the usual saloons and "grocery" stores, including that of the infamous Rosanna Spears. But tonight only one place of business on the street interested Jacob Hays. It was easy enough to spot; its lights were brighter and its paint fresher than the rest.

*The Great Republic Oyster-Cellar, by C. Washington,* stated a sign-board; and continued, *Fresh and Pickled Oysters, Clams, Hard-shell and Soft-shell Crabs, Garnished Lobsters. Fringed Hams, Fresh Country Fruit.*

The interior was neat and clean and contained several tables, a row of booths along one wall, and even the unusual glory of a glass-fronted show-case in which reposed half of a fringed ham, a huge platter heaped high with fried soft-shell crabs, bowls of fruit, and part of a roasted pig with a lemon in its mouth. A whitewashed keg displayed the necks of bottles of ginger-beer, porter, lager-beer, and mead, the rest of the bottles being concealed by cracked ice. On the rear wall were large steel engravings of Generals Washington and Jackson, and a smaller one of Governor Clinton.

It was, indeed, "rather a dicty place for Collect-street." It could not very well have been furnished and provisioned on the savings from a seaman's wages.

Present in the room were a Negro couple, evidently the proprietor and his wife, and several white couples, the men and women dressed in clothes which managed to look at the same time both flashy and bedraggled. The customers glanced up from their refreshments, sat for a moment transfixed at the sight of Hays and Breakstone, tensed, exchanged glances, and then as it was made obvious that the door was not being blocked and that none of them was engaging the attention of the law— relaxed somewhat: that is, if slouching in their seats and hiding their faces with arms propped on elbows may be considered relaxing.

The proprietor, a powerfully-built man in his early middle years, pressed himself back against the wall with something clenched in his fist. His wife retreated wordlessly to a corner.

"Cudjo Washington," said Hays, advancing and holding out his staff, "I call upon you, as a citizen of this city, to lay down that oyster-knife." The implement fell with a clatter.

After a second Washington said, "Before the Lord, I didn't know it was you, gentlemen. I thought—" He ran his tongue over his lips, then came forward to the counter with a mechanical smile and an attitude of well-practised deference. "What will you gentlemen be pleased to have?" he asked.

"A few words with you in your back-room. Your wife can stay here to wait on the patrons." Breakstone posted himself outside.

"Well?" asked Hays. It was dark in the room. Only a small piece of candle burned in a saucer.

"I didn't know what they was up to, Mr. High Constable. I never found out until it was too late." The man's voice was low, but it came from a huge chest and throat, and rumbled out into the shadows. As to what he meant by what he had said, Jacob Hays had no idea at all. He generally avoided opening a conversation with a suspected man in terms of accusing him of a specific crime. *Well?* was usually opening enough. Often the single syllable put mind and tongue to something quite different from what the High Constable had been thinking of, something of which the High Constable had known nothing. One could, after all, always take up later the matter which had prompted the inquiry in the first place.

"He hadn't no right to keep hold of my papers. No right a-tall," Cudjo was saying. But this was not exactly what Hays was expecting him to say. Ah, well, wait a bit. Let the man talk. But all the talk, it became obvious, was on lines other than the first comment. Had Cudjo realized that he had started to give himself away? And, so considering, Hays realized that he himself was no longer thinking in terms of a simple murder.

He *would* have to lead the conversation, after all. Well, so be it. "What were they up to, Cudjo, and just when did you find it out?"

The man's eyes seemed red in the candle-light. Was there cunning in them? "You says—what, sir?" Hays repeated his words. "I mean to say," Cudjo evaded, "what was he up to, keeping my papers? Now, they was mine, legal. So—"

"So you killed him."

A confident laugh. "Cap'n Pierce? No, sir! He too mean to die!"

"Not when he'd gotten a knife in his throat, he wasn't." The laugh ebbed away, the man scanned Hays's face. His huge chest swelled. He shook his head dumbly. "Mr. Breakstone! Send the woman in here. . . . Now, what time did your husband come back tonight?"

"Why 'twas about—" She checked herself and looked at her husband. But he sat still, utterly still. Her voice dropped a notch, became uncertain. "Why, master, he was here all night. He never go out." She looked from Hays to her husband, pleadingly. But neither offered aught for her comfort. She began to wail.

Cudjo accompanied them quietly to the Watch-house.

"If you didn't kill Captain Pierce," Hays asked, and asked over and over again, "then why were you so afraid when we walked in? Why did you pick up the oyster-knife? You said, 'I didn't know it was you. I thought—' *What* did you think? Who were you expecting? Who are the 'they' you talked about? What was it you 'found out they were up to'? Why was it 'too late' by then?"

Then, still getting no response, Hays put to him the brutally suggestive, but terribly pertinent, question, "Cudjo, have you ever seen a man hanged?"

Sweat popped out on the man's broad face. He began to shake his head—and continued to shake it. It seemed he could not stop. Soon his whole body was shaking from side to side. He essayed speech, but his voice clicked in his throat. Hays brought him a mug of water, and he swallowed it greedily.

"I will tell you, master," he said, after a moment. "I see there is no help for it. I will tell you everything. It begin two, three months ago."

———◆•◆•◆———

Two or three months previously, Cudjo had been living in a corner of a room in the Shambles tenement on Cherry-street, in the Fourth Ward. He had had no job in a long time, and only the pittance which his wife earned by peddling hot-roasted corn through the streets kept them from actual starvation. Captain Lemuel Pierce came and offered him a berth for a coasting voyage, and Cudjo had jumped at it.

"You got your free papers, don't you, Cudj?" There had been no slaves in New-York State since the Emancipation of 1827, and Cudjo had been free even before then, for his owner had brought him North and manumitted him. He knew that Captain Pierce must be referring to his seaman's papers.

"Yes, sir. I got'm. We going South, Cap'n?"

Pierce smiled, showed yellow teeth. "We ain't goin' to Nova-Scoshy. Better hand them papers over to me for safe-keeping, Cudj. That way, I c'n take care."

Pierce was obliging enough to advance $2 on wages, which were given to Phoebe Washington, and to promise warm clothes as soon as they got aboard. The two proceeded to Staten-Island, where the *Sarah* was lying off a small creek which emptied into the Kill-Van-Kull. Roaring Roberts was first mate. Tim Scott and Billy Walters made up the rest of the crew. They put out to sea on the next tide.

"He never come out of the cabin till the second day," said Cudjo. "But I knew his face."

"Whose?" Hays asked.

"Mr. Jones's." And who was he and what did he look like? He was a big man with a red face. Cudjo had "seen him around"; more he knew not. Mentally Hays ran over all the Joneses he could think of, from Ap Jones the cow-keeper to Zimri Jones, who sold woollens. None fitted the picture.

The *Sarah* was dirty, but Captain Pierce had kept her in good shape otherwise. He and Mr. Jones had had words right from the start. Jones, who apparently had chartered the sloop, objected to any one's—particularly the Captain's—drinking "until the job's done." Pierce had said that he was master aboard his own vessel and would drink what and when he pleased; forthwith he applied himself to his demijohn.

Neither Cudjo nor any of the three White sailors had any idea of where they were bound, except that it was, in Pierce's words, "Somewhere South and warm." It was after they had passed Cape Fear that Pierce and Jones revealed their destination to him. "They had to," Washington said. "They needed me. Cap'n Pierce knew I was born in Brunswick and had sailed all those waters."

"You ought to know St. Simon's Sound pretty well, I guess," said Pierce.

"Oh, yes, sir. My old master—"

"Damn your old master!" said Pierce. "Do you know where Remington's Landing is? You do. All right. You'll pilot us there."

They lay well off shore till dark, then entered St. Simon's Sound, then Tuppah Cove. Remington's Landing lay up an inlet into the Cove. The moon was full and bright. Captain Pierce, aided by the winds, had planned well.

"Take care, Cudj," he said; and then a while before they came up to the wharf, "you—no noise!"

The ship's-lamps were extinguished. Silent as a ghost ship, the sloop moored. The shed by the wharf was full of baled cotton. Without words, directed by gestures, they all set to work loading it aboard. Even Pierce and Jones took off their coats and pitched in.

After a while—Cudjo didn't know how long—they became aware that some one was looking at them. It was the Negro watchman. Evidently he had been taking a nap on one of the bales. He stared at the scene—and an eerie scene it must have been, too—the six strange men toiling silently in the pool of moonlight. His voice, when he spoke, was tremulous.

"What—what are you White men doing with that there cotton? It belongs to Master Remington, and I know it ain't done been sold!"

They could have told him some lie and kept him silent, Cudjo said, recounting the story to Hays. Tied him up, maybe. But Jones pulled out a knife and at the sight of it the watchman turned and was off like the wind. He had no chance, of course. They were on him before he could cry out. Cudjo, standing aghast, saw an arm rise and fall twice. Then the five men dragged the body aside into the grass. Cudjo was still standing, numbly, when they returned, and gestured him back to work.

They were at sea again by dawn.

"What happened to the cotton?" Hays asked.

It was hot in the Watch-house; the wick in the whale-oil lamp needed trimming, but somehow he could not put his mind to asking the Night Constable-in-charge to take care of it. Here, then, was the story of the theft of the Sea-Island cotton in Georgia, of which he had been notified weeks back. It had been carried out by men recruited under his very nose, so to speak: Billy Walters, Roaring Roberts, Tim Scott, Captain Pierce, Cudjo Washington. Who had been behind it? Mr. Jones. Which ones were still alive? Cudjo Washington and Mr. Jones.

"What happened to the cotton?" Hays asked again. He knew well enough what had happened to the men.

The proprietor of The Great Republic Oyster-Cellar shook his head. "I don't know, Mr. High Constable. We put in to Philadelphia—didn't tie up, though, just lay out in the river— and Mr. Jones and Captain Pierce rowed ashore. They come back inside of an hour and Mr. Jones had a sight of money with him. I expect he'd been to the bank. They paid us off and told us to get our gear together and go ashore. Not to come back. He warned us—Mr. Jones, I mean. 'Don't let me see you in New-York,' he said. 'I'm paying you extra for that,' he said, 'so you better not try to fool me.' Said to me, 'Send for your wife. Don't go back for her.' He had a mean look to him. A hard man."

"And you took the money? The proceeds of the stolen cotton? For you knew that's what it was, for all he paid you in advance."

Cudjo nodded. "He said I had to take it. Said he'd kill me if I didn't. 'You're in this, too,' he said, 'the same as the rest of us. If I were you I'd go far away.' So I took it. And I was afraid to say any thing. I could've thrown it away, all but my wages. But it was more money than I'd ever seen, almost. I thought, I'll hold on to it for a while and study this. Then—'Send for your wife,' he said. I can't write and she can't read. I come up here to see her and study what to do. And when I saw that rat's-hole we were living in—in the Shambles—and her tired out from crying hot-roasting-ears up and down the streets—"

———

HE HAD SUCCUMBED to the temptation and had used the money to fit up the oyster-cellar. A sailor's life was hard, and usually, not a long one. The rest of the story was easy enough—in part—for Hays to imagine. One by one the three other sailors made their way back to New-York in defiance of "Mr. Jones's" warning. One of them must have preferred to spend his share of the crime in Philadelphia, or—Hays remembered the worn, worn shoes found on another's feet—or in some other place no closer to New-York.

"Jones" must have been a fool to think they would stay away. As soon as their money was spent they must have tried to blackmail him—tried alone, almost certainly, not in concert, for each had been killed alone and separately. Perhaps Jones hadn't even known that Cudjo had returned to New-York.

"What happened on the sloop tonight?" Hays asked. Somewhere off in the city a church-bell sounded the hour. How quickly the night was passing!

Washington had forgotten to ask for his free papers in Philadelphia. Presently he remembered, but did nothing. If he needed them, by some dire chance, to go to sea again, he could get another set. Chiefly, though, he worried about their remaining in the hands of Captain Pierce—Captain Pierce, whose evil reputation he knew as well as Hays did, and whose evil nature he knew even better, having sailed under him. But Pierce was off in Perth-Amboy, having the *Sarah* over-hauled.

"Are you going to wait in your cellar till he picks his own time and come to kill you, like he did the others? Well, I'm not," Pierce had said. "You'd think he'd know better than to threaten me, wouldn't you? You'd think he'd speak sweet to me, but no. 'Stay out of New-York, Pierce. I warn you!' " Cap'n Lem had mimicked "Jones." Cap'n Lem had been drinking, in his little cabin there in the sloop at Bayard's Wharf. "Well, I don't fancy staying out of New-York, see? And I don't relish the idea of being killed on some dark night. No, Cudj, I tell you: there's only this—*kill him before he kills us!*"

But Cudjo had had enough of that. Four men were already killed, including the slave watchman down on St. Simon's-Island. It was Cudjo's belief that the White men would still be living if they hadn't tried to get more money out of "Jones." All that Cudjo wanted was his free papers back. And Captain Lemuel Pierce refused to deliver them. He showed them, he laughed, he drew them back. They were to be the price of Cudjo's assistance in the death of "Jones." They had quarreled, the master of the *Sarah* grew ugly, Cudjo had snatched at papers and torn them from Pierce's grasp. Then he had run off. That was all. That was his story.

Hays was rather inclined to believe him.

But who was "Jones"?

---

A FEW HOURS' sleep, and the High Constable was up and on duty again. As soon as breakfast was over he stalked down-town, on his way to Ter Williger's place of business. Old Nick would be pleased to know that the matter of theft of the Sea-Island cotton from St. Simon's had been solved.

And then, as if his thoughts had become tangible, the word "Gloves" appeared in front of his eyes. Hays stopped short, looked carefully. There it was, in the window of that little shop. *D. MacNab, Leather and Leather-Findings. Cobbler's Supplies. Saddlery and Harness. Books Bound. Gloves Mended. Fire-men's and Watch-men's Helmets.*

Hays passed under the wooden awning and walked up three steps. A bell tinkled as he opened the door.

"What can you tell me any thing about this glove?" he asked.

"That it's no' yours, Mr. Hays."

The High Constable laughed shortly. "I know that. And if *you* do, it must mean that you know whose it is, Mr. MacNab."

"Och aye? Must it? It's nae muckle thing to ken whose hand fits a glove, and whose doesna." And, as Hays digested this, and ruefully admitted the man was right, MacNab said, "But it sae happens that I do ken whose it is, for I mended it masel'. And what's mare, I mended another for the same mon—slashed across the palm it was—and handed it back not an hour syne."

Not trying to conceal his excitement, Hays leaned across the counter. "What's his name, MacNab?"

But MacNab said, "Och, that I dinna ken. A big man, wi' a sonsy red face on him. He didna come in himsel', this time, he sent the coachman wi' the money. 'Mak' haste,' says the coachie, 'for he's complainin' we won't get to the Battery in time to catch the packet-ship.' So I took the siller and gave over the glove, and that's all I ken aboot it."

Calling his thanks over his shoulder, Hays ran out.

It took three cabs, one after the other, to get him to the Battery without the horses foundering. And all the clocks along the route displayed each a truly Republican and Democratic spirit of independence, no two agreeing. He was in constant agony that he might not make his destination in time. He pondered, not for the first time, on the absurdity of the head of the only effective police-force in the State (if not the nation!) being dependent on common carriers to convey him wherever his own feet could not. He allowed himself the uncommon luxury of a dream: a light carriage, the property of the Watch, drawn by a team of swift and strong horses, ditto. But it was only a dream. "Economy in government" was the official policy—except, of course, where official corruption was the cord. So far, at any rate, the sachems of the Tammany Wigwam had refrained from taking over the Watch. Which meant economy.

Blocks before the Battery he began to groan, for the crowds streaming away meant that all the farewells had been said and the ferry for the packet-ships had already left. The spectacle of the speeding cab (though devilish little speed could it manage in these crowded streets despite the fact that Hays was standing half-up and gesturing other vehicles aside) attracted the attention of the crowd, and there were loud comments—most of which contained the words *Old Hays!*

He leapt from the cab as soon as it drew up at the wharf, and dashed through the lingering groups of people. A corner of his eye observed three known pick-pockets, but he did not stop. That is, he did not stop until he saw that the ferry had gone, gone so definitely that he could not even pick it out amidst the thronged shipping of the harbor. As he drew up short, dismay large and plain upon his rugged face, a fierce and stalwart young man, with cold blue eyes and a rather hard-looking mouth, appeared out of the crowd and demanded, "What's up?"

"Oh, Corneel—I've got to get aboard the packet-ship before she leaves—"

"Which one? Two bound for Liverpool, two for New Orleans, and one each for London, Havre, and Charleston. Take your pick, I've got a steam-launch."

Which one, indeed? Liverpool was the cotton-port of England, and Jenkins had done business with the Captain of *one* of the Liverpool packets, at any rate. But, through the noise and clamor, he heard, as if in his ear, the voice of Mrs. Jenkins: *Mais, ooh, la belle France!*

"The Havre packet, Corneel! That'll be it! But can we make it in time?"

With a flurry of oaths Corneel declared that he would soon

put Hays aboard her, and ripped out orders. Almost at once a small, trim steam-launch appeared and they tumbled into it. Corneel took the wheel himself, and in another minute the paddles were thrashing and the whistle was screaming.

"Damn my tripes!" Corneel shouted. "This is like the old days! Remember when I was Captain of old Gibbons's steamer, hey?"

Hays nodded. "In open violation of the monopoly that New-York State had given Livingstone and Fulton," he pointed out. "Wherefore, it was my plain duty to arrest you. I told you I'd do it if I had to carry you ashore. I *did* do it and I *did* have to carry you ashore!"

Corneel roared with laughter, damned his tripes again, and various other things, swore luridly at the pilots of any vessels which did not instantly veer out of his way at the sound of his whistle; and in very short time they had beaten a white, frothy path across the blue waters and were in the cool shadow of the huge ocean-goer.

"Ahoy, the *Hannibal* packet!" Corneel shouted, his crewman seizing the ladder—which was still down to let the pilot off—with the boat-hook; then quickly fastening on with the line.

A row of curious faces looked down at them from above. Corneel and Hays clambered up the ladder and confronted the somewhat astonished Captain. Hays lifted his staff of office. His eyes picked out one face from the crowd, and a thickly-packed crowd it was, too; for few had chosen to go below and miss the passage down the Bay and through the Narrows. It was a face easy to pick out, once it had been described. "A big man with a red face," Cudjo had said. "A sonsy red face," was Mac-Nab's description. Hays wondered at his never having made the connection.

"What brings you aboard, Mr. Hays?" asked Captain Delano.

"A desire to ask a question or two of your passenger, here—" Hays stopped in front of the man, who greeted him with the same affable smile he had worn at their previous meeting.

THE IMPORTANCE OF TRIFLES

"Good morning, Mr. Hays. Have you had any success in your quest for information about Nankeen?" he inquired.

"Good morning, Mr. Jenkins. Yes, I have. Do you know this glove?"

For just a fleeting second the smile seemed to slip. "No, I'm afraid I don't."

"Try it on," said Hays. "Let me have your left hand."

Jenkins drew the hand away and Hays caught it. For a moment they stood face to face, breast to breast, hand in hand. A little breeze blew across the deck. No one else spoke. Jenkins was a large man and a powerful one. But, still, slowly but surely, inch by inch, Hays drew his right hand back, and clenched in his right hand was the left hand of Mr. James Jenkins.

Suddenly Jenkins laughed. "An odd jest, sir. But I'm willing to oblige you."

His resistance ceased, and he held out the reluctant hand, clad in a fawn-colored glove. For all his amiability he moved slowly, but the fawn-colored glove came off and the glove Hays held out—one of grey leather—went on.

"Now, sir, are you content?" Jenkins demanded, still smiling.

"Perfectly." Hays held out his High Constable's staff. "James Jenkins, alias Jones," he said, "I take you into custody on a charge of having murdered Billy Walters, Tim Scott, Henry Roberts, and Lemuel Pierce, all in the City of New-York; and one Negro man, a slave, name unknown to me, on St. Simon's-Island in the State of Georgia."

The smile entirely left Jenkins's face, which had gone white—then the color came flooding back, but not the smile.

"Captain Delano," said Hays, "I trust you will render whatever aid may be necessary."

Jenkins had found his tongue, and turned it glibly on the Captain. "I've never heard of any of these men, sir," he said stoutly. "Nor have I ever been to St. Simon's-Island. What is this nonsense about gloves and murders? I know many passengers will vouch for my character."

"There are those ashore," said Hays, "who can vouch for it, too! Went South not long ago to buy Nankeen, did you? Never a bit of it! Chartered Lem Pierce's sloop to go South and fill it full of stolen Sea-Island cotton is what you did! And killed the poor Negro who was guarding it! No wonder you got rid of the bales so fast—sold them to the master of the outward-bound Liverpool packet just by good luck? Never a bit of it! Planned, planned! Every step of the way!

"But you hadn't planned on your accomplices returning to blackmail you, did you? Still, you drew up a plan soon enough for that: you lured them to dark places under pretense of payment, and there you killed them. Billy Walters was the first one. He was found with a piece of cotton in his mouth. Raw cotton—Nankeen—such as you dealt in, Jenkins. What was the cotton doing in a dead man's mouth? Here—"

Hays plucked the grey glove from the hand in which Jenkins, having taken it off, was holding it.

"Roaring Roberts, another of the lot, was found dead in the Old Brewery, and this glove at the entrance to his room. And Tim Scott, the third sailor of the crew of the sloop, was strangled to death in an alley off South-street. What is the connection in the circumstances of their deaths? Why, this—on Scott's neck were the marks of only nine fingers. Where was the tenth?"

In an instant Hays had seized the left hand of James Jenkins and held it up for all to see.

"There is no tenth," he said. *"Jenkins has only four fingers on his left hand!* That is why he always wears gloves! Look at the little finger of this glove: it has no creases. If I were to turn it inside out you'd see how the leather is darkened by use on the other four digits—but not on this one! And to hide the fact of his missing finger even more, Jenkins always stuffs the empty digit with raw cotton fibre. Look at this—"

Hays held out the fawn-colored glove. Four of its fingers hung loosely, but the fifth stayed as plump as if it had a flesh-and-blood finger inside it. Hays fished inside and the little finger went limp as he pulled out a piece of cotton stuffing.

Some thing like a sigh went up from the crowd.

"Now, examine the little finger of this first glove again," Hays continued. "See how the thread at the end is a lighter

240

THE IMPORTANCE OF TRIFLES

color? Why? The end had been mended and the thread hadn't yet worn as dark as the rest. But why did it need mending? Because when you, Jenkins, attacked Walters, he bit your hand, tearing the glove open and forcing the cotton stuffing out through the rip his teeth made! And before he could spit it out, his neck was broken, and he was a dead man! And in your fight with Roberts you lost the glove and were afraid to go back for it, weren't you?"

Jenkins, unsmiling now, said nothing.

"You had Duncan MacNab mend the first glove. He did his job well, so when you killed Captain Lem Pierce and found the palm of the glove that you had on then had been slashed by Pierce's knife, you took it to MacNab, too. And just got it back to-day. Let's see the other glove to this fawn-colored pair, Jenkins."

Jenkins thrust both hands deep into his pockets. There was a hard, ugly expression upon his face. "Let's see your warrant— Leatherhead!" he demanded.

Hays shook his head. "None needed to apprehend a fugitive fleeing the State to avoid prosecution."

Jenkins sneered, "You don't know much law, Leatherhead. Your jurisdiction ended back at the Battery."

Hays said calmly that they were still in New-York State waters, and that if it became necessary, he was prepared to make a citizen's arrest. Jenkins had something to say about that, but there was an interruption.

"Damn my tripes! Are you trying to keep us talking till we're out past the three-mile limit? Belay that!" And Corneel rushed forward, seized Jenkins around the waist and threw him over the side of the ship. He fell, screaming and kicking, while the ladies shrieked and swooned. Without even waiting for the splash, Corneel clattered down the ladder, Hays behind him.

Jenkins surfaced, and screamed in terror. "I can't swim! Help me, I can't swim!" He grabbed at and caught the boat-hook and was hoisted aboard the launch, where he lay, sodden and sobbing.

"If he makes any trouble, Corneel, hit him with the boat-

<section>241</section>

hook—the blunt end." Hays craned his neck upward. "If Mrs. Jenkins wishes to come ashore," he called, "we'll wait for her." They waited several minutes. Then a steward pushed his head over.

"She won't come, sir. She's locked the door of her cabin and she says she won't come out."

Jenkins's face swelled.

"Cast off," Corneel directed.

"The trull!" Jenkins said, his voice thick. "The slut! I'd never have done it if it weren't for her. 'When are we going to have a house of our own, Mr. Jenkins? When are we going to have a carriage of our own?' And now the dirty—"

But Corneel told him to mind his tongue and not speak that way of ladies. Jenkins looked at him with his red eyes. "Who in the devil's name are you?" he asked.

"Cornelius Vanderbilt. *Not* at your service, except as the High Constable directs. Killed five men, did he, Hays?"

"Three sailors and a sea-captain in New-York and a slave down in Georgia."

Corneel took off his cap. "May the Lord have mercy on their souls." He clapped it back on again and blew his whistle and damned the eyes of the pilot of the New-Brunswick ferry. There were death and evil in Jenkins's face as he looked at them, but Hays held the boat-hook, and all around them were the deep, deep waters.

The crowd at the Battery, far from having dispersed, was larger than it had been. Word of the High Constable's chase and his dash across the harbor had evidently gotten around. No one could any more believe that Old Hays had gone hunting off to Europe than they could believe it of the Battery itself. Every spy-glass in town seemed to have followed the steam-launch, and there were cheers as they stepped on shore.

They'll cheer at the hanging, too, Hays thought, for hanged Jenkins would certainly be. Not even a member of the Cotton Exchange could get away with four local murders. Cudjo would get off, though, if he turned State's evidence; as he would have to in order to avoid extradition on the Georgia charge.

There were four Constables waiting to take the prisoner

into custody. One of them was young Breakstone. "Now we know the answer," he said, "to who has nine fingers and kills sailors." But Jenkins said not one word.

An officious, well-dressed, and over-fed man slapped Hays on the back. "A marvellous job of work, High Constable!" he crowed, as if he had directed it himself. "You may well congratulate yourself that it's done. Now it's up to the judge and jury—your job is over!"

Hays looked at the man's pompous and moon-like face. Then he looked out over the teeming harbor, and then back to the city almost hid behind the forest of masts along the waterfront; the city ever growing, thronged with new-comers from Europe and America.

As he thought of its swarming and wretched tenements and its corrupt administration, the High Constable reflected that crime—as witness Jenkins—was found in high places as well as low, and that greed and vice would go always hand in hand. Hays shook his head sadly.

"No," he said, "it's not done. It's not even begun."

The plump citizen seemed to feel a response was expected of him. He chuckled. But a slight blankness on his bland countenance seemed to indicate that he did not quite take in the High Constable Hays's meaning.

GRANIA DAVIS has lived around a lot. She has dwelled in a mountain in Mexico, on a primitive sandbar in Belize, and on a beach in Hawaii. She has taught in Tibetan refugee settlements in India, and worked as a military historian in neon-lit Tokyo. Her extensive travels inspired a series of fantasy novels based on the myths of the Orient. *The Rainbow Annals* is based on Tibetan legends. *Moonbird* uses Balinese myths. *Marco Polo and the Sleeping Beauty*, written with Avram Davidson (who is himself a legend), is set in China. Her many short stories reflect her sojourns abroad.

She was married to Avram Davidson, and collaborated with him on short stories and novels, and a son. Since Avram Davidson's passing in 1993, she has devoted herself to publishing his immortal works.

She has settled down recently, dividing her time with her family between Marin County, California, and on the north shore of Oahu, Hawaii.

RICHARD A. LUPOFF is the author of more than thirty popular books, including science fiction novels, histories of popular culture, biographies, fantasy novels, an elusive paperback penned under the name "Del Marston," and seven Marvia Plum/Hobart Lindsey mystery novels. He is also a veteran of the radio industry: he began his broadcast career writing the evening news at WIOD, Miami, in 1955, and recently passed the twenty-year mark as a talk-show host at KPFA, in Berkeley, California.

MICHAEL KURLAND has been the editor of a magazine even more idiosyncratic than himself, a seeker of absent persons, and guest lecturer at numerous unrelated events. He has also written over thirty books straddling a variety of fields. His nonfiction works cover topics as diverse as forensic science, criminal law, espionage, amateur radio, and the history of crime in America. Currently in print are *How to Solve a Murder: The Forensic Handbook* and *How to Try a Murder: The Handbook for Armchair Lawyers.*

Kurland's crime novels include *The Infernal Device*, which was nominated for an Edgar and an American Book Award, and the Alexander Brass mysteries *Too Soon Dead* and *The Girls in the High-Heeled Shoes.*